RANGER'S CALLING

THE FIRES OF WYNCHELL

RANGER'S CALLING
BOOK ONE

RAYMOND KEITH

ISBN ebook 979-8-9892608-2-9

ISBN paperback 979-8-9892608-3-6

ISBN Hardcover 979-8-9892608-4-3

Cover design: GetCovers.com

Author photo: EAH Creative

Maps created using: Inkarnate.com

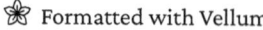 Formatted with Vellum

To my brother,
John
I could not ask for better siblings than the ones I have been given. No greater bond could we ask for than the one we have. We have lived great adventures together: in fantasy stories, in real life, and in seeking the deep things of God. So much of this story is because of our love for one another.

ACKNOWLEDGMENTS

"First and foremost, I thank the LORD, the Creator of all things and Master Storyteller, with whom we share His creative expression. He has given us His Word, the Lord Jesus Christ, Who found me and saved me when I wasn't even looking for Him, yet needed Him desperately.

I would also like to thank:

My wife, Judy Rae, who loves books, but does not like fantasy. Thank you for reading many pages of my works and the vital feedback and encouragement you have given.

My beloved brother, John, who despite his busy life, always takes the time to read my drafts and give me his feedback and share in his creativity. I love how you explore the English language. And also to his wife, Kathy, who also always encourages me and for gives insightful advice.

Nora Lee Taylor, my friend and fellow author, who encouraged me to write down and share "the stories that God has given me" and introduced me to her editor. I need to now also add her mother, Linda, who also encouraged me and took the time to read through my drafts.

Kimberly Lord, my friend and wise counselor, who also helped as a beta reader with encouraging feedback. Plus, you share my love of The Lord of the Rings.

David N. Alderman for his quality editing services. My novel is far better because of your expertise.

To my daughter, Katey, my brothers and sisters, and to all my family, who always love and support me.

The great talents at Getcovers.com

To Thomas Umstattd Jr and all the folks at AuthorMedia.com who help so many of us independent authors find success. I am successful most of all because of your wisdom.

All those at Realm Makers, who encourage us all to be better in every way for the Glory of God.

My Launch Team, my wonderful followers who have been so supportive and helped me reach all of you. D. T. Powell, Nancy Fagan, Debbie Harris, P. R. Allen, Jackie Allen, Davie Williams, Laurie Robertson, Xavier Schwindt, Raeleane, Debbie.

My Kickstarter campaign supporters who helped me reach well beyond my goal: Glenn, Susan, Dale, Teresa, Faye, Mike, Bobbi Jo, Joan, Leroy, Cammie, Melissa B., D. T. Powell, J. A. Webb, JR Schell, Xavier Schwindt, Kathy Brasby, Christy S, KL Wagoner, John Gilligan, Z.R. McCormick, Brian Grimes, Andrew Schell, Josiah DeGraaf, Matthew B. Dawson, Camy Tang, Kimmy, Lee Alexander, Gerald P. McDaniel, Jack Arvidson, Rosa Thill, David DeHaan, Starr Z. Davies, Chris Frank, Becky Gunsolus, Ethan Eshleman, Dale Speicher, Richard Kirschner, Martin Cerda, Phoenix 17, Peter, Justise Briones, Barde Press, Malcolm Coon, Meredith Carstens, Barry & Denise Craigen, Chuck Kutchera, Jackie, Tom, Susan, Peter, Glenda, Kyrie, Krisan, Dylan, Kim, Diane, Heather, Kelly Jo Wilson, Mustardseed Realms, Clair, Morgan G.

You, my readers, who have taken the time to read and hopefully enjoy this story."

Note:
Copies of the Maps and more can be viewed on the website.
https://authorraymondkeith.com/veardalan/

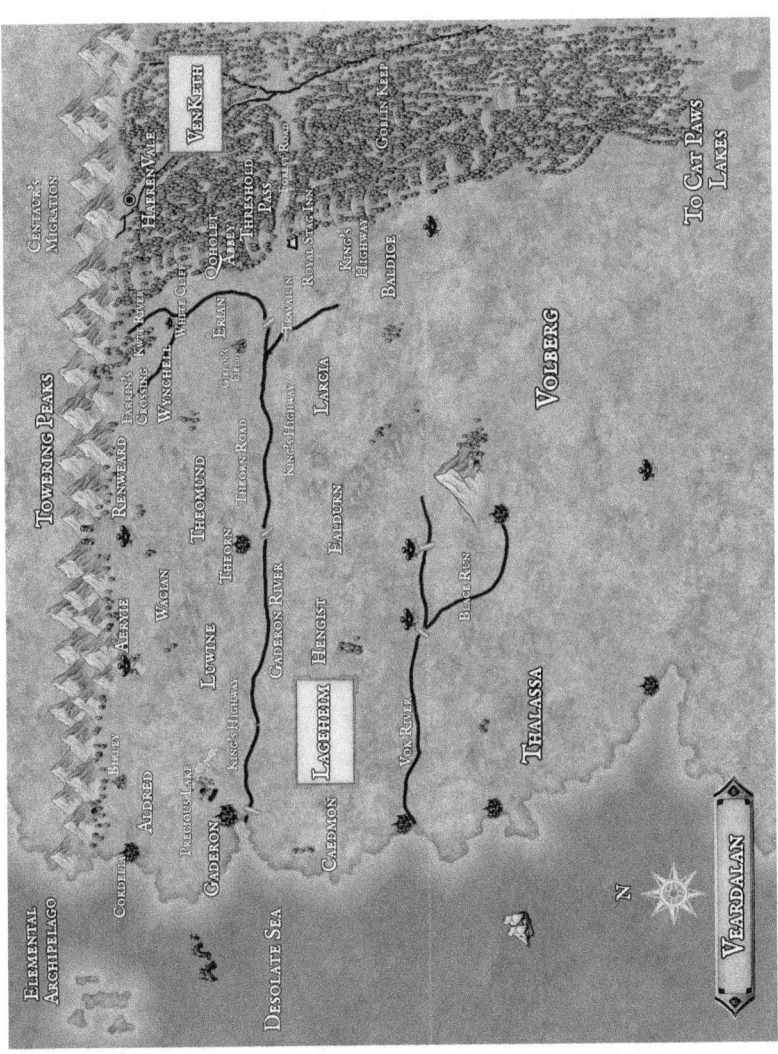

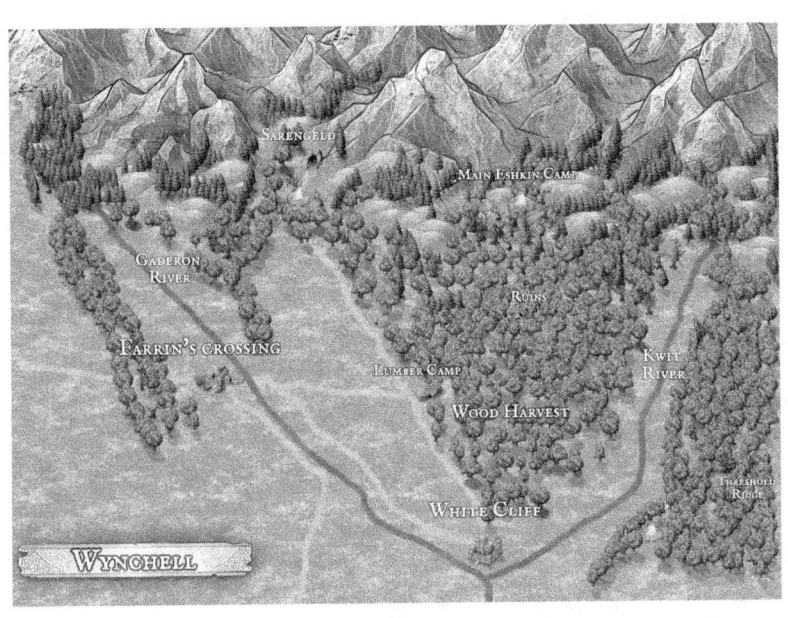

SARENGELD

MAIN ESHKIN CAMP

GADERON
RIVER

RUINS

FARRIN'S CROSSING

LUMBER CAMP

KWIT
RIVER

WOOD HARVEST

THRESHOLD
RIDGE

WHITE CLIFF

WYNCHELL

CONTENTS

CHAPTER I
BLACK AND GRAY

My father was a heartless man, and I did everything not to be like him.

He pillaged, murdered, and enslaved. My mother, one of his last victims, named me after him. *N'ethilion* means, 'son of the wicked man' or 'son of the fallen' in her native elfin tongue. But she gave me another name, a human name, because we lived in the world of men. *Galieb* means 'beloved' in the local dialect. She wanted to proclaim her unconditional love for me, despite the circumstances of my conception, despite what others may say or do.

But I never doubted. I knew she loved me. Every deed and sacrifice confirmed her maternal devotion.

Many resent the fate of their situations in life, like growing up without a father or being an outsider, but I never did. I always accepted my life for what it was. I felt my situation built character and maturity that I found lacking in others. Later in my life, I realized not having a father also had its disadvantages. Frankly, it all seemed so providential—like it was part of some complicated plan.

1

I wasn't missing much, not having someone wicked in my life. And there were plenty of good men to fill the gap growing up.

Now I have a better understanding of why things are the way they are. I understand now it was not really my mother that named me, even if she spoke the words at my birth. Even if she had her own personal reasons. My name is part of my calling.

But this story is not ultimately about me. It is also about 'He Who Is', and the One He has sent. To this, I bear witness. I am just a small piece of the much larger narrative. An epic that stretches across all the ages of history.

My part of the adventure starts in the Hidden Valley, tucked between the mighty Lageheim kingdom and the vast VenKeth, the Venerable Woods. In the Hidden Valley is the Qoholet Abbey, a training ground for elite ranger sages. I spent my entire youth here.

The Hidden Valley was all I knew the first nineteen years of my life.

My first routine patrol took me along Threshold Ridge, the eastern boundary of our valley. The mountain ridge stretched from the Towering Peaks far to the north, all the way to the Ven Marshes, many leagues to the south. Everyone expected this patrol to be uneventful, including me. Few problems occurred during these patrols. But anything could happen in the VenKeth, especially on the edge of the Fae Lands.

My life changed forever when I saw boots sticking out of the ripening blueberry bushes. No one alive would lay head first with branches digging into his back. A falchion lay nearby, glinting in the fading moonlight as it dropped lower on the horizon.

The entire scene put me on edge. It felt like a test my mentors had set up, but this time, it was real.

I fiddled with the throwing axe stuck in my belt as I looked around me. I was not sure what to do at first, so I moved closer to the body to get a better look.

It was a dead male. Pale foam had dried around his thin lips and yellow stained tusks, which jutted up from an excessive under-bite and square jaw. For armor, the creature wore tanned skins and chunks of fur over a leather cuirass. It was nothing I had ever seen before. He was not a human or elfin, and he did not look like a goblin, the creatures claiming part of the forest south of here. The skin looked ashen gray in the setting moon's light. Contrasting the skin, patches of blackened flesh had corroded the neck, the right hand, and the left thigh. A tiny needle-like shaft remained embedded in his thigh, seemingly the source of the corrosion. No rotting stench touched my nostrils, only the raw odor of sweat-infused leather.

This one died most unpleasantly just a few hours ago. I knew who killed in such ways, and it caused me alarm.

Gripping my recurved war bow, I raced forward, anxious about any upcoming encounter. Sweat trickled into my budding beard and soaked the linen under my brigandine armor despite the cool morning air. Fearing what I was going to run into, I concentrated on keeping my steps light, touching the ground with only my toes. My feet avoided noisy debris yet maintained as much speed as possible.

Gliding through the woods unnoticed is what rangers are known for.

Having elfin blood, my eyes do not need light to see as the moon dipped below the horizon. I could see even with no light at all, but then only in shades of gray and only about sixty paces at most. But I did not need my elfin vision, for by the time I reached my destination, the first rays of the sun raced horizontally between the dark trunks. The morning light highlighted the large array of mushrooms spread out across the forest floor that I sought. Fungi of many colors, shapes, and sizes sprung up from dark soil, creeping across half buried rocks and climbing the sides of massive stumps. All were beautifully arranged into a stunning garden. I knew the colony that worked the garden would be active with the rising sun.

As I approached, I took notice of many crushed mushrooms before two flashes blinded me.

"Wait! I am from the abbey! Are you safe?" I stumbled to a halt, grumbling as I squinted in pain, hands covering my eyes.

"Stay back, archer! We are on high alert!" a male voice called, barely audible if it had not been near my ear.

"I am Galieb! A ranger on patrol!"

"If you value your life, be silent! Notify the queen!" As my eyes recovered, I found myself surrounded by dozens of tiny elfin-like creatures with prismatic dragonfly wings. Faeries. A few were male, but the majority were female, no taller than the length of my hand. The males held spears or swords. The females armed themselves with bows. Tiny tunics of green covered their bodies, though of what material I could not tell. Each one's hair was a different color, the hues matching the seven bands of the rainbow. Faeries, like bees, were almost all females except for the consorts to the queen, and the females were all her children.

In the center of the fungal colony stood the largest, most brilliant toadstool, its circumference equal to a round tavern table, its height reaching to my chest. From underneath its rim came the queen, a tiny but stunning female surrounded by eight maidens and two males, weapons prepared.

"Stand down all. He speaks true," the queen commanded. "He comes from the abbey. And one does not forget a half-elfin. Lord Devarim always speaks highly of you, Galieb."

I shifted my feet, trying to remember proper faerie

etiquette, before bending at the waist in an awkward bow. Formalities always made me uncomfortable.

"Are you patrolling alone? Are you no longer an acolyte? Have you passed the tests?"

"Yes, as of last week." All the consorts flustered at me for forgetting her title, causing my face to flush. "Uh, your Majesty. I saw a gray corpse laying among the bushes. I knew he had been here. Did he harm anyone?"

"Be at ease, young ranger," the queen replied. "And you may call me Reyowin. During the night, a patrol stumbled upon us and attacked. My warriors defended the colony. After seeing that one's fate, the rest of them fled. They still damaged some of our homes and crops before we chased them off. Thankfully, we all escaped injury. In all my long years, I have never seen eshkin in these parts before."

Eshkin, as I guessed. My mentors spoke of them often, but I never encountered one. Eshkin are humanoids driven to excessive wickedness by their god, Eshek. "How many, if I may ask?"

"Four is all we saw," the queen answered. "A small patrol. They came from the north, and the rest fled back the way they had come. With the elfin kingdom to our northeast, most likely they came down out of the mountains."

"I trust your wisdom, your majesty—uh, Reyowin." It just seems a far distance for them to travel. The Towering Peaks are many leagues to the north. Hopefully, it was just a small raiding party that wandered too far.

"My lady, how can I help?"

"Nothing for you to do here for us, young ranger. We can manage. The villages below are your concern, however."

"Yes, your majesty. I will continue north. If they threaten Woodhaven, I will find them. If I am able, I will notify you of any other danger."

"They won't be back here after seeing the effect of our

poisons. And my warriors," she added with her chin pointing out. "Be safe, young Galieb. Next time you are here, I have some morels for your mother, Edhelwen. I am sure she is proud of you."

"I did not know you knew my mother, my lady. Proud, yes, but sad, too. Half-elfin age fast—like humans. Too fast for elfin mothers." Few at the abbey knew her elfin name. Most in the valley only knew her by the human name she chose, Sadima. Only my mother would have told her true name to the queen. My mother was the master gardener for the abbey, having the gifted ability to enhance growth. She started that garden from scratch. Now I understood where the mushrooms came from.

"Faerie queens know many things, young Qoholet. Our years rival those of the elfin. All the Fae understand the passing of time in ways similar to the elfin." She paused before adding, "Be careful, Galieb. For her sake. Eshkin are dangerous, and you are still a youth."

"Yes, my lady."

I continued following the ridge, leaving the faerie colony with my eyes alert and my war bow in hand. Studying the terrain, I could see signs of the eshkin: a newly broken branch here and there, overturned pebbles in the packed earth.

Once I found my first partial boot print, I took a moment to study it. Using my bow to measure, I calculated the length of stride and size of the foot. Following these prints resulted in more discoveries, such as distinctions in strides and foot sizes.

How many times did my mentors drag us acolytes up the ridge to look at tracks in the blazing sun and blowing snow? How many times in the middle of the night? But endless hours of training paid off, as always. These skills will save lives. How could I not find satisfaction in that?

The tracks confirmed three booted walkers.

After a few hours of travel and tracking, I slowed my pace due to the tracks looking fresher this far along.

Faint clanks came up from the valley below. Touches of smoke tickled my nose. Woodhaven was the settlement farthest north in the Hidden Valley. Were these the signs of everyday activity or new destruction? My hands turned to sweat at the thought of the village in danger. People I knew popped into my head: Reeve Fredric, Orrick, and Orrick's flirtatious young daughter, Elfrieda. They treated me kindly during my last visit. My mind split between wanting to rush down the mountain to check on the villagers and feeling it may be wiser to follow the boot prints. Would the tracks lead me down there? Were there other eshkin about?

Other sounds suddenly caught my ears from the ridge in front of me. Guttural sounds. The harsh speech of the eshkin. The sound stood my hairs on end, and my heart pounded. I used controlled breathing to keep calm. Three enemies seemed too much for just one unproven youth.

My nerves demanded that I just let them walk away, but the Qoholet taught not the ways of cowardice.

I crept upon them like a woodland shadow. No leaf stirred, no root snared, no twig betrayed. They seemed not to fear an attack but argued without a lookout, standing in a circle. Blending myself with trunk and brush, I closed the gap until their words became clear.

Studying them seemed wise. All three were bald with ash-gray skin, similar to the corpse.

"I want to check out that village," stated the one with a falchion hanging from his belt.

It helped I learned the eshkin speech, though it did not come easy for me. Thankfully, the old centaur, Vollyr, insisted on it.

"And I say we wait!" the largest one answered. An axe

reached from shoulder to hip next to his quiver of javelins. "If those cursed faeries had not killed Grunch, I would agree with you. But we have enough trouble already."

"And I say we go to the village. I'm hungry. Roasted pork sounds great," the first one countered, clacking his jaws twice.

"Ha! it would take hours for you to roast a whole pig, Colb. You would starve!" stated the third one. He also sported a long axe and a quiver on his back. "But a few slabs of bacon over some coals would do."

"Sounds good, Nark!" agreed Colb, his left hand resting on the hilt of his falchion.

"Not today," barked the big guy.

"Come on, Dolf!" Colb protested. "Bet they're just scrawny farmers. Like up north. Easy pickin's. Or we could just steal a squeaker or some mutton. No need to rally the entire valley."

Dolf exploded, punching Colb in the face with all his might, crushing his nose before sending him to the ground, dazed. "I'm tired of yer tongue!"

Dolf clacked his teeth and jutted his lower jaw out. That seemed to indicate some type of challenge. Dolf placed his foot on Colb's chest and pressed down as the eshkin gasped. Dolf's right hand gripped a long dagger shoved in his broad leather belt.

Was he going to kill his companion right now? The sudden brutality of the entire scene unnerved me. I had heard of this type of senseless violence, but seeing it was different. Eshkin seemed to have no regard for life.

"Both of you shut it!" Dolf's gaze drifted between the two. Colb wheezed, trying to breathe with Dolf's foot on his chest.

Neither took the challenge.

Dolf removed his foot, and Colb scrambled to his feet, eyeing the others through slits. His hands clenched and unclenched, the right twitching towards his falchion. Bright red blood dripped from his face onto the front of his iron-knobbed leather cuirass.

"You in front, Colb. Back to camp," Dolf barked, then clacked his jaws once.

The three started off again, walking in a line, heading north. After that encounter, I feared even more for our villages. These creatures seemed brutal and heartless.

I followed them.

I let out a breath when we passed the Wolf's Nose, a rock outcropping at the top of the ridge just beyond Woodhaven. The rangers considered "the Nose" the corner of our boundary, but I continued after, worrying they may turn aside or stop. Not feeling the need to stay close anymore, I slowed down, and created more space between us. No point in giving them a chance to notice me.

It did not take long after that for Nark to drift behind. My instincts told me something was happening, so I stopped behind a young tree. He slipped his long axe off his back. Dolf looked over his shoulder and started to turn when Nark planted the head of his great axe in the eshkin's skull. Dolf collapsed like a cooked noodle without even a grunt.

The coldness of the act caused me to swallow hard. I was not rid of them yet.

Colb spun, feeling for his sword.

Nark stared at him, axe in both hands. "I'm in charge now," Nark stated, then clacked his jaw twice. "Let's see if we can find a squeaker down in the valley."

Colb laughed at Dolf's demise. I did not like the sound of its callousness. "How about its mum? I could eat a whole pig myself."

"Maybe find a woman, too. Make her a breeder," Nark added. He set his axe down, but keeping it within reach. He snatched Dolf's dagger to cut off his victim's ears. After removing the iron ring and other decorations stuck in the over-sized lobes, he strung it on his belt, stacked against a few other smaller shriveled pieces.

"I've been admiring this dagger of his," Nark commented as he stuck it in his belt. "This is man-steel. Took it from some lobeless round ear."

'Lobeless' was apparently a slander for humans.

"Yeah, me too," Colb replied with an expression of envy. "Good blade." The two eyed each other warily, Nark retrieving his axe from the ground, but nothing happened. They searched their comrade's body, stripping it of valuables, including a few coins.

Leaving their companion to the scavengers, they started off again. This time, they turned around and headed right towards me.

Dragon's breath! Now what am I going to do?

CHAPTER 2

A SHAKING OF THE SOUL

I froze, my mind blank. Years of training 'went with the leaves,' as they say. The two warriors pocketed their booty and spit on the corpse before turning.

This skinny tree provided little cover.

"If you are going to follow eshkin, better have a plan," I muttered to myself, my mind racing faster than my heart. Or as mentor Horten drilled into us, 'Better know how to bake it before you crack the eggs.'

The eshkin still chuckled to themselves as they took the first steps in my direction. The hairs on my neck told me to run.

My brain spit out ideas, first telling me that if I moved, they would immediately see me. If I stood still, they would walk right by me and see me, anyway. Then I would have to bolt like a frightened rabbit and probably fight both, hand-to-hand.

As they continued my way, they looked right at me. My bow would be useless up close. My Qoholet training is top-notch, but nothing prepares you for the real thing. A confrontation was inevitable.

You need to calm yourself, I scolded my mind. *They trained you for this!*

The invaders walked at a normal pace, but still closed the gap rapidly. My nerves calmed as I worked my breathing. A dozen ideas flitted through my mind as I dismissed all of them.

Creeping eastward out of their path, I lowered my center of gravity, taking precise steps, feeling every pebble under my feet, my eyes never leaving the two. My arm pulled three arrows from my quiver in a timed motion before I even realized the shafts were in my hand. The warriors continued straight, step by step, without changing course.

Notching one arrow, and holding the other two ready between my fingers, I called out, using Merchant's Common— the language between races. No reason to let them know I understand eshkin speech.

"Halt! You are not welcome here! Head back up to where you came from!"

Maybe I should have just planted a few arrows in them before they even realized I was there. Combat was familiar to me, but killing was not. At least beyond deer and small game. Still, they were humanoids, not just animals. Many societies considered the eshkin part of the 'Accountable', that is, beings responsible for their actions before the Creator.

"Who's that?" Nark said, looking my way, still gripping his bloodied axe.

"There! A hunter!" Colb pointed at me before reaching for a javelin. "Eshek's favor! First lobeless we've seen! This may be more fun than I thought! His ears are mine!"

"There's just one! Killing blow gets the ears! Spread out!"

Nark also reached for a javelin, but I had already released the arrow. It slammed into Colb's right shoulder, piercing hides, leather, and torso. He dropped the javelin with a curse.

Satisfaction swept through me as I notched the next. My confidence grew just a finger.

Nark got his missile launched, but I had already shifted right. Fear and uncertainty fled as calm and coolness took over. My mind took in every bump under my feet. I felt every vane of the feathers against my cheek. I noticed every ridge of my bow's grip.

Both eshkin charged me. Colb still had my arrow sticking out of his shoulder. I drifted back to keep my distance, conscious of the terrain under my boots. I pushed out the fear of rushing enemies and focused on the gaps in Colb's armor, putting a second arrow into the warrior's throat.

Nark was upon me, swinging his long axe. Dodging heavy cuts, I dropped my bow and the last arrow. My heart pounded, but I felt nothing. Years of training took over. I scrambled left and right, the axe head swishing past me. My sword and throwing axe appeared in my hands before I realized it.

When Nark saw Colb gurgling on the ground, he paused, now cautious of me. His large swings turned to quick slashes with the axe head to test my skills.

Taller, broader, and stronger—not to mention more experienced—Nark seemed to have the edge. My only advantages were agility and speed. Even with my brigandine, one hit from that heavy axe would finish me. I saw what it did to Dolf's head.

Changing my grip, I shifted to a rapier fighting style, giving me the reach to match his long-handled axe. He swung, and I jabbed, making minor cuts in his arms as I used the trees to keep him at a distance.

He did not tire easily, as I hoped. Maybe mind games would help. "There is still time to flee," I said.

"Ha! Flee from you, little half-blood?"

"I heard you fled from those tiny faeries."

That did it! His jaw tightened and his eyes bulged. The cuts came faster and harder, but wilder.

"All your companions are dead," I continued. "No one will know. Except you."

"Shut up! I'll split you!"

"You'll know. Dig in your mind, won't it? Running from little women."

Was he ever going to tire? He surprised me with a one handed thrust, just grazing my skull, causing me to stumble back, dazed. Another fierce attack came with an arcing swing downward, but I redirected it towards the ground as I jumped sideways, my head still rattled.

The warrior took advantage of me being off balance and planted his feet for another big cut.

Retreating would have put me right in its path. Anticipating his moves, I stepped forward into a thrust, focusing all my strength on piercing his neck above the thick leather. The axe blade came down behind my back, the handle connecting with my sword arm.

The point didn't sink in deep as planned, but skipped off an iron knob of his hardened leather and then tangled in the hides, just nicking the skin below.

Shock flashed across his face. The wound spooked him, but he quickly recovered. His hot breath washed against my cheek.

Panic rushed through my body, so I chopped my axe deep into his knee before he could react. His long axe dropped behind as he collapsed onto me, both hands grabbing at my arms.

The two of us now grappled on the ground, my sword trapped between us, useless. He bit into my left arm, tusks sinking deep into the muscle. I screamed and punched in reaction.

Punching his left ear did nothing. He hammered blows into

my ribs, and even though the metal plates of the brigandine armor took much of the force, the strikes drove the edges of the armor platelets into my skin through the linen between.

Even with blood pouring from his leg, I feared being on the losing end of this encounter. Desperation flooded me. I fumbled around for anything, finding the coveted dagger taken from Dolf.

Releasing his teeth from my arm, Nark pushed up on his one good leg. As he raised his fist to smash my face, I jammed the dagger into his armpit, yanked it out, and did it again, praying it pierced lung and heart. At first, he just stared at me, but then his eyes went blank. He collapsed on top of me.

My heart pounded for several minutes. I took big gulps of air. It finally dawned on me it was over, and I was still alive.

Swelling black eye, ribs bruised, and arm bleeding, I crawled out from under my enemy. I gazed at both bodies, making sure they were dead. I then peered around me, all my senses alert. The woods reeked of silence.

I am alive. All my enemies are dead. My heart slowed down, and my breathing finally returned to normal. My clothes dripped with sweat.

Good thing it wasn't Dolf I had wrestled with, if these two were so afraid of him.

I cut a piece of fabric off Nark's attire that I could use to slow my bleeding, my hands trembling. Years of hard training could not prepare me for this experience. I stared at both eshkin as I wrapped my wound. Killing a humanoid, even in self-defense, even heartless eshkin, shook the soul. It was not the same as hunting a deer or wringing a chicken's neck. That wrenched the heart enough some days.

I trained to fight evil and wicked creatures most of my life. I survived this ordeal. Now what? Could I still do it? Is this what I wanted to do?

Unsure, I gathered my weapons. You never know when something else may come along in the VenKeth.

The sun almost reached zenith, leaving me half a day still. It was time to get going. My assignment had been to patrol to the Wolf's Nose and return. But I needed to check on the village. I should make Woodhaven by early afternoon. But first things first: I needed to heal my wounds.

I pulled a linen cloth out of my pouch and unfolded it to reveal the comfrey leaves inside. Taking one leaf, I put the rest away. I waited until my hands stopped trembling. With my right hand facing up, I circled my palm thrice with the leaf while holding the stem in my left between the thumb and fore-finger. You had to be careful to do it just right for the most potential, or the spell may fail. I set the leaf flat on my palm and then placed my palms together with the leaf in between. Cupping my hands, but keeping the fingertips and wrists together, I slowly removed my left hand. On my right hand were seven bluish white, perfectly round, pearls. I ate them all.

Within minutes, I could feel my strength returning and my wounds scabbing over. My body repaired itself naturally, but the berries sped up the process and provided all the nutrients I would need for the next few hours.

As I rested, eyes closed, taking deep breaths, I allowed the magic berries time to repair my body.

Once I felt ready, I searched the dead for anything useful. I found a few foreign copper and silver coins I did not recognize, so I took them, along with the coveted dagger and anything else I found useful, including Dolf's ears. I needed to show something distinctive to the Council.

Smoke touched my nostrils again. Were there more raiders? With the berries still working their effects, I hurried down the slope to the village.

CHAPTER 3
THIS DAY WAS COMING

Woodhaven seemed eerily quiet as I moved downhill through the forest canopy. The only sound I made was a faint rustle across the leafy floor. Quiet, I hoped, was a good sign. Glimpses of gray smoke rising from the village caught my eye through the trees. That was not a good sign. Visions of burning homes flashed through my mind.

Hidden Creek tumbled north through the bottom of the valley unconcerned, and I followed it south towards town. I took the briefest scan of the water for clues, but nothing revealed itself.

The first buildings came into view between the trunks, revealing logged walls with few windows and no doors, for most faced towards the town. I had no notion yet of the condition of the town, but at least the buildings still stood. The stressed voices of bleating sheep touched my ears. Bow in hand, I worked my way from bush to bush, and finally to the closest building, a small livestock pen made of logs. The smell of burning wood increased, and I could hear the creaking of the water wheel at the mill, but little else. The sheep went silent.

What is going on here? Am I too late? Have the eshkin already been here? Or is it nothing at all?

Moving around the pen, I slinked forward along the property, trying to get a better view of town. If any eshkin were about, I wanted the advantage. I still had a limited view, so I scurried up to the corner of the small fence.

An explosion of squawking greeted me as three startled chickens flew in every direction, feathers flying. A young girl feeding them shrieked at their reaction.

"So much for sneaking into town, you fool!" I muttered to myself and twisted my head back and forth, watching for charging enemies.

"What are you doing?" the girl scolded, hands on her hips. "You scared the life out of me!" Suddenly, a big smile crossed her face as she tucked blonde hair behind her ear. "Ranger Galieb!"

"Elfrieda! What's going on? Are you alright?" The fifteen-year-old daughter of my host family a few weeks ago, Elfrieda had tagged along with everything I did, including finding lost livestock in the woods. She was a little smitten with rangers, but overall, she proved to be a good helper.

"I heard you passed the tests. I am so happy for you! A sworn ranger! How exciting!"

"Elfrieda! What's that smoke? Has there been any trouble here?" I questioned as I stepped past her, scanning the village. It seemed nothing had happened, but I needed to be sure.

"Trouble? What trouble? What are you talking about? Are you injured? What happened to you?" She touched my face, her brown eyes studying my bruise.

I stepped back. Best not to encourage her. She did not seem to be listening. "What is causing that smoke?"

"The mill is burning scraps. They do that sometimes. What is the matter with you?" Her scrunched eyebrows made her look annoyed.

"No danger in the village?" My worries subsided as I felt the tension drop.

"No. How did you get that black eye? And what happened to your arm? I see dried blood! I need to get some water!" Her eyebrows lifted into concern.

"That's good. I need to—"

"No, blood is not good!" Her eyebrows were back to being scrunched.

"Elfrieda, I am fine. Please take me to the reeve," I commanded, not wanting to deal with a dotting girl.

"Alright! Are you not glad to see me?" the girl pouted with her chin against her chest.

I relaxed and focused on the pretty girl before me. All seemed quiet, except for the annoyed hens. Time to make up for any rudeness. I was just a few years older than her, but she was still too young. "Yes, I am glad to see you. You look nice, as always. But I need to speak to the reeve. Right away."

Pleased, she turned to lead the way. "So, why did you chase my chickens?"

"Never mind." My face flushed for just a second.

As we walked, passing by the log homes and people working, listening to Elfrieda tell me about all that has happened since I was here last, I realized this is why I trained among the Qoholet. This village, these people—and many others—is why I wanted to be a ranger. Would I fight to protect them? All the doubts I had on top of the ridge left me.

The town remained blissfully unaware of the eshkin patrol wandering nearby, at least until I showed up bloodstained and bruised.

Fredric was the man appointed overseer of Woodhaven by

the Qoholet Council and given the title of reeve. His salt and pepper beard marked him as middle-aged. A fair and kind man, he took his responsibilities seriously. Upon seeing me, he invited us both into his home. A log structure larger than most in town, he brought me into a front room used for meeting the public.

Elfrieda left to get a pitcher of water and a cleaning bowl as I informed Reeve Fredric. The lines on his face increased as I spoke.

"We can send a message to the abbey. I have a vek right here," Fredric offered, pointing with his thumb.

My eyes followed his thumb over to a large cage in the next room. The vek lounged on a branch, the snake-like body draped like a rope on either side. Four tiny legs gripped the bark. Dragonfly wings stood straight out from the middle of its back. Its dragon shaped head didn't move, but I know he also studied me with the slit pupil on this side of his face. As a boy, I learned the hard way to take care of what you say in front of a vek because of their ability to memorize short messages and repeat them.

I did not approach it. Veks are notoriously choosy about with whom they bond. A small pouch for rolled messages hung next to the cage.

"Just that one? No, you may need it in case any eshkin do come here. Can I borrow a horse? There is no danger yet, and I can be there by nightfall. You need to form a watch tonight."

Fredric agreed to a horse and the watch. He sent for a horse as I washed up in the bowl Elfrieda prepared for me.

With promises to return the animal, I rode off with haste. Elfrieda was sad to see me go. They were simple villagers, but hardy, and each knew how to use the sword, spear, and bow. With the families of the village now prepared, they no longer would be an easy target for any raiders.

The smooth dirt road skirted the Hidden Creek as it wound its way south under the majestic maples and oaks. I maintained a fast pace, switching between galloping and trotting.

Before the sun touched the western ridge, I reached the Hidden Lake. My path took me along the eastern shore for two miles under weeping willows and broad sycamores before the village of Lakeside came into view. Fishermen in small boats dotted the lake as their wives prepped for their return in front of buildings of wattle and daub. My horse huffed as it climbed a rise in the road going past the waterfalls pouring over the red shale and into the lake at its south end.

The village of Lakeside disappeared behind me and the maples gave way to open pastures of grazing cattle and sheep. A few miles farther, the pastures changed to vineyards, orchards, and planted fields as the sun fell below the ridge, reducing the light and heat.

After another eight miles, the village of Stonecrest came into view and I knew I was almost there. So did my steed as she raced the last few miles with dedication. Beautiful homes crafted with fieldstone sat tucked among the cherry trees lining both sides of the road. Candles and lamps illuminated the wood-framed windows as the evening crept in. Once I passed through the village, the abbey came into view.

The Qoholet Abbey stood almost at the very south end of the Hidden Valley, tucked back under the overhanging shale cliffs of the eastern ridge. Water seeped out of the cliffs to run down on either side of the stone structure constructed of matching red shale, following grooves carved into the cliffs by dwarfin builders. About twenty feet from the bottom, the water dripped melodiously into pools below, each of them filled with white water lilies my mother had planted. The water then spilled out of the pools and ran together to start the Hidden Creek's long journey to the Gaderon River. The building itself was the tallest structure in the valley, standing three stories high, peaked with a prominent bell tower in the front. Additional halls ran deep into the mountain inside the abbey, but none of the acolytes knew how many or how deep.

It was here where I trained and took my oaths. It was within its stone halls that the council met and where rangers brought scrolls filled with wisdom from around the world to add to its library shelves. The Qoholet were sages as much as they were warriors.

I spent my entire life around that majestic learning center tucked under the cliffs. Years ago, the chief ranger, Devarim, had brought my mother to this place to recover from her ordeal. She never left.

After a long, hasty ride through the valley, I arrived at the abbey late that same evening. The stables sat on the south side of the abbey, built along the very end of the valley. Despite my haste, I took care of my exhausted steed first. The stable master told me I could find Devarim in the library. The twin pools reflected the starry sky as I hurried across the small wooden bridge to the main door of the abbey.

The library was the largest room in the abbey, with its high ceiling and rows of shelves filled with books, scrolls, and maps. Most acolytes did not realize what wealth was at their fingertips.

The room was lit by magical glowing balls floating near the ceiling, giving off a soft light. Striding in, I spied the chief ranger sitting at a long table with an oversized book before him. A lamp sat next to it. Even at ease in the library, Devarim exuded strength and wisdom. The silver gray in his beard and dark hair only added to the impression. His eyes betrayed intelligence and sophistication beyond his rugged exterior.

He did not study alone, but several other council members reclined with him, enjoying tea and cookies. Next to him sat his wife, Lady Valda. Across from Devarim sat the ancient gnomin and headmaster, Maistren Sabbis Lilke. Next to Lilke and across from Lady Valda sat Sabbis Horten with his wolf companion, Skelbrader, who stretched himself out under the table.

"Something happened," observed Horten as I strode into the room, his good right eye following me all the way. Over the left eye was a dark woolen patch. He crossed his arms across his light summer tunic of sienna brown.

Devarim stood at the sight of me, his lips tight in concern, not expecting me back until sunrise. "Galieb, is everything alright? Are you injured?"

My welfare came first. That is why everyone respected this man. As Wise Protector and Chief of the Qoholet Council, he cared about each of us the same as his own sons.

As I stood before my mentors, I gave my full report.

"I found these coins on them," I finished, putting the coins on the table. I continued standing, waiting for their questions. The ancient gnomin, Maistren Lilke, peered over the pince-nez on his bulbous nose at the coins. Half the size of men, gnomin are a race of humanoids prized as tutors among the nobility and known for mechanical inventions. Everyone revered the Maistren Sabbis, the Headmaster. His full name was actually much longer: Maistren Sabbis Lilke Obed Stavewielder Murnig Skholfounder Treestumbler Gottson... and many more we guessed. He was the only one who knew all of them. To be agreeable, he just used the first three names.

"You did well to take on two eshkin," Devarim encouraged as he smiled at me. "Few with your experience would have survived. Do any of your wounds need tending?"

"All healed up. Just exhausted from the long day. If not for the boost from the healing pearls, I would not have returned so quickly." *Hungry too*, I thought as I eyed the tea and cookies.

The magical berries sustained me this far, but the effects were waning.

"Really? Still a little purple around the eye. And your breathing seems strained," commented Lady Valda, Devarim's wife, eyeing me sideways as she smoothed out her full-length robe.

"Ribs may still be a little sore." I admitted.

"Good thing Sadima taught you healing spells despite the Council's rule," Valda added, referring to the forbiddance of teaching acolytes how to use magic. Devarim's wife never trained as a ranger, but learned the magical arts herself. Delving with passion into her studies, even the reputable wizard societies of Lageheim recognize her as a proficient mage. As part of the council, she researches the best magical spells that will enhance the strength of the Qoholet.

"Please sit as we examine this situation," The Wise Protector said. Skelbrader, Horten's white muzzled wolf companion came and licked my hand in sympathy as I settled into a chair I pulled from another table close by.

"Now, let us get to the matter at hand. I never heard of eshkin this far from the mountains. That's a concern." Devarim's hand moved to rub his bearded chin. The sleeve of his simple summer tunic sliding down his forearm.

"It has happened once before." pondered Lilke, fingering a stubby cane with his knobby hand. His words came slow and precise. "During the reign of Rodulf the First, I believe. He was the fourteenth ruler of Lageheim. Eshkin poured out of the mountains, stirred up by Havik the Cunning. A brilliant general for an eshkin. Brilliant even by human standards, for that matter. But Rodulf scattered them in the end." He bit into a cookie, followed by a sip of tea.

"Maistren, are you saying this is a sign of another surge?" I asked, not liking what he may be implying.

"Most likely just a lost patrol," Horten said after he finished chewing. His words seemed rushed after Lilke's comments. "They wander the Towering Peaks sometimes. Come down seeking plunder. Before the demon cursed me, I chased a few eshkin back into those mountains. More than once." Losing an eye and crippled in one leg, not even the high clerics of Lageheim could heal him. A prophet told him one day a true healer would come to make him whole again.

"Maybe. But we are many leagues from the Towering Peaks for wandering eshkin." Devarim stated. "Their pattern is to establish larger camps and scout from there. That raises more questions. Is there a raiding party close to Woodhaven? How is it that the elfin did not stop them? Why follow the forest ridge when the Protectorate of Wynchell has villages vulnerable to plunder?"

"And why haven't we heard about this before?" Lilke added, scratching at the wisps of gray behind his long, narrow, pointed ears. "Another mystery is these coins. The kingdoms that mint these are east of the VenKeth. Seems a long way for eshkin to travel. Whom did they pillage to get them?"

"Kjell's still in the valley," Horten said. "Let's send him north with Meinrad, beyond Woodhaven. Kjell can handle a vek. If there is anything to report, the rangers can send it to us right away."

"Yes. Good idea," Devarim agreed. "I will send them at first light."

The others approved the plan.

Devarim stood and put his hand on my shoulder. "You protected Woodhaven. Who knows what would have happened there if you had not engaged those raiders? Today, you proved your worth as a ranger. Well done."

I flushed at his words. I waited my entire life to hear such praise, especially from him.

"How are you—in here?" Devarim pointed to my head and then to my heart. "Killing, even in self-defense, even if it's eshkin—it changes things. Not everyone can handle it."

I did not answer right away, but ran a hand over my hair and glanced sideways. "It hit me in my core. But I feel—justified. I'm... okay. Thank you for asking."

"We will talk more later. Before you go."

"Go?" My heart started racing.

"You are among the sworn now. Free to stay or go. You owe nothing to the Qoholet except to fulfill your vows. Do as you wish. However, I have something in mind if you are interested. Are you ready to leave the valley and go on your own?"

The thought thrilled and scared me at the same time. "Yes!"

"Your mother will not be!" Valda reminded him, brushing back her thick reddish brown hair that tumbled down onto her shoulders. "Especially after all that happened already. I remember how hard it was when our sons left the first time."

Devarim looked at me straight, his lids half closed, head tilted slightly. "Go to Wynchell in Lageheim. See if they know of any eshkin raids. Send back a report."

"And stop eyeing the cookies and just eat one already!" Horten added, leaning on his crutch to bring the plate to me. "Take two! I made plenty!"

I'm going to miss his cookies, I thought as my taste buds sighed with pleasure.

~

"GALIEB! I HEARD SOMETHING HAPPENED." My mother's lithe frame stood in the doorway of our home, her blue eyes full of concern. The two of us lived in a quaint, three-room cabin west of the abbey. A large garden filled most of the space between the buildings. She must have been working in the garden earlier, judging by the simple brown dress she wore, and how her hair was up in a bun, which made her pointed ears more prominent. "Look at your eye! And you look exhausted. Here, sit. Rest." She stepped back to let me into the main room of the cabin, pulling out a wooden chair from the kitchen table. She took a second chair for herself. Her pale features reflected the orange glow from the lantern on the table.

"I am fine. I ran into two eshkin. Well, three actually."

"Eshkin! Three of them? By yourself? Oh, Galieb! Amilye's care! Are you hurt? Tell me."

It fascinated me how she fell back into elfin expressions when excited, which was a rarity. She no longer followed the elfin goddess, Amilye. Like all Qoholet, she now searched for the Yett Sorr, the Self-Existent Eternal One. The One that logic demonstrates is the source of all creation, including beings like Amilye.

"Reyowin's consorts killed one, Nark killed Dolf. Then Nark and Colb saw me, so I had to fight. I killed them both."

"Nark and Colb? Dolf? Did you break bread around the campfire with them first?"

She made me laugh out loud. Chuckling hurt my ribs. She's usually so calm. "No, mother! I followed them for a few miles. Listened to them talking. I'm fine. Truly! Nark beat me up a little, but your healing pearls worked. Thanks for the comfrey leaves."

She hugged me, then sensed something more. "What else? Devarim is sending you somewhere, isn't he?"

"Yes. To Wynchell."

Multiple facial expressions flashed across her thin face before she spoke. "Wynchell!" She exclaimed, almost standing up again. "So far? After almost getting yourself killed right here? What is he thinking?" After the outburst, she regained

27

her composure. She brushed the honey blonde strands away from her face. Silence hung between us as she stared at nothing for a moment until understanding came upon her. She worked with Devarim for too long and knew his ways. "They're concerned about other eshkin raids. But why you? I know you took the oaths, passed the tests...Do you feel ready?"

"I believe so. It's time for me to go. Explore. Find adventure. Fulfill my calling, whatever it is. You knew this day was coming." It tore my heart to tell her, but ever since Devarim had mentioned it, I felt there was something ahead of me I needed to do. Perhaps my calling awaited me in Wynchell.

She gave a sad nod. "I think we all feel that way when we are young. A sense of purpose. I did in my youth. Here I am and I know now this is my purpose—raising you and teaching here. Creating these gardens. Being assaulted and coming here was not my plan. My life was not what I thought it was going to be. Life can be strange with its twists and turns. But I am content here. Your purpose may not be what you think it is, either." Sadima sighed. She took a human name when she came here, putting aside her elfin name, Edhelwen, among the humans. "I do not know if I am ready for you to go. Humans move so fast through life—and it seems my half-human son does too. A mother is never ready, I guess."

Many elfin thought it strange that my mother settled among humans after being abused by men, but she found peace and comfort here. My father was a heartless man, and so were his gang of cutthroats. But the Qoholet protected and served, working to make the world a better place. Men could be one or the other, good or bad.

She gave a somber smile. "I am giving you a whole bushel of comfrey leaves to take with you. And any other herbs you'll need. Just don't forget to come back."

CHAPTER 4

PREPARATIONS AND GOODBYES

The thought of finally going out on my own was thrilling, but also frightening. Even though part of our training included overnight patrols in the VenKeth, this was going to be a whole new experience. I did not know when I would be back. Purchasing what I needed along the road might not be practical. I had saved up some money over the years as an acolyte, but my funds were not excessive. Thankfully, the abbey had all I needed, as long as I did not forget to take it. I also hoped to find some source of income along the way. My mentors did all they could to help me prepare.

Standing in my room by my bed, I looked over everything I planned to take one more time. I had gathered a week's worth of food, such as dried fruit, jerky, and bread, and stored it in my small backpack. Midsummer was too hot for my woolen hooded cloak, but I rolled it up and strapped it to the pack. The gray-green tone blended well with the forest colors and it would keep me dry in the storms, too. I also added other things to my pack, such as a tinderbox, candles, and a healing kit. My mother gave me a robust supply of various herbs as well, which I stuffed into pouches.

My weapons, however, became my highest priority. I had spoken to the fletcher and he filled my quiver with a score plus three of arrows. Most had the heavy bodkin tips for battle, but he recommended I take a few barbed heads, too. The last arrow was of silver, and held the power of my vows.

Holding either end of the arrow with my fingertips, I gazed at the shaft, the ceremony still fresh in my mind...

DEVARIM STEPPED FORWARD *with a beautiful silver arrow in his hand, his fingers around the shaft near the middle, the tip pointing towards me. He touched both of my shoulders with the point, then held it before me. "Galieb, take hold of the arrow before you."*

I did as commanded, my fingers wrapping around near the middle, my hand touching the Chief Ranger's, enhancing our bond as ranger brothers.

"Repeat these words if it is honest for you to do so. I, Galieb N'ethilion, heartily swear to do my best to abide honestly by all the Tenets put forth by the Qoholet and to seek wisdom throughout my life. I will share what wisdom I have obtained with the Abbey and with those that have need of it. All my life, I promise to seek for the Yett Sorr, the Creator, the Eternal One who is the true cause of all things. I vow to do what is good, stand up for justice, and defend the truth."

As I repeated the words, I could feel the weight of the vow. It was more than a vow; it was a covenant before my mentors and the Creator.

"Stand, Galieb, take the arrow, and may it serve you always as you serve the good in this world."

I stood, and we looked each other in the eye. Devarim let go of the arrow and my eyes dropped to the shaft. It has a bodkin tip of pure silver. Silver also overlaid the ash shaft with white goose feather fletching. But what had caught my eye was the royal blue handprint of Devarim etched into the silver where he had held it.

I shifted my grip, using only my fingertips, and saw the same was true of my handprint—minuscule ridges etched into the arrow in the same blue. As I moved my hand about, no more changes occurred. My eyes focused back on Devarim, who walked back to stand with the other councilors. They all nodded knowingly, for each owned a similar arrow.

Devarim spoke again. "Your vow is etched into the arrow, a daily reminder to you. The power within the shaft will wax or wane with your commitment. Use it wisely."

I stuck it in my belt as they brought forth more gifts.

"The other gift you are to receive is this silver brooch for your cloak. The brooch features the design of the Qoholet symbol. A sword represents our stance against evil and the scroll symbolizes the seeking of wisdom. Whenever you find this symbol, know that the Qoholet sanctioned it."

The brooch was in the shape of a "Q" overlapped by a rolled scroll. The pin of the brooch was shaped like a sword, the point forming the "tail" of the letter when the brooch was closed.

I slid the shaft into the quiver, hoping I would live up to that vow.

Next, I looked over my war bow. I made this weapon myself, as required as part of my training. The war bow was the ranger's defining weapon and my most constant companion throughout my entire life. The Qoholet studied the art of war from many cultures. They concluded that centaurs made the best bows for rangers, surpassing all others in archery skill. The centaurs themselves had trained my mentors, teaching us their secrets. A shorter, but powerful composite bow, it was effective in the forest and the open field, on horseback and on foot, good for distance shooting and rapid release.

I set aside the war bow and picked up my cut and thrust sword. *Angedon*, I named it: 'the Undone.' The blade had once been owned by my father and used for plundering. Devarim kept it all these years for a reason he could not explain.

When the time came for my testing, the Council asked Stakhiljan, the abbey's dwarfin artisan, to reforge the weapon. He reworked the entire sword.

I brought the blade close to my face, using the sunlight coming through the window to reveal the fine dwarfin weave running down the blade with hints of blue. The blade matched that of an arming sword, but tapering the entire length to a sharp point for better thrusting. My fingers touched the intricate but tiny runes of seven dwarfin blessings marked at the top of the blade on one side. I flipped it over to see Stakhiljan's mark and the blade's name stamped on the other. Stakhiljan had also removed the half-basket hilt and the cat paw pommel, replacing them with a swept hilt and an apple-shaped pommel. I admired the sweeping curves of the protective hilt with its finger rings, designed to be held for both cutting or thrusting.

The weapon, previously used for wickedness, was now transformed into something new. Hence its name.

Once I took my vows, the Council gifted it to me. Angedon is the finest blade I had ever held. I had spent the morning carefully honing its edge to sharpness and polishing every cranny. After I wiped off my fresh fingerprints, I found great satisfaction listening to the blade slide back into its custom scabbard.

Lastly, I inspected my hand axe and dagger, both also freshly sharpened. Even the sturdy back spike of the axe pricked my finger.

I ran my hand over the brigandine armor hanging on the wall, my finger tips riding across tiny steel knobs and soft brown linen. The small overlapping steel plates beneath had protected my torso a few times already and would do so many times in the future. This type of armor offered proficient protection while still allowing for the flexibility of shooting a bow or wielding a sword.

Every warrior needed to find the right balance of armor, weapons, and traveling comfort. The ranger also needed to consider stealth and speed. The Qoholet trained us in various weapons to make us proficient in each, but each of us chose our own combinations and specialties. Mine was bow, sword, and axe, with brigandine armor.

Feeling as prepared as possible with supplies, I now needed to gather information.

RANGERS KJELL and Meinrad returned before I left, reporting that they found no live eshkin. Only the dead ones I encountered. They discovered the remnants of a recently abandoned eshkin camp about a day's journey north of Woodhaven, however. For whatever reason, the raiders packed up and returned north without their dead comrades. Perhaps not finding anything civilized to plunder, they moved elsewhere. The council became even more concerned about what may be happening with our human neighbors to the northwest and the elfin lands to the northeast.

Horten and Skelbrader met me in the library to assist with

my planning. The impaired ranger hobbled over to a shelf in the library using his homemade crutch and pulled out a long, rolled parchment. Since his injuries decades ago, he agreed to become a mentor at the abbey, earning the title of Sabbis, or teacher. My mother's caring values always made me want to rush over and assist him, but the ranger always insisted on doing things himself.

The wolf, Skelbrader, sprawled across the floor with his head against a bookshelf in the most relaxed fashion, but his pupils never left the aged ranger.

Horten sat down before he unrolled the parchment onto the table to reveal a large, colorful map. The hand-painted masterpiece was of the mighty kingdom of Lageheim, but it included our Hidden Valley and other surrounding lands.

"I know you have never traveled far beyond our valley, except for maybe going to the inn. Is that true?" Horten asked.

"Basically true. I have tagged along on patrols with other rangers to the south, a few miles beyond the Pass. And I travelled a few miles along the Forest Road. My mother took me to HaerenVale when I was young. I lived among the elfin for a few months." Barely able to find our valley on the map made me feel naïve of the world. I had traveled so little in comparison.

"That's right, I remember now. I guess it did not go well with the elfin?"

"I made friends but did not find a close friend. The elfin did not treat us harshly, just seemed disinterested. I was not one of them and lived more in line with the pace of men. The elfin of HaerenVale are not kin, but my mother stated she did not expect any better reception if we traveled across the VenKeth to her home. Elfin differ from men."

Horten looked at me with compassion. "I know elfin do not tolerate mixed unions. Humans are more tolerant, but most also consider it improper to marry because offspring are rare and usually sterile. But your circumstance is not from rebellion on your part, and we here at the abbey have always considered you one of us. Some would even say special. You belong here with us."

"Thank you. I know that. I have always felt the abbey is my home."

"Good. Now let's look at this map." Horten pointed out the various features as he spoke. "The Kingdom of Lageheim is divided into thirteen dukedoms called Protectorates, named after the former sub-tribes of Tyria. Fourteen if you count the Gaderon region. King Reinhart rules from the city of Gaderon. I hope you know this already or I failed at my teaching. The Protectorate of Wynchell sits in the frontier region against the Towering Peaks and by the north corner of the VenKeth. The rivers Gaderon and Kwit, which come together at the southern end in white cascades, define the region best. White Cliff is the principal city, which stands high above the junction of the rivers on pale limestone cliffs. I haven't been there in many years, but it is a lovely place."

"How far away is that?" I asked as I studied the map.

"About the same distance as the elfin kingdom, over here to the east. The artist did not mark the elfin territories on this map, but it is in this region of the VenKeth." Horten swirled his finger over the forest region next to the mountains. "It will take about ten days on foot to get to Wynchell, no matter which way you go."

"Should I travel the Threshold Ridge, like I did on my patrol? That is the way Kjell and Meinrad went." I felt uncertain about what to do.

"Rangers prefer the wilderness routes, I admit. You could follow the Hidden Creek to where it turns west and cuts through the ridge. It eventually spills into the Gaderon River about here, in the Protectorate of Erian, south of Wynchell. But that area is mostly uninhabited and there is no way across the river, except to swim. Maybe you could wave down a lumber boat heading downriver, but they would probably suspect you are a bandit and will not stop. Or perhaps they may even think you are some Fae creature trying to lure them into the forest. It should be faster to take the highways through Lageheim."

"The wilderness sounds like an interesting route, but I will do as you suggest. No matter how I go, it will be a new adventure," I said.

"It would be a good idea to find out any news at the inn first. And get some of Enna's honey cakes for the road."

That convinced me!

It took me a few days to prepare before leaving for my big adventure, but then I set off early. Each of my mentors gave me a few final tips and made sure I did not forget anything. My mother went over various herbs and their uses to be sure I remembered, though she had taught me my entire life.

Finally, she gave me a hug and wished me safe travels, making me promise to send word back.

Another delight came from Gwyn, my mother's garden assistant. Though I courted her, she ended up choosing a respectful villager from Stonecrest over this sterile, half-elfin adventurer. She wanted a secure home and a family, and she knew I would leave eventually. I could not blame her, I guess, but my heart still ached. She gave me a long hug and wished me a successful journey. I peered into her smiling face, etching the memory into my mind.

The last words of wisdom came from Maistren Lilke, as he leaned on his staff. "Remember, young Galieb N'ethilion Half-elfin, son of Edhelwen, we send you not only to fight eshkin and not to win personal glory. We send you to do good as we, the Qoholet, humbly understand it. A universal morality that is embedded into creation itself. We send you to grow in wisdom and understanding, seeking to find the Yett Sorr, the One who is eternal in existence, and the source of all things, both seen and unseen."

CHAPTER 5
KNIGHTS AND HONEY CAKES

The worn but pleasant trail from the abbey to the remote Forest Road climbed up over the ridge out of the Hidden Valley as it meandered south. It took me hours of hiking with a full pack to reach the junction (hidden by brush) with the Forest Road. From there, it was just a few short miles west and out of the forest to reach my destination.

The sun sat lower in the sky as I reached the inn, all the trees casting long shadows across the grasslands. The summer afternoon waned, but I had a few hours until darkness fell.

The lone building of pale stone stood defiantly on the edge of the wild, far from its nearest neighbor. Mighty hardwoods spilled down off Threshold Ridge and crept onto the grassy plains, with a few of the twisted oaks cluttering around the tavern as if claiming it for their own. The beautiful structure seemed both an outgrowth of the forest and the last reach of civilization, yet aloof from both. One of the tall, twisted oaks came into view first, the white giant's overhanging canopy bringing to mind a mother hen brooding over its stony chick. A low branch spiraled out in angular bends at just the ideal height, appearing coaxed into the position by a master gardener. Maybe it was. One never knew about elfin. A wooden sign hung off the ivory-colored branch, suspended on two dull brass chains. Carved into the center of the sign stood a leaping deer painted in a chestnut hue, its chin set regally. A crown of bright gold sat upon its head, encircling the base of impressive antlers. *The Royal Stag* read across the bottom, etched with a gold hue.

"The Inn at the Forest's Edge," as it is named in songs, is no longer a quiet place since the Goblin War a few years back. The story of the stable boy's rescue of the elfin princess from the goblin king spread a new fame of the tavern and the Venerable Woods. Adventurers and bards of all kinds came from far and wide to learn the tale or to seek their own glory under the ancient canopy.

The fools.

Others came just to say they stayed at the renowned tavern. Johann, the heroic stable boy of these tales, now lives among the elfin, exploring the Fae Lands with the hornless unicorn, Silvian. According to the bard and the innkeepers, Johann continues his martial training, and they say that one day his skills will match any elfin in HaerenVale.

The overflowing stables around the back told me the place was not only busy, but at peak capacity. I almost did not go inside, for I preferred the quiet woods and quaint villages of the valley. Crowds of unknown persons were intimidating and made me feel vulnerable, not that I could claim lots of experience with such things. Being a half-elfin outsider did not help. But the lure of honey cakes and the need for news caused me to open the door with reluctance. After all, both were the reasons I came.

The heavy wooden door swung open on near silent iron strap hinges. Burning wicks and roasting stew invaded my nostrils. Loud chatter mixed with the occasional ringing of metal assaulted my ears. It felt warm and stuffy compared to the open air, but the room seemed well lit. Candles sat on the tables, dim lanterns adorned the walls, and elegant glowing orbs hovered against the ceiling, sustained by elfin magic.

Standing just inside the closed door, I assessed my situation. A few eyes glanced my way, but most focused on the sword fight on the far side of the room. Such events happened regularly here. The elfin Baralas is not only a bard, but a master duelist. He pays out coveted gold pinnacles to any challengers who beat him, but it only ever happened once. I never wasted my meager wealth on the challenge, but many young adventurers did, hoping to win the heavy ten-gold coin. Not to mention basking in the glory that would come from besting the notorious entertainer.

Minted by the Merchants Lords to the south at the Cat Paw Lakes, pinnacles were the largest and most prized coin in the world, as were all coins minted by the Lords, for all known civilizations desired them. I guessed that each Merchant Lord owned chests full of the pinnacles, but it took a simple laborer most of a year to earn the worth of one.

The duel ended in shame for the young swaggering rogue. His companions laughed but patted him on the back as the rest of the patrons cheered the bard. Observing their clothes, I guessed the youths came from Thalassa, a neighboring kingdom to the south, seeking excitement.

At another table sat two dwarfin, most likely from the Underhalls of Volberg. Leaving their extensive halls was a rare thing. Morgrim, the dwarfin stable hand, stood chiding them like old friends.

Plenty of travelers filled the seats. One of the most intriguing was a small band of well-armed adventurers. The middle-aged woman with cropped blonde hair stood out as their leader. The abundant years of hardship exposed by her eyes weakened the once attractive face.

A few other travelers sat in long robes of summer wool, with scrolls sticking out of pouches, ink and pens hanging from their belts. It was obvious even to me, despite my sheltered life, that they were Lageheim clerics. Law Speakers. Scholars who memorized and interpreted the Law, known as the Lage, and spoke in the courts of the kingdom.

The Lage or "the Law." The foundation of this mighty kingdom of Lageheim. Centuries ago, Walferd the Just discovered the Law among the Shepherd Kings of the south. Committing himself to their ways and their God, he brought the law back to his people and named it *the Lage* in the local dialect. After uniting all the clans, they crowned him king of Lageheim. That was eight hundred years ago, and none dared to challenge Lageheim's might.

An overabundance of locals and commoners crowded the bar stools or leaned in corners. There seemed to be more of the duke's soldiers present than usual, too.

And that man sitting alone in the abacot cap and fine linen robes, with numerous pouches across his belt? Is he a wizard?

Something was afoot.

At a table along the back wall sat two large men in linen gambesons, and tabards of blue and gold. *Lageheimers, for sure, but not from the Protectorate of Baldice. More than just knights of the realm. Sworn paladins of some order.*

The tall, young one waved me over to the empty chair at their table. I took it. The only other choice was the wizard's table, and I didn't want to sit with him. Apparently, no one else did either. If you can't trust a knight, who can you trust?

As I settled in, their eyes ventured to my ears, then my beard. Yes, I am a half-blood! The conversation I just had with Horten came to mind. My face soured a little, I am sure, despite my efforts to be unreadable. The older man frowned, but the younger tried to be polite.

"Greetings, uh, sir." The younger stumbled, not sure how to address me. "I am Erik Blackmane. It is most pleasant to have your company."

Wow! One of the Blackmanes. The Blackmanes bred the finest war horses in this part of the world. The most expensive, too. A thick, black mane of hair covered his head, but the family name came from the distinctive horses, not the other way around.

Brown eyes peered into my blues as we assessed each other.

"Galieb at your service. I appreciate your kind offer of a seat in such a crowded place."

His age seemed comparable to mine, so perhaps he has not taken his oaths yet. Even seated, he was half a head taller than everyone else in the room.

"Galieb, this is Sir Lucian Radbourn, my commander," Blackmane said as he motioned to his companion.

Another influential name. Radbourns are close relations to the wealthy Duke Theomund, a close relative to the king.

"Greetings," the commander replied. "Would it be too bold to state you are a ranger? One of the Qoholet?"

"You know of the Qoholet?" My surprise seeped through my voice, and I forgot the formalities. We didn't like being noticed. *Maybe I should not have admitted that yet. Another mistake! Being out in the world differed from going through training.*

Sir Lucian gave a chuckle. "I cannot speak for Erik, but I've encountered a few rangers in my time. They all impressed me. I am disappointed to learn they allowed such—unnatural unions, however." He frowned again at my ears. "Our Law dissuades such marriages. But I forget my manners. You seem

42

young despite your beard. Are you a full ranger, or still an acolyte?"

"I passed all the tests," I confirmed between clenched teeth, irritated by his comment. *Maybe the wizard would like some company.*

"Sir Lucian, we must be gracious. We all fall short of the Law. Please, Galieb, we mean no offense," Erik said in an attempt to smooth over his lord's bluntness. "We know not the circumstance of your past."

"Tis true." Sir Lucian gave a deep sigh to control himself. "I upset myself with all that we have seen in recent days. It seems too many forget the Law and follow strange ways. We even encountered a sacrificial altar for a foreign god. Blasphemy! Not to mention rumors of this brown robed wanderer questioning the Lage."

"Galieb, are you familiar with this? Others tell us of an old, robed man called the 'Wandering Eye' going from town to town preaching contrary philosophies. To see our own citizens doubt the goodness of the Lage weighs on our hearts." Erik added.

I responded with a negative as the elfin innkeeper, Erdan Silverfrond, interrupted to take our orders. I ordered my favorite meal here: the beef stew with fresh baked sourdough bread smothered in hand-churned butter. The knights each ordered the house specialty of seasoned pheasant. Erik asked for a hearty ale while Lucian requested an elfin wine. Drinking alcohol sparingly, I preferred their specialty elixir made by the elfin from flower nectar, grapes, and berries. Few knew that the best cuisine served here came from the elfin kingdom of HaerenVale. I also ordered enough honey cakes for all, hoping to appease these newcomers to the inn.

Time to turn the conversation. "I assume you are knights of Lageheim. May I ask what order your colors represent?"

"Defenders of the Lage," Sir Lucian responded with an air of confidence. "Defenders answer only to the Law and the Lag Giefan, that is the Law Giver. We have also sworn allegiance to the king, of course, as long as he follows the Lage."

"I heard you are the best," I said out loud as I searched my brain to remember what I knew about this Order. Several popular stories tell of heroic Defenders defeating giants, basilisks, dragons, hordes of goblins, and even demons. Who knows how much was true, but they won many of the king's tournaments.

"Ranger Galieb, may I clarify?" Erik asked. "I have not yet taken my oaths. I am still considered a squire. They have not yet fully accepted me into the order."

Sir Lucian grunted. "Such modesty. Soon, Erik. Remember his name, young ranger. Erik Blackmane will be one of the finest paladins since Walferd the Just knighted Sir Reinhart. And Erik is more gracious than most, including myself."

"You are too kind, sir." Erik nodded his head at his mentor.

I had to admit that I liked Erik. "What brings you to this inn?" I asked. "A quest? Testing your resolve against the dark creatures of the VenKeth?"

"Nothing so adventurous, I fear," Sir Lucian stated, waving in dismissal. "Lady Zebah of the Lakes, daughter of the Merchant Queen Chennai, will pass this way. She is to marry Lord Archibald, the son of Duke Theomund in the coming days. Many say she is the most beautiful woman alive. We plan to become part of the Lady's escort."

My eyebrows went up. *Most beautiful woman? Daughter of the merchant queen? This would explain the crowd and the soldiers. Still, this inn seems to be in the middle of nowhere for knights and wizards to watch a parade.*

"I would expect such noble paladins to greet the lady at the

Duke of Baldice's castle or at the crossroads of Giefanfeld," I inquired.

"Our Order does not approve of this unholy union." Sir Lucian's frown returned, and his eyebrows furrowed. "I spoke against it to the duke. Who knows what gods she worships? What law she follows? 'Queen' Chennai," he spoke the title with disdain, "will not say who the father is. She never married, but most suppose she frolics among the men of her court. It's not surprising for the Merchant Lords to act in that way. All is permissible along the Lakes. They care for naught but wealth and power. I fear the duke may have forgotten as well. His already substantial worth will more than double with this marriage. His influence, too. Both him and his son seem completely smitten with the maiden since their journey to the Lakes. I fear for the kingdom. If it ever falls, it will fall from within." He finished his short tirade with a fist on the table, but then calmed himself. "Forgive me for my poor manners. I must stop before my rudeness gets away from me and I dishonor the order."

"Your frustration is understandable, my lord," Erik assured his mentor. "None in the order want to see our ways forgotten. The Law made our kingdom mighty. Perhaps she desires to learn the Lage. Our own good Queen Adeline, many blessings upon her, trained as a Druen, worshiping nature in her former days. Now she sees the wisdom of the Lage and the Law Giver."

"We can only hope," Lucian muttered.

A young barmaid in a blue sleeveless dress approached with our food. The short puffy sleeves of the white undershirt brushed my face as she placed the food and drinks on our table in the crowded place. As she wiped her hands on her stained apron and left, we all focused on our plates.

Sir Lucian spoke a rote blessing before we ate.

Erik turned back to me as Lucian ate in silence. "To answer

your question, we desired a pilgrimage to the famed tavern. Does a knight need an excuse to visit a place where such noble deeds occurred? We will join her procession from here. To aid with protection, yes, but mostly to learn more about her. The Lady has her own elite guard, as well as the soldiers of Duke Theomund and the local lords. I also hear she is a gifted magic user."

That piqued my interest, causing my eyes to focus on his. Magic does not come easy for most humans.

Erik turned the subject back to me. "So, what of yourself? If not to see the Lady, then what brings you to this remote inn? What are the duties of rangers?"

The maid returned with a basket of golden honey cakes. "Enna's honey cakes always bring me here," I said with a smile to lighten the mood as I selected one of the tasty treats. "I hope that is something you both will appreciate. News is another. Rangers spend too much time in the wilderness and don't always know of noteworthy events, such as a nobleman's wedding. But I have another concern. Are you good knights aware of any eshkin raids anywhere in the kingdom?"

"Eshkin raids?" Erik asked. "None that we have heard. The Lord Defender mentioned it not before we left, and no one on the roads spoke of eshkin. Why do you inquire about such things?"

Lucian paused his fork halfway to his mouth.

"I encountered a small party north of here a few days ago," I said. "Along the forest's ridge. If they are near here, Wynchell may be next, if they have not already attacked there."

"What became of the ones you encountered?" Erik asked.

"They are dead."

"Impressive, ranger!" Erik exclaimed.

"Not all by my hand. I only killed two, and I almost didn't make it."

"Still a respectable feat," Sir Lucian said. "Not everyone who meet eshkin survive. Most likely they were just a small party out of the Peaks. My experience of them—and I have encountered a few—is that they cannot stay organized. I am sure the knights of Wynchell can handle any raids. Rare, but not an unheard of hazard along our northern borders." He focused back on his food.

Someone plucked the strings of a lute, and all in the tavern hushed. Baralas now sat on a stool and enchanted all with one of his ballads as only an elfin bard can.

IN WESTERN LANDS, against the seas,
    Abundant waters and rich in trees,
    Mountains guard the northern flanks,
    And lush fields touch the River's banks.

TYRIR ONCE RULED this wealthy realm,
    With hounds and hawks and a mighty helm.
    In joy, he chased both boar and deer;
    And feasted much from his spear.

THE MEN of old served him fair,
    Portions to their god, with little care.
    Twelve tribes arose, with each in strife,
    Craved much in deeds, but cared less for life.

FROM HERE CAME FORTH, one of their own,
    A knight quest bound, name now renowned;
    Walferd the First, a wanderer bold

Sought with his heart, wisdom of old.

MOUNTAINS, jungles—many lands he roamed
    Far east and west, for truth, he combed.
    Mystics he sought, and elfin lore
    But no peace he found in his deep core.

IN DRY PLACES far south of here
    Wise men he met that had no fear;
    Shepherd Kings' wise ways, he learned,
    their Laws in hand, to his land returned.

EALDURN FIRST CAME to see law's light
    While other tribes held fast the night;
    Through truth and honor and might of deed
    And by the Giver's grace, he did succeed.

SOON KNOWN to all as a noble knight
    Judgments he made both wise and right.
    All crowned him now Walferd the Just
    For in his Law they now do trust.

TYRIR NO LONGER RULES this land
    The scepter rests in the Giver's hand.
    No longer do men live with much strife
    The kingdom rules with abundant life.

CHAPTER 6
A COT WITH A VIEW

Baralas sang all the chords of the saga of Walferd the
Just, the first king of Lageheim, each verse lifting us to
faraway lands and heroic times.

After the bard finished, I opened my mouth, prepared to
excuse myself and leave. Before I could do so, the lone wizard
approached our table, adjusting his robe and cap as if overly
concerned with his appearance. The robe itself was of rich
scarlet linen threaded with gold. He kept both his wavy straw-
berry blond hair and his beard neatly trimmed. His posture
was precise, walking with a straight back.

The Defenders stood to greet the man. I followed their
lead. Elfin can sense the radiance given off by all created things
more acutely than men, and even as a half-elfin, I noticed an
overabundance of magical energy around the wizard. Far more
than any other human I had yet encountered. Lady Valda, the
only mage I knew, seemed no different than any other human.
A confusing, yet unique experience indeed.

"Greetings, good sirs," the newcomer stated. He had an air
of nobility and confidence, his body looking a fit middle-age,

but behind his eyes he seemed ancient. "Please call me Aurel. It seems many are here to see Lady Zebah. Do you plan to escort her entourage to Theorn?"

"My lord, yes, that is our intentions," Sir Lucian said. He then introduced us all. "Please join us. Perhaps we have similar plans?"

"I regret my plans take me elsewhere. Forgive me for eaves-dropping, but I overheard part of your conversation and have an inquiry for the half-elfin, if I may?"

I stiffened. Catching the attention of a wizard is rarely wise. *Maybe I need to wear my hood up.* Rangers never appreciate being noticed, but drawing the eye of a wizard in a crowded tavern made me feel like the bard's next act. The entire tavern must be watching.

I nodded, but avoided his focused gaze.

"Ranger Galieb, you mentioned encountering eshkin, I believe?"

I nodded again with a glance at his face, and his eyes seized mine.

"Where was this, and how many were there?"

"In the forest, north of here. Along the ridge. I saw four." To not answer truthfully seemed foolish under his scrutiny. Not that I had planned otherwise.

"And they are all dead? You killed four eshkin? I have my doubts, young Qoholet."

"Forgive me for the confusion, good sir." I said, trying to remember proper Lageheim mannerisms. "One lay dead, so I followed their trail to the others. I only killed two. As for the fourth, his companions killed him when they fought among themselves."

"As is always the case. Two eshkin is still impressive for one so young. The reputation of the rangers precedes you, and you uphold that notoriety. My compliments to your mentors and yourself."

"I only defended myself."

"Are you aware of any other raids?" the wizard said, continuing his inquiry. "You seemed concerned about Wynchell."

"I do not have any news. That is all I can tell you." His eyes released me and I focused my gaze on the wood grains of the table.

"I will pass this information onto those who need to hear it. Thank you for defending the realm." A gold coin appeared in his hand, which he placed before me on the table. Stamped on the side facing up was the silhouette of King Reinhart. A gold crown, minted by the royalty of Lageheim. On the other side was a stamp of a crown, hence the name. "Honest information is always worth the price, even from a miser like myself. Now, please forgive my intrusion. It is time for me to retire to my room. Good evening, gentlemen." I looked at the coin before slipping it into my pouch. It was the first gold coin I ever owned. As valuable as it was, ten of them would not quite match the pinnacle the bard put up as a prize.

I breathed a sigh of relief and used his departure to thank the paladins and scamper for the door. Despite the added gold, in my pouch were my meager life savings, and I did not waste it on a room, but knew of a place to camp closer to the King's Highway. Many miles lay ahead of me yet, and every step counted.

"It was a delight to have met you. Let me walk you out, my new friend." Erik stood and reached out his hand to let me pass first. "I pray we break bread together again, soon."

"Do not let his manners fool you, Galieb," Sir Lucian commented. "He cannot let two hours pass without checking on his horse. Such are the ways of Blackmanes. Safe travels, young ranger."

IT TOOK me three uneventful days to reach the Seven Arches Bridge by foot. Formed of cut limestone, the bridge spans the Gaderon River at its easternmost crossing. Almost all the waters of Lageheim are tributaries of the mighty Gaderon, which flows harmoniously across the land before endlessly feeding the Desolate Sea. The great river itself starts its journey in the heights of the Towering Peaks, skirts the VenKeth on its way south before sweeping west across the center of the kingdom, dividing the land into two unequal halves.

Standing on the banks of the river, I grimaced at the currents flowing under the bridge, carrying barges, fishing boats, and various waterfowl with it. A high stone tower stood over each end of the bridge, designed with a gated tunnel with which everyone desiring to cross must pass through. Apparently, the guards of Seven Arches are less familiar with rangers than knights and wizards because they refused me passage across into the Protectorate of Erian. With the approach of the Lady Zebah, I was too heavily armed for their liking. If I assassinated the fiancé of Lord Archibald in the Protectorate of Baldice, that was the Duke of Baldice's problem, but it would not happen in Erian under these guards' watch.

So, I stomped back to Travailin, a large town just a mile or two south of the bridge, to spend some of my limited coin and figure out a way across.

Maybe I should have gone through the wilderness after all.

Travailin grew around the crossroads of the King's Highway and the Theorn Road. Not a large settlement by any means, but all three villages in the Hidden Valley combined could fit inside of this town. Such bustling places intimidated a wilderness wanderer like me. I could not imagine what large cities would be like.

Half-timbered structures of wattle and daub with red-tiled roofs overhung narrow cobblestone streets. Humans in the hundreds clopped about on errands unknown, including merchants, farmers, craftsmen, soldiers, knights, and clerics. An occasional elfin, dwarfin, or gnomin mixed among the humans with little trouble. Moving about the open streets made me feel exposed, so I hugged the buildings as best I could and avoided the center. I felt surrounded as I walked with one hand wrapped around my coin pouch with continued glances over my shoulder. Civilized places such as this had reputations of abundant thievery to those of us in the countryside.

One of those glances revealed two men in drab, off white tunics several paces behind me. One had an eager grin on his face, which stood out from the preoccupied countenances of everyone else. Further glances revealed that they still followed and worked their way closer, passing signals to each other. It did not take the local thieves long to mark me as an outsider and chose me as a target. Just before their sticky fingers reached my valuables, I twisted to plant my back against a wall as my eyes bored into their souls. Hovering too close for polite society, they avoided my glares with sheepish glances in all directions. Like shadows in a dark alley, they quickly blended once again into the crowd. I knew they would be back. Along with more skilled rogues. The abundance of soldiers on every street did not deter them.

A sympathetic baker in the market pointed out a pleasant tavern on the main avenue, which I ducked into, hoping to calm my agitated nerves. The place was less than half full, many folks being out and about during the daylight hours. The rest sat nursing drinks as if waiting for something.

"Welcome!" stated the innkeeper, a portly man with thinning hair. He wiped his hands on his apron and pushed up the loose sleeves of his red under-tunic out of habit. "Looking for a room?"

"Anything available for someone of my limited status?"

The proprietor looked me over, one side of his mouth raised. He scratched at his sideburns and pulled at a heavy mustache, which seemed to be the latest fashion among the middle class in these parts. "I have a cot in the attic. Three copper commons for a night.

I guess I looked as frugal as I implied, despite my weapons and armor. Everyone prized the Lake coins over those minted in Lageheim, but most people in this part of the world still valued the royal currency. The lowest valued coin was the 'common,' a plain copper with a large 'C' on it. Five commons made a 'daily,' or a half-silver piece that was the standard wage for most workers: one daily per day. It was enough to provide for a small family, but one would never become wealthy by honest means. Two daily's or ten commons equaled a full silver called a 'noble.' Most of the everyday activity of the realm used these three coins to conduct business. Among the wealthy, gold was more plentiful, like the gold 'crown' the wizard gave me back at the inn. The crown equaled ten nobles, not to mention a hundred commons, or twenty daily's, to give the idea how long it took to earn the value of one. The realm produced a five gold coin known as a 'mage,' but they were uncommon, as those who had such wealth preferred the currency of the Lakes.

I had several pouches of commons, daily's, and nobles, so I could spare a few coppers for a cot. "Sounds reasonable. I will take it, I suppose."

"Just so you know, a man rented the cot a few days ago, but never showed up. I will tell him I gave it to you if he does."

"I do not want any trouble." Civilization was already becoming too much trouble.

"I do not expect him. It has been three days. So, are you in town to glimpse the Lady of the Lakes?"

"Just passing through."

"They say she is the most beautiful woman you will ever see. And one of the wealthiest. I do not want to miss that!" He lowered his voice. "Please refrain from mentioning my excitement to my wife."

I nodded. "Have any stew?"

"The Chicken and dumplings is warm."

"Sounds great. Any bread?"

"I have some left over from yesterday. I will give you a few slices at no cost."

"Much obliged. When is the Lady supposed to arrive?"

"Any time now!" The innkeeper blushed with excitement.

Rats.

My best efforts to stay ahead of her train and get to Wynchell as fast as possible were to no avail. Thinking of attractive women brought to mind two beautiful young lady friends from back at the abbey. Both the acolyte Derika and my mother's assistant, Gwyn, had chosen others over me, so the thought of encountering a highborn woman too aloof to notice this backwoodsman stirred up some past resentment. I tried to focus on my current problem of getting past the bridge guards, or at least convince them of my innocence.

I found a corner of the dining area to hide in and kept my back to the wall. After finishing my dumplings, I grabbed the attic key and climbed up the stairs to find my bed. A closed door on a side hall revealed a second set of steps leading to the attic. I found the door unlocked, but locked it behind me to keep everyone else out. The street thieves made me more cautious. Up in the attic, my room comprised nothing more than a cot, a cold, half-melted candle, and a small dresser, all behind a dusty curtain. The roof slanted down at a steep angle, making the space even smaller. Extra bed frames, extra dressers, and chests full of linen, all covered in a thin dust, cluttered the rest of the attic, giving it a musty odor. At least there was a small window off the end of the building, right next to the bed.

I threw my pack, war bow, and quiver on the cot, and enjoyed a good relaxing stretch. I opened the shutters to let in some clean air and light. The window opened right over the wide main street. My view comprised the busy cobblestone streets below and the roofs of the facing buildings.

Across the street, and two buildings west from my room, a man in a hood watched the streets from a small window similar to mine.

As I took in my setting, a distant trumpet sounded to my left, drawing everyone's attention. People poured into the already crowded streets, including the innkeeper, a woman I assumed was his wife, and his staff.

"Much better view from here, and no crowds. No cutpurses, either," I muttered to myself.

Men dressed in mail and metal caps—most walking, but some on horses—came round the corner first, pushing the crowds to the sides of the wide street. One-handed arming swords, and tabards of red and white marked them as local men-at-arms. The parade followed close behind and soon came into view.

Following behind the men-at-arms, at the front of the column, a man rode with an open-faced helmet and half plate armor that reached down to his thighs, all shining bright like a mirror, trimmed in genuine gold. Five indigo swan's feathers decorated his helm, marking him as someone of higher rank. He was an officer of the elite mercenaries known as the Kiavonians, the personal bodyguards of the wealthiest Merchant Lords on the Cat Paw Lakes.

At his hip bounced a one-handed sword. Though it was too far to see yet, I knew it was a half-basket hilted sword with a bronze pommel shaped into a cat's paw.

My hand wrapped around the hilt of the fine sword on my hip.

Quality weapons by any human standards, but the Kiavonian smiths cannot match the skills of dwarfin artisans. Angedon had once been a Kiavonian blade. My father had served as one of these same guards before he turned bandit and slave trader. Distaste for these men grows, though I do not know them except by reputation.

Kiavonians had a reputation for coldness and professionalism.

The procession drew closer, bringing me back to the present. Next to the first officer rode a knight in full armor, his helm hanging from his saddle. A long sword, mace, and heater shield also hung from his horse. The red and yellow of his tabard marked him as a knight from the Protectorate of Theomund. Behind the two leaders rode six more Kiavonian guards in pairs, armed with their signature swords, pikes, and crossbows, and dressed in similar armor to their captain, their faces just as expressionless.

After a small gap in the procession, an ornate carriage rolled slowly along the street. A Kiavonian with a crossbow in hand sat next to the driver, and two attendants stood perfectly straight on the back. Hawk-headed steeds the size of draft horses pulled the carriage, their fierce gaze causing the crowds to shrink back as they approached. More fearless than equines, and far more dangerous, they tended not to be skittish, making them a rare prize among the highest elite.

As I watched the procession through the window, I heard the squeak of the door hinges at the bottom of the stairs.

I thought I locked that. Did the innkeeper have another key? I could see the man and his staff in the streets, so it could not be them.

The steps creaked as someone moved up the stairs towards me.

Perhaps the other guest showed up after all. He must have had the same idea I had of watching the procession away from the crowds. But where did he get a key?

I turned to greet the man as his hooded head rose from the stairwell and became visible above the floor.

For just one second, we stared at each other without moving. At first, nothing suggested he was anything other than a local commoner, although I imagined him being too hot under the hood.

"The innkeeper—" was all I got out before he lifted a crossbow and fired at me.

I dodged as best I could in the small space, landing on my side on the floor, the dart sinking deep into the windowsill.

The man cursed as he dropped the crossbow and slid a long but slim dagger out of its sheath.

I shifted my feet under me to stand, but the assassin got there first. He stood over me and struck downward with an overhanded blow.

Using my left hand, I blocked and twisted his wrist as I pulled him down next to me. I tried to get the advantage by rolling on top, but we ended up grappling on the floor, punching and kneeing each other.

We collided with the dresser, dropping the candle on top of us. Our faces got tangled in the dusty curtain, causing us both to spit and cough.

Neither of us managed an advantage until I grabbed his right elbow with my right hand and yanked towards me, still twisting the wrist with the dagger in it with my left. He screamed in pain as his arm dislocated from the shoulder.

I snatched his dagger and almost instinctively stabbed him in the heart. That is how they drilled the training in us. Checking my actions, I stuck it in my belt instead.

He glared at me as he held his arm. I rolled him over on his stomach and tied his hands behind his back with his belt, bringing more screams. The entire fight only took a minute. Too much noise came up from the street for anyone to hear.

I caught my breath and allowed my heart to slow down. From the corner of my eye, I noticed the other hooded man I had seen earlier in the window across the street. His hood matched the one my prisoner wore.

A crossbow rested in his hands as well.

The captain and his knight companion reached the front of the inn. Grabbing my bow, I notched an arrow, taking aim at the second assassin. He held the loaded crossbow out of the window, pointing it down at a target behind the carriage.

I hesitated.

Killing eshkin in self-defense was one thing. Shooting a human who didn't even see me was another. My mind raced between various actions. What would happen if I did not stop him? This man planned to murder someone. Just like the one at my feet tried to murder me. Was there another option that did not include death?

No.

Sweat poured off my forehead as I screamed, "Assassins!" out the window.

My arrow caught the hooded man in the torso, pushing him back into the room. The bolt released as the crossbow dropped to the crowd below.

I stumbled back into the room as two other bolts shot upward, hitting the shutters next to my head.

My prisoner tried to get up and scamper away as men burst

59

into the inn and rushed up the stairs towards us. I planted my foot on his back, bringing forth another scream.

I held my bow over my head with both hands as the men-at-arms came up, crossbows and swords pointed at my chest.

"Hold! I am not your enemy!" I shouted.

"Give up your weapons!"

"Here is the man you want." I nudged his arm with my foot, causing him to cry again. I set my bow on the bed, making slow movements and keeping my hands open.

"Ranger Galieb, is that you?" Behind the men-at-arms stood a fully armored man with his sword drawn and his visor open.

"Erik! Tell them I am not an assassin!"

"I thought you were going to Wynchell?"

"It seems delays are my fate."

After confiscating all my weapons, Erik lead the way as the Kiavonian guards escorted me and the prisoner down to the excited street.

"Someone help!" a man in the streets pleaded. "We need a healer! Our daughter! Help us!"

Men-at-arms and guards surrounded the luxurious carriage, swords and crossbows in hand. Behind the carriage crouched a crying mother, holding a small girl covered in blood and struggling to breathe. A man stood weeping behind them with his hand on the mother's shoulder. Next to them kneeled another woman, dressed in white and gold, with a headdress of indigo swan feathers.

My chest tightened. *Did I cause that?* I started forward to help, but guards restrained me.

"Whose this half-blood? Another assassin?" sneered the officer from the head of the column. The knight of Theomund stood next to him.

"No, Captain. He is the one who alerted us to the attack,"

Erik stated matter-of-factly as he moved next to me. "Ranger Galieb disabled this assassin here and most likely saved the lady's life."

"How well do you know this man, squire?" the knight of Theomund challenged.

"If Erik, an esquire of the Defenders of the Lage, says it is true, take him at his word, good sirs. I always do." Sir Lucian turned from standing over the woman with the headdress, his long sword also unsheathed. Both the Theomund knight and the captain eyed me sideways, unconvinced.

"She's alive! Our sweet Odell is alive! Thank you! Thank you, my lady!" the father shouted as he hugged his wife and daughter. "Truly, we are all blessed with your arrival!"

We all turned back toward the scene behind the carriage as a stunning young woman stood to face me. Her milk-white hair poured down to the small of her back like cream from a jar. Eyes as gold as the bracelets on her wrists stared out of a stunning countenance of soft brown. Framing her face was a headdress of indigo swan feathers attached to a golden circlet with complimenting earrings. Her knee-length linen tunic matched her white hair and golden eyes. Blue tights revealed shapely legs, and leather wrapped sandals covered her feet and calves.

Magical grace radiated from every pore. Truly, before me, stood the most beautiful woman alive. Even a backwoods ranger could see that.

CHAPTER 7
THE MOST BEAUTIFUL WOMAN ALIVE

"Ranger Galieb, your quick thinking saved lives."

When Lady Zebah of the Lakes spoke, it was as if angels were singing. My eyes locked on her lips as they moved, they too being speckled as if with gold dust.

"I would be pleased to have you join us on our journey to Theorn."

I could feel her charm wrap its arms around me and draw me in. Images of intimacy danced across my mind, dreams of eternal love. No other could compare to this woman who stood before me. Perhaps here was one who would truly love me as I am. Desire pounded against my will, pulled against its grip, whispered in my ears.

But as I imagined many beautiful futures with Lady Zebah, deep down, I knew it could not be true. Such women do not settle for ones such as me, but marry the richest, the most powerful, and the most handsome.

Hope lingered, but doubt overwhelmed it, breaking the spell. Elfin naturally resisted magical charms, or I would have been hers.

Shaking myself from the dream, my emotions crashed from the euphoric ideal, and my head swam. My heart pounded. My knees faltered but did not buckle. Running all the way to Wynchell would have drained me less.

I regained myself before answering.

"I, uh, I would...be honored, my lady. However, need takes me elsewhere. I will gladly accompany you as far as I am able."

Everything in me told me to flee before I did something foolish. But in the back of my mind, I knew I still needed a way across the bridge.

"Don't insult the Lady!" the captain threatened, drawing his sword half out of the scabbard. Sir Lucian turned red with anger, and even Erik scowled. Every soldier and guard within earshot glared at me, ready to cut me to pieces.

Zebah gazed at me with uncertainty for just a moment, then the confidence returned to her eyes. "Calm yourself, captain. I need you to find every assassin and execute them. Immediately."

The men all stood uncertain at the sudden command, ready to defend their lady from my perceived insubordination, yet knowing they must obey her order.

Erik cleared his throat before speaking. "Forgive me for speaking out of turn, my lady. Perhaps we should question these assassins. Find out who hired them."

"Hired by rivals who dislike our alliance, I am sure, good squire. Such is life on the Lakes." A stern face turned to the leader. "Immediately, Captain. We need to send a message."

"Immediately, my lady!" The captain snapped and several men rushed to do her bidding.

"Ranger Galieb, stay with us until you must depart." That sultry voice probed for a weakness in my defenses. "Return his weapons to him. We may all need them again." She smiled with her golden eyes still on me.

My heart pounded. *Run, you fool!* But I did not. "I am honored," I stated, hoping not to get knifed in the back for any clumsiness on my part, but everyone relaxed at her words. It felt better to be armed again.

"What is the delay?" A woman twice the age of Zebah shouted out of the open door of the carriage. A loose, short-sleeved silk dress reached to her feet as exotic striped furs hung across her shoulders. The bright colors complimented her dark skin.

"A peasant girl was injured, Queen Mother," Zebah responded.

"Well, get her out of the way! Call the healers. They can help her. We need to continue!"

"She is being cared for. We are leaving now, Queen Mother. Captain, are we ready?"

"Yes, my lady. All as you commanded is done."

Erik, concerned for the injured girl, checked with the family, but the girl now smiled and laughed and praised the lady.

I tried to settle with the innkeeper for any trouble I brought to his business, but Sir Lucian interrupted. He paid for the damages and arranged for cleanup, making sure the Lady knew of his generosity. The innkeeper, speaking of his delight and honor at seeing the Lady and somehow being a part of the rescue, loudly refused any payment at first, but Sir Lucian insisted. Since Sir Lucian paid for everything, including my cot, and they had made no arrangements for me at their lodgings, I just stayed the night at the inn with plans to meet the procession at the edge of town at first light.

As the procession moved again, the crowds began chanting,

"Hair milk-white and eyes of gold!
Truer love than in tales of old!

Almond skin and healing hands,
Great beauty, come bless our lands!"

GOLDEN EYES HAUNTED my dreams all night. No matter what the scene, the Lady's face appeared somewhere. Though her charm spells failed, feminine beauty still has its natural temptations for a young male alone in the world. But I also noticed another presence on the edge of my mind and dreams, though I could never quite sense who lingered there. The presence did not seem threatening, just observant.

I left the tavern at dawn after eating a quick breakfast of sausage, fried eggs, and fresh biscuits. I arrived before the Lady and her procession, but the wait wasn't long. They found a horse for me to ride at the Lady's insistence. Keeping the same order as the day before, the column moved forward. Sir Lucian rode beside Lady Zebah, following her mother's carriage. Erik and I rode close behind them with a dozen men-at-arms and Kiavonian guards bringing up the rear.

Erik sat regally upon his namesake steed, making it apparent that he spent his whole life in a saddle. His stallion stood tall, having the powerful neck and shoulders of a war horse. The horse was pure white, except for the mane, tail and nose, which were a deep black. The way the squire and his steed interacted, 'companion' seemed a more accurate term. Sir Lucian also rode a matching Blackmane stallion, colored the same except for the black feet.

As the town fell away behind us, I grumbled to Erik about my encounter with civilization. "Assassins, pickpockets, and surly guards. And Travailin is just a moderate sized town. What are the large cities like? It is no wonder I prefer the wilderness. A bear or a griffin may want to eat you, but I understand them. Too many people here. You never know what cunning is in their hearts."

"Not all are bad," Erik replied. "Some people are like the griffin, some are like the ants, some are like your steed. Some see you as prey, but many serve each other in peace. For instance, I recently found a ranger at an inn. A most interesting fellow, to be sure. He seems to be a good person, but I cannot be certain yet."

I smiled at the comment. "Maybe. I will need to ponder that." Changing the subject, I inquired, "Sir Lucian seems to have changed his mind about the Lady. You both have."

"Yes, now that we met her, it is impossible not to be charmed. Sir Lucian is just as smitten as the others."

"Well said."

"Her beauty is extraordinary," Erik said. "And a delight to anyone who meets her. But she also demonstrates modesty, intelligence, and courtesy. She seems to live up to all Lord Archibald stated of her."

"A great first impression."

"We all saw how she healed the young girl. A compassionate heart. Compare the coldness of her mother, Queen Chennai. Was the Lady not gracious to you as well?"

"Yes, she was. I could be lying next to the assassins. Very decisive, too."

"Yes, well. I must admit, my friend, that command made me feel uncomfortable." Erik furrowed his brow. "The Lage tells us all the Accountable are not to be murdered, but are subject to justice. Execution was inevitable for those assassins. Though I prefer to see the proper procedures carried out. I have yet to hear the lady speak of her beliefs. We can only observe her actions. May I encourage patience and grace until we understand more? The Lakes present dangers we do not grasp."

"I cannot help but be impressed by her, along with everyone else. Just be prudent, my friend," I cautioned. "I believe she enhances her charm."

"What do you mean?"

"She tried to charm me with magic. It seemed unnecessary with one so naturally beautiful already. But elfin are difficult to charm. One benefit of elfin blood. Do you know where she learned to heal? Is she a cleric of some kind?"

"As I have said, I have not discovered her background or beliefs, including her magical abilities." Erik seemed unsettled by my comments. "I will keep all of this in mind, Ranger Galieb. Sir Lucian and I will not go against the Lage, nor its Giver, for anyone."

"Though I just met you a few days ago, I truly believe that." Erik had a sincerity I trusted. I doubted it more with Lucian.

It took less than an hour to reach the Seven Arches Bridge. Many people already stood on the sides of the road hoping to glimpse the Lady. The guards cleared the bridge so we could cross without incident. Our procession thinned momentarily since the soldiers of Baldice stayed behind as we crossed into the Protectorate of Erian, whose men-at-arms took over. Some guards from Erian recognized me from the day before as I passed, but they said nothing. My expression may have been a little too smug in contrast to their frowns. I guess I could not blame them for doing their jobs. Such providential acts may have saved the Lady's life.

Once across the bridge, a full day's ride was before us to reach Giefanfeld, the principal city of Erian.

Erik and I continued riding together, but we dropped back to the rear guard.

"So, how did you break the assassin's arm?" Erik asked. "Killing eshkin, subduing an assassin. Two assassins! I can only hope to live up to such glory."

None of it felt very glorious. Just intense, life or death decisions with little time to think. I ran a hand over my hair at the uncertainty.

"Folami is the name of our master-of-arms," I answered, drumming my lips as I remembered the exhaustive training. "It means, 'he who commands respect.' Some call him 'Legend.' The man lived up to both of his names. He fought in the arenas of the Merchant Lords and survived. Not just survived but became a champion."

"He was a slave? The pits seem abominable." Erik scowled with disgust as his left hand gripped his long sword pommel.

"No, a freeman who chose on his own to enter the arenas," I explained. "He's Ugalorian. They are a warrior race of people that live somewhere south of the Lakes. He tells tales of fighting opponents of every race. Dwarfin, elfin, even gnomin with their exotic inventions. Folami was so successful that the Merchants feared him. They attempted many times to murder him in the arena. They sent eshkin, minotaurs, saber-tooth cats, griffins, even a young dragon. He defeated every one. But all that slaughter weighed on his soul more and more. Most of these creatures never had a choice in fighting."

"Forgive my doubts, but a dragon? That is unheard of." The one side of Erik's mouth raised.

"Ugalorians specialize in weaponless combat and live for one-on-one duels. Wrestling, strikes, punches, locks, takedowns. They fight each other naked. Just man against man. But he knows weapons, too. At our summer games, using a spear and a shield, he kept five armed men at bay." My voice raised in admiration. Ugalorians have a passion for all martial arts.

"Impressive." Erik ran his fingers down his long mustache.

"One thing he taught us is what he called the nine weaves against the dagger. Drilled it into me since my youth. When that assassin attacked me, I just reacted." My left hand fiddled with my axe.

"You must have learned the lessons well."

"We received excellent training, but I am too inexperienced for a skilled assassin. He may have been just a street thug for hire. "

"Rangers have a humility that matches that of the best paladins, I see." He smiled at me as he patted his horse.

Maybe, I thought to myself. But that man in the attic was no professional or I would be dead. Perhaps the Lady, too. The whole encounter felt off now that I gave it some thought.

Long shadows stretched beside us as the procession reached the capital of Erian. Trumpets announced our arrival. The procession would head west from here, following the Theorn Road to its principal city and the Lady's waiting groom.

My travels took me north, and I had hoped to slip away without passing under the gate. But then Erik, Sir Lucian, and the Lady herself insisted I stay the evening with them.

How could I refuse?

CHAPTER 8
THE WAYS OF
THE COURTS

Twenty-foot walls of cut stone surrounded the town. A whitewashed castle sat on the hill at the north end, reflecting yellow with the lowering sun. I thought Travailin bustled with life, but Giefanfeld was twice that place, yet small compared to what I heard of other cities like Theorn and Gaderon. I could not imagine so many people living in one place.

The duke of Erian heard what had happened in Travailin and was determined that no assassination attempt would happen in his Protectorate. Men-at-arms moved about every-where, and the Kianovan guard had crossbows armed in hand. The duke himself came to meet the Merchant Queen and the Lady to see them safely inside the castle.

Many hooves clopped on cobblestone as our procession moved through the wide street up the gradual slope to the castle on the far side of the city. People gawked at us. Some even called out, but the seriousness of the men-at-arms and the people's respect for their duke kept them more subdued than at Travailin. We all remained alert, shifting our gaze between the crowds and the surrounding windows.

We passed through another gate to reach the castle proper as the sun touched the horizon. The moon would not rise for some hours. It surprised me when the duke provided a small guest room for me and extended his invitation for the evening's festivities. I expected to sleep with the men-at-arms or in the stables.

Frankly, the whole idea of eating with the upper class touched my nerves. An attendant even prepared a bath for me. I did not know how to handle such attention.

At least I had some time to be alone and rest before facing all the aristocracy. I looked around the room. A small book shelf contained about a dozen books. The first one I picked up had the title: *The Lineage of the Kings of Lageheim.*

I also found: *The Lage, The Complete Law and Its History.* Though my training included the history of the kingdom and the basic tenets of their law, I flipped it open:

Treat any man you meet as you would want for yourself.

Give generously. If you see a person in need and do not help, you have failed the law.

Use honest weights and measures—do not cheat your neighbor or any person who comes to do business with you.

The Lag Giefan, the Law Giver, alone is to be honored. Worship no other gods.

I put the book back, for I was too nervous about this evening's banquet to sit and read anymore. Instead, I honed all my blades until it was time to go to supper.

Putting aside my gambeson and brigandine, when the dreaded moment came, I donned the clothes assigned to me: a light summer tunic of forest green that reached just past the knees, with full sleeves, pleated at the armhole with the ends turned back to form cuffs. It buttoned down the front, from the suffocating collar to the belt. Cloth leggings of gray covered my legs and soft leather slippers adorned my feet. The scarlet cap they provided stayed in my room, ignored. I tucked my dagger into my belt, even if it was unfashionable. I did not like being unarmed.

As I reached the massive dining hall—at least massive to me—the guards stopped me and pointed at my dagger, but the captain waved me by. An impressive hall opened up to me. The ceiling was three times my height, and enormous tapestries covered the walls, daily life in the fields being the most common theme. Local nobility cluttered the room, chatting in small groups, most in brighter colors than I wore. The men all wore caps, tunics, and tights of varying degrees of quality and color, depending on wealth and status. The ladies wore full length dresses, with a wide degree of hairstyles, some so complex that it must have taken hours to prepare. Minstrels strummed on stringed instruments. I did not see anyone I knew except the wizard from the inn talking to some high-ranking clerics. He had introduced himself as Aurel, if I recalled correctly.

I slinked into the corner, trying to go unnoticed. I just wanted to eat, thank the duke, and go to bed. They shut the city gates for the night, or I may have even found a pleasant camping spot farther up the road instead.

As I cowered with my back against a wall, eating mush-room caps stuffed with spiced trout, a dark-haired man with a trimmed beard approached me. My whole body stiffened in panic and my eyes turned to the ground. *Dragon's breath! Where's Erik when I need him?*

"Galieb? Is that you?" the man asked once he reached me.

Astounded at first that someone knew my name, I peeked up at his face. "Ottokar? What are you doing here?"

The man chuckled. "What am I doing here? Why to meet

the lady, like everyone else! This is what I do. I am the third son of a noble, you must remember. And I am an outlander for the abbey. The question is, what would a young hunter be doing in the Duke of Erian's court? Did Devarim send you to find me?" He sipped wine from a goblet made of cow's horn, and wood.

I forgot about Ottokar being an "outlander," or a liaison for the Qoholet. An informant in some sense, too. He came back to the Hidden Valley during the Spring Games every year, or if urgent news required it. I knew him to be a skilled ranger, despite being dressed like the nobility, in a similar tunic and tights, but with brighter colors and more embroidery. He wore the scarlet cap matching the one I left in my room.

"No. I am heading to Wynchell. Somehow, I got tied up in the Lady's procession. She insisted I come here. This is the last place I want to be."

He chuckled again as he rubbed his pointed goatee. "You do appear out of place, and not just your ears."

I could feel my face getting hot. I sighed. *Maybe I should have worn the cap.*

"Yes," Ottokar continued, "some have commented about you already. Not to worry. If the Lady invited you, few will have the courage to challenge your presence. I will make sure you do not embarrass yourself. Not too much, anyway. I never thought I would see you in such fine clothes. Green suits you. Though you seem to be missing a cap?"

He was enjoying my discomfort way too much, but I was grateful he was here.

"It is best to learn that poor fashion draws just as much attention as pointed ears," Ottokar said, his smile leaving his face. "A noble must be able to navigate the courts much like a ranger moves through the wilderness."

I nodded.

"Congratulations on taking your vows." Ottokar's smile

returned as he put his hand on my shoulder, a large ring on the middle finger. "You will make the Qoholet proud, I do not doubt."

I appreciated the encouragement.

"Now, let me remind you of the hierarchy of the courts to lessen your blunders," Ottokar continued. "The dukes that rule each Protectorate answer only to the king. They are all equal in authority, but of course, some have more influence than others. Erian does not have the status of some, such as Theomund, who is next in line to the king. Outside the little prince, Wilhelm, of course. But Wilhelm will not be eligible to reign for another decade, at the earliest."

Ottokar paused as a servant in a simple blue tunic and a round green cap filled his goblet. I took a goblet as well.

"The title of earl is given to the sons and any brothers of the present dukes and are next in rank. Their wives, however will have the title of countess. For instance, when Lady Zebah weds Archibald, she will be named Countess Zebah. Keep in mind, however, when the present duke of Theomund passes away and his son, Earl Archibald, is sworn in as duke, Lady Zebah will become the duchess and have more influence than all the other duchesses. All the nobility understands this, thus many are here to win favors before she even marries. Such are the challenges of court life."

"Sounds confusing," I said as I ran a hand over my hair.

He took another sip before continuing. "Below the earls are the barons and their families, who are the baronets, like myself. Of course, you will find the knighted freemen and other wealthy people of influence mingling with nobility."

Erik finally arrived and joined us. "My apologies for tardiness. Stedgyr, my stallion, needed a little extra attention this evening. He does not like a few of the men in the stables. Honestly, I do not find them agreeable either. However, the stable manager seems an honest fellow, and I do not want to disparage on the duke's gracious hospitality."

I introduced Ottokar to Erik, almost forgetting their titles in my awkwardness.

"So how did you two meet?" Ottokar asked.

"Well, first at the inn, then again at Travailin when he subdued two assassins." Erik bragged on my behalf. Others took interest in our conversation at the word 'assassin,' eyeing my ears as they sought to eavesdrop.

"That was you? The entire court is a buzz about the assassination attempt on the Lady." Ottokar laughed again. "Well done, lad! You already fulfill your calling."

All attention turned to the doorway as Queen Chennai and Lady Zebah entered with their captain standing right behind. The queen had changed into a more luxurious, even more colorful silken gown accented with exotic skins and feathers. Lady Zebah, however, wore a white full length linen dress, accented with gold, in a similar style to the tunic she wore earlier. The swan feathered headdress and earrings also adorned her head. Every eye fixed on her. She radiated beauty and grace without seeming pretentious. As they moved forward to mingle, I noted the captain wore all his weapons.

The boldest and highest ranked nobility all moved to greet them while the rest of us lesser beings waited our turn.

"There is something about Lady Zebah, Ottokar," I whispered.

"What do you mean? I am told she is extremely charming," he responded, not turning to look at me, but observing the women.

"That is why she is so dangerous. At least to me."

Ottokar chuckled at my youthfulness, not taking my warning seriously enough. "I would be pleased if you introduced me to her," Ottokar said to both of us.

Erik agreed when I hesitated, leaving me standing alone once again.

The duke entered with his wife, and a servant announced all to be seated soon afterwards. Each of us had an assigned seat around the enormous U-shaped table. The wooden table itself spanned ten paces on each side, handcrafted of the finest cherry wood. The queen and the lady sat next to the duke and duchess at the center of the table. Thankfully, Erik sat with me near the south end, while Sir Lucian and Ottokar sat with those of their ranks. As I approached, I noticed the chairs and the corner legs of the table sported intricate carvings of wheat and apples and other fruits. Heavy cloths of the finest linen covered the tables. Dyed green, white, and blue, the linens reminded me of the summer sky over lush fields. Maple wood bowls and plates awaited each seat. Goblets of cow's horn with maple wood stems, matching to the ones we held, sat next to the plates.

After a heartfelt toast to King Reinhart III, the beloved ruler of Lageheim, acrobats, singers, and poets performed for us as we ate crab chowder imported from the coast. Shark fillets followed with parsley potatoes and greens, accompanied by wheat bread and grape jelly. Elfin wine and dwarfin mead filled the bronze goblets.

"Any noteworthy news from the lakes, Queen Chennai?" the duke asked as we ate, and the entertainment took a break. "I hear your business thrives." Chennai held no official title, but only named herself queen as she controlled a significant portion of the Cat Paw Lakes.

"Lord Jonas lost two ships last month. Apparently, a giant octopus locked onto one of them, pulling it under. When a companion ship came to assist, a dragon turtle attacked the octopus. The ensuing battle damaged both ships. The entire crew and all the merchandise of both ships now rest at the bottom of the lake, lost. No one has seen anything like that in a hundred years."

Everyone gasped at the tragedy.

"That sounds dreadful," the duke responded.

"Dreadful for Lord Jonas. I took over two of his trade routes because of his failure." Her words displayed the cutthroat ways of life on the Lakes.

"Are you not worried about your own crews and ships?"

The queen waved her hand as she continued to nibble at the food on her plate. "Such occurrences are rare, but it is a risk. That is why it cost so much for your nobles to get silk and spices from the far east."

"I did not know such dangerous creatures truly existed. I thought they were just excuses for the high prices," the duke responded. "Why did the giant turtles attack the octopus? Do these monsters often attack ships?"

"Dragon turtles," Lady Zebah interjected, "eat the giant octopus, my lord. Very fearsome creatures." At the sound of her voice, all turned to listen, the murmuring dying off. Her mother's words and that of all the others came across as crass in comparison. "Though I have never heard of one preying on an octopus as it attacked a ship. As for the vessels, an octopus sometimes preys on the sailors by pulling the ships over."

"Oh, my!" a few ladies exclaimed.

"Let me assure you that our crews are always our primary concerns." Zebah's voice captivated all who heard her. It was like the sound of songbirds greeting the dawn despite the dark subject of conversation. "Such attacks on ships are rare. However, we train specialized mages for such things, and the ships travel in pairs for this reason, armed with harpoons. Dragon turtles also prey on sailors, but that is even more of a rarity, thankfully, as we have fewer ways to defend against such an assault. Most of the time, we just need to avoid hitting their hard shells with our ships."

A silence took over for a moment, before the duchess spoke up. "Such an enlightening conversation. We know so little about your business or even your culture. Tell us, Lady Zebah, about your lovely headdress. Where do you get such blue feathers? Are they dyed?"

"Not at all, duchess. The azure swan is another unique creature that frequents the shallow coves around the lakes. They are a symbol of our people. There is a small bay next to our palace that the swans nest in during the spring. We have servants that care for the creatures and collect the feathers. We use them for many things, including for adornment and in our ceremonies."

"They certainly enhance your abundant natural beauty," the duke responded. I guessed that every man in the room, including me, thought the same as her golden eyes and alluring smile drew all gazes to her. "Your presence will most certainly bless the courts of Theomund. And all Lageheim."

"To serve and bless your kingdom is why I came. It will be an honor to see our two cultures unite and grow."

The duke toasted the idea, and everyone followed suit with much enthusiasm.

"Yes, that is why I agreed to this arrangement. It should be very profitable. For both parties." Queen Chennai smiled as she sipped her wine.

Though most seemed smitten with the lady, as I gazed around the room, I noticed a few individuals looked concerned, including the wizard Aurel. Ottokar also looked thoughtful as he peered over his goblet. Something felt off, but a longing for feminine affection muddied any reasoning.

After dessert, I wanted to leave. I found Ottokar and Erik to say goodnight so I could slip off to bed as soon as possible.

"Galieb, our friendship has just budded, and I am sorry to part," Erik said. "Yet I feel our roads will cross again. A premonition perhaps."

"I feel the same. The ideals of paladins have always had my admiration. To find you striving so earnestly to live up to them gladdens my heart."

WHEN MORNING CAME, I rose early, ready to continue. It felt good to be in my own clothes again and to have my weapons back. Not as comfortable as the tunic and leggings, but a brigandine and a bow suited me better.

The night before, I snuck a few rolls from the feast to serve as my breakfast, to avoid the need to raid the kitchen first thing.

As I scurried along the stonewall of a side courtyard, a silky voice stopped me in my tracks.

"Ranger Galieb, leaving already?"

I followed the voice over my right shoulder to see Lady Zebah standing by a bench of carved cherry wood, dogwood trees and red roses on either side. Those golden eyes drew me in as the melody of her voice carried me away.

It took all my strength to respond. "Alas, Lady Zedah, my duties call me elsewhere."

"Yes, rumors of eshkin raids to the north," she said as she drew closer.

"That is what I am to uncover, my lady." I found court pleasantries difficult enough as a simple woodsman interacting among the nobility, but this beauty stressed me more than any other. "What brings you down here so early and by yourself?"

"I come to speak with my father."

"Your father? So you know your father? Is he here?" As soon as I spoke the words, I wanted to take them back. Sir Lucian had stated at the inn that no one knew who her father was. This woman flustered me, but she only looked amused, not insulted. I ran a hand over my hair.

"Yes, I know him. He gave me these bracelets." Her smile faded as her golden eyes looked away. "As for where he is, he constantly wanders about, caring only about his mission."

"His mission brings him here?" I did not understand, and it made me feel even more foolish.

"Not right now, but I can feel him through these bracelets. I talk to him, even if he does not listen." Her smile returned, and she looked up at me. "What about you? Is your father human or elfin?"

"Human, but I never knew him. He died before I was born. It sounds like it was better that way."

"And your mother?"

"Elfin. She is back home, worrying about me, I am sure."

"That sounds so freeing. You can do whatever you wish." Her hands wrapped around the bracelets and she stared far off.

"My lady? Forgive me. I do not understand."

"No, you do not and cannot. Both mother and father use me for their own purposes. But I have my own plans." The smile disappeared and her eyebrows formed a line. Her jaw tightened.

My hairs stood on end though I could not explain why. "May all go well with you," felt like the right thing to say.

She drank me in with her eyes and I got lost in their depths. I wanted to grab her hand and tell her to run away with me, but I did not. Neither of us said anything for a moment.

"You honor your order, despite your youth. It seems wise to learn more about rangers." She paused as her smile grew. "And half-elfin are a rarity not forgotten. Are you sure you don't want to come with me? I can find a place for you."

Every nerve wanted to flee, yet my knees almost buckled, pledging eternal servitude. I had no response in me but to bow, just to get away from those golden orbs and her ever-present radiance if for no other reason.

Her gaze shifted to something behind me. "Lady Zebah!" a woman's voice called. I recognized it as the duchess.

"I cannot." Was all I managed.

Anger flared across her face, but then her composure returned. I was not sure if it was because of my rejection or the duchess' interference. "Safe travels, Galieb. May we meet again. Soon."

"The honor would be mine." Though I prayed to never see her again.

And with that, she walked over to the duchess, the power of her aura leaving with her. I leaned against the wall, drained.

CHAPTER 9
TWO CAMPS

As I moved north, houses fell away and the farms became more scattered. Erian produced a multitude of crops like wheat and corn, the road taking me beside the green fields in the summer sun. Other travelers passed me, going both directions along the road. Peasants pushing wooden hand carts, farmers in horse-drawn open wagons, and merchants in fancier enclosed wagons, some in small trains with bodyguards. I also saw men-in-arms riding in pairs, an occasional knight on horseback, and even a few dwarfin in small groups.

It only drizzled on me for a few hours the second day. The journey did not have the beauty of the woods, and it was too hot on the open road, but it was still a pleasant walk.

It took me another four days to reach the border of Wynchell, which was nothing more than a creek crossing with a few men-at-arms stationed in a small stone tower. I inquired about eshkin and they affirmed hearing an increase in raids between the rivers among the lumbermen and the dwarfin mines.

"Between the waters?" I asked, not sure what he meant.

"Aye. 'Between the waters,'" one man answered. "The best part of the land. Most of Wynchell is east of the Gaderon River and west of the Kwit River. Folks around here call that area 'between the waters.'"

Wynchell produced grains, hay, and hardy livestock, but was better known for lumber and iron ore. Clumps of wooded plots now interrupted the fields as the road increased in elevation. A bit of snow remained on the Towering Peaks in the distance in front of me. I caught glimpses of White Cliff, the principal city of Wynchell, rising above the trees far to the northeast. The lofty, white washed towers gleamed in the sun as they stood tall and thin on the edge of the pale cliffs as the foaming cascades of two rivers tumbled down on either side and out of sight.

Just a few miles past the crossing, I found a clearing under a stand of hemlocks that looked like a soft spot to lay my bedroll. Maybe I would sleep better here. Lady Zebah had been invading my dreams nightly since I met her. Perhaps the effects of her charm spells still lingered.

As I settled in for the night, a small fire flared up in the distance among the trees. That could mean many things. *Was someone else camping? Could there be eshkin this far south? Or maybe bandits?* A wildfire also crossed my mind. I watched it for several minutes, trying to decide if it was a campfire or something else. It burned fiercely at first, like oil thrown in the flames, but soon settled down.

I thought it best to investigate before crawling into my bedroll. I did not want bandits stabbing me as I slept.

Finishing my cold supper, I moved deeper into the forest towards the flames, listening for any sounds on the breeze. My boots touched no twig or leaf. The distance to the fire stretched farther than it first seemed, and the flames burned lower as I approached.

A few more paces ahead, the orange of dying flames against the purple twilight drew my eyes to a small clearing. Devarim's scolding voice in my head caused me to stop, look around, and listen for anything around me before proceeding, but I noticed nothing.

By the time I entered the clearing, all that remained were glowing coals. The red-hot embers huddled on a small altar of piled stone built under a majestic ash tree. Upon closer examination, I noticed among the coals smoldered the burnt remains of a fawn. Little was left of the animal except for the hooves, charred bones, and a few strands of hair. Stuck in the ground next to the rocks was a small, handcrafted stick. Someone had tied a crude flint point onto the tip and accented it with chicken feathers, making a poor replica of a spear.

Not something I would expect to find within the borders of Lageheim. I do not think Sir Lucian, Erik, or any of the clerical orders would approve of this. Probably why they hid the altar here in the trees. Unattended fires during the heat of summer lead to dangerous wildfires, which also annoyed me. I studied the area, but it was too dark now to learn much more about the altar or its builders.

Not eshkin. Too neat. Just some locals dabbling in the occult? Maistren Lilke always says such things are dangerous. Never know what spirits you will draw in.

I hesitated, then tore it down, breaking the mock spear before throwing it into the trees. I struggled with destroying someone else's property, but as a ranger, I could not allow someone to draw in unknown spirits.

Probably just rebuild it, but this will send a message. I blurred my tracks with a branch, just in case, before heading back to my camp.

A few days of travel north brought me to the Gaderon River once more, the towers of White Cliff now behind me and out of sight. The river swung east to skirt along the VenKeth, while the Road to Wynchell arched westerly as it journeyed north. But here they met once again, and I looked for a suitable place to camp in this remote setting.

Not as wide as at Seven Arches Bridge far to the south, the river was still many paces across and moving with a fair swiftness as it sought the edges of the wild to the east. Herons and other waterfowl dotted the shores. I soon found a delightful spot for fishing hidden from the road along the river, with quieter pools away from the main current. Freshly cooked food sounded delightful, and fish fillets would be an agreeable change.

I waded into the river, leaving myself plenty of time for fishing before darkness was to set in. Using an arrow, I made attempts at spearfishing some of the trout.

After multiple attempts that ended in me catching only one fish, I considered making a light fishing bow out of reeds. My war bow was just too powerful to catch fish.

Just then, an older man dressed in a simple brown robe entered my camp. Sturdy but plain boots poked out from under the bottom hem of the bland robe. He stopped when he saw me, and he leaned on a boar spear decorated with eagle feathers, the point of the weapon reaching just above the crown of his head. Ancient, blackened runes marked the ashen handle.

He said nothing, just gave me a hard stare with his one eye. A leather eye patch covered his left eye, just like Horten. I really did not want any company, and I guessed by his frown that he did not like me being here. His look matched that of the assassin in Travailin just before he fired his crossbow. This time, my bow and sword lay on the shoreline, out of reach, but I still had my axe and dagger tucked in my belt, though he did not appear threatening.

"Greetings! I am Galieb." I smiled as I stood knee-deep in the river, trying to be friendly.

"I see someone else has discovered my favorite fishing hole in all of Tyria," he finally responded. No introduction followed, I noticed. Calling the land by its ancient name seemed unusual.

Before I could invite him fully into my camp, he made himself at home. He threw down a small squirming woolen sack and sat down on a short log lying next to a fire ring set up by a previous camper. The spear lay next to him within hand's reach. He adjusted the hunting knife stuck in his belt as he sat. It was the only other weapon I could see.

His arrogant air added to my annoyance.

"You have the look of a Lilke protégé. A Qoholet rambler and babbler. Half-blood, no less." The man stroked the twin braids of his beard as he spoke, the bronze tan of his skin contrasting with the colorless gray of his wispy long hair and beard.

"Do you know Maistren Lilke?" I called, not sure what to make of his comments or the sack.

"Know of him. I would never name him 'Master.' His intellect matches his gnomin stature. And he is not who he says he is."

My annoyance started to turn to outright anger at the slander of my friend and mentor until I suspected he was baiting me on purpose. "I caught two trout so far," I said. "I'm willing to share what I catch. It may not be much."

"Avoiding my challenge, I see. Is that a Qoholet habit or just your own?" He studied me with his one all-encompassing dark eye. "Very well. What if I just take the fish from you? What would happen then?"

I found my hand fingering my axe blade as I assessed him with the water lapping around my calves. The man was wide across his torso, and he had broad shoulders, looking strong as an ox despite age, like someone who had worked hard in the fields his whole life. In height, I guessed him to be about average for a man of Lageheim, making him just a touch taller than me. The back of my neck told me there was more. I sensed something extraordinarily powerful about him.

"Is there some way I can address you, sir?" I avoided the questions, doing my best to be perfectly gracious instead of annoyed. *Don't play his game. Be above it. Confrontation could be fatal.*

"Once again, you choose social graces instead of answering troublesome questions. Does not Qoholet mean 'Gatherer of Wisdom' or 'Collector of Proverbs?' Have you no proverb ready for every response? And do not call me 'sir.' I wish no association with any of those tin soldiers that took over this land."

This monk seems well informed and extremely intelligent. He finds pleasure in probing. I cannot quite grasp the reason. Did he just like to test people, or was there another motive? Like hatred of rangers? I just want to fish and camp in peace, but my unnamed visitor refuses to let that happen. Maybe if I satisfy him enough, I can find a reason to slip away.

"The Qoholet have collected many proverbs and have tenets we live by. One of our highest tenets reads: 'Continually promote what is truly "good," whether such "good" is expressed in an idea, an action, or a being.' Whatever can be established as truly good, help that to increase. I consider it good to share with you any food I have, including the fish I catch." I watched his reaction before adding, "Do you prefer something other than 'sir'? May I honor you with a proper title? Treating others with respect is also a Qoholet practice."

"Ah, using my own game against me." The plain robed monk gave the slightest chuckle, seeming less aggressive. "People call me many things. The Wandering Eye, Biting Fly, Brown Robe, among others. Some names are quite nasty. Derleik is what I call myself."

"Nice to meet you, Derleik."

"You may not think so later."

I avoided his stare and concentrated on the water, staying close to my sword. I hoped he was finished with his probing.

But he was not. "So 'Beloved'—sounds like your mother named you. Besides collecting proverbs, do not Lilke's lackeys also study philosophy? Logic? Seek truth?"

"We study many things," I said, dreading his response. *Maybe he was trying to get me to move on so he could have his camping spot?* I braced myself for what may come next. Apparently, he knows the ancient Tyrian language well if he could translate 'Galieb.' I stabbed at a fish, but missed.

"Yes, like swinging swords and bending stringed sticks, by the looks of you. Not spearfishing, obviously. Tell me, what is the meaning of life according to your order? And do not misquote the tenet this time. Earlier, you left out: 'good as defined by the Universal Moral Law.'"

I felt the flames of his tongue. Fishing was not my best skill. And he caught that I had left out part of the tenet. He already knew what we taught. My face flushed with uncertainty. "It sounds like you are already very familiar with our ways. In summary, 'do good, reduce suffering, seek truth.' Are you disagreeable with any of our tenets?"

He smiled, but I was uncertain what to make of it. "Of course, everyone is a 'do-gooder' in their own eyes. Can you even define 'good?' Is fishing good or evil? Is sword fighting good?"

I wished Maistren Lilke was here to answer for me. He could handle such things easily. I waded closer to shore, still looking at the water. My mind felt cluttered, many ideas all racing together with no coherency. My pulse increased along with my doubt. I breathed in and out to gain focus. "It depends on intent. What is the reason I am fishing? To destroy life? To feed myself? That I may feed others? What are the reasons I am fighting? To murder, or because of selfish anger? Or perhaps I am protecting a helpless child. The act itself may be good or evil, depending on the motive."

"Now we get to the heart of things," he said. "So, what makes killing someone to protect a child better than killing a man who slandered you? Where do such rules come from? Different cultures and different ages have different definitions of 'justice'."

My answer was reactive but reserved, even if not wrong. "Some would say the gods. The Lageheim king and his knights say the Lage, the law given to them by Walferd and Shepherd Kings. They all claimed it came from the Law Giver."

His eyebrows raised, but it seemed rehearsed, as if he already knew the answer before he asked. "So, the Qoholet follow the Lage?" Anger came through his voice as he continued. "What or who gives this king or his ancestors the authority to decide how others live? Thieves and backstabbers, all of them."

Something riled him. I felt riled, too. I did not know what it had been, but best to not feed that. *Calm yourself Galieb! Keep it a friendly discussion.* "Someone must establish order to keep from chaos. The Qoholet have their own tenets. Similar to the Lage, but not the same. We seek the Yett Sorr, the Eternal Self-Existent, the source of all other things. The One who has always been and has no cause. One who must be all-powerful, all knowing, and perfectly just. We seek this Eternal's moral law, the universal moral law that is part of the created order. Logic has led us to these conclusions. Do we err in our logic? What guides you if such ways are not agreeable with you?"

"My own, same as everyone!" he shouted. Then his anger passed. "Ultimately, the mightiest make the rules, even by your own standards." He paused. "In the end, it matters not. Whatever this first source may be, even if your logic is sound, it does not care." He pointed to the sun as it touched the treetops. "Time rolls on endlessly without care. The sun rises and sets again, returning the next day. A generation comes and passes away. We revere them for a season, but then we forget them. It matters not what they have done. It matters not if someone does good or bad, no matter how a culture defines those terms. Does justice really exist or is it just a hope when we are wronged? Human, elfin, dwarfin, gnomin, eshkin–they all return to dirt. Even the gods rise and fade away. There is no meaning. There is nothing new that has not already been done. All things are full of weariness, with no end."

The monk no longer focused on me, but his eye stared at the flowing water. *The Qoholet had answers to such comments,* I wanted to say. *All the intelligent races seek more than mere existence. We seek for meaning in our lives, so there must be something more beyond the material world. Someone who placed meaning within us. We did not invent it, but desperately seek it.*

But I decided not to draw him back to me. I made my way out of the water and collected my weapons. His eye focused back on me.

"I assume rangers can start a fire?" Derleik asked, but it felt more like a command.

My eyes never left him as I complied, using my tinderbox and the wood I had gathered earlier. As I settled on a rock to clean the fish, the sun dipped behind the trees, warning of the coming twilight.

As I sat down, a man of rich dress entered our camp.

He glanced at me before addressing Derleik. "What have we here? Did you gain a servant?"

He appeared a nobleman or some upper class, wearing a gaudy and colorful silken tunic that reached to his ankles. A cloak lined with ermine hung from his shoulders. His appearance suggested he was not from Lageheim. Perhaps a traveling merchant, though I heard no wagon or even a horse. I couldn't imagine someone so wealthy wandering about on foot in such a remote area.

"Ha, no. Servants betray you," Derleik said. "This foolish youth decided to fish in our meeting place." He waved at me as I set my trout to cook over the building flames.

"Oh? Shall I remove him?" The newcomer responded nonchalantly.

The hairs on my neck stood straight. It did not sound like a jest, though I saw no weapons on him. *A wizard, perhaps?*

"No, he is entertaining enough. At least for now. Any news?" Derleik asked the newcomer, reaching for the squirming bag.

"All is going as planned." The man seemed to wear a permanent smirk, like a joke that only he knew. His dainty hand caressed a thin beard of reddish orange accented with white, which matched his closely trimmed hair.

"Good," was all Derleik said.

Strange enough, the richly attired nobleman seemed subordinate to the brown-robed pauper.

Satisfied, Derleik stood and gripped his spear in one hand.

What was he going to do? Tired of debate, did he wish me gone from his camp? My body tensed, various options racing through my mind. Fighting seemed more foolish than fleeing, but nothing appeared hopeful.

He did not approach me. Instead, he grabbed the sack and pulled out a squealing piglet, held up by the back legs.

"A dirty piglet?" the noble protested. "Where did you get that?"

"A gift from a local follower. Though it took him too long to see it that way."

Without hesitation, he ran the edge of the spear blade across the neck of the piglet. Blood poured out, but none of it reached the ground. The intricate designs on the well-crafted blade drank every drop. When he set the blade aside, it appeared as clean as before he used it.

"Drinker needs blood every moon, or it gets too unwieldy even for me." Derleik said.

He tossed the carcass directly into the fire, and the pair watched it burn.

Derleik took a deep breath, closing his eye, seeming to find satisfaction in the aroma of the burning flesh. "Lekhash, we have other things to discuss. Without the youth."

"As you wish." The nobleman stood with his continual smirk, the flames dancing in his beady, black eyes. But he no longer appeared as a man. In his place stood an upright fox, complete with a bushy tail, dressed in expensive clothes. He placed pince-nez on his pointy nose and reached into the satchel strapped across his chest full of scrolls and books.

I remembered nothing else.

CHAPTER 10
BLOOD AND MUD

I woke up where I had sat the night before, collapsed by the fire ring, cold and hungry. My muscles and back ached from the hard, uneven ground and awkward sleeping position. Overnight, the ground drained my body heat, giving me the shivers. I stood, stretched, and stomped my feet to get the blood pumping. The morning sun broke over the distant ridge, and I relished the added heat, though the sun would become overbearing soon enough.

I looked down and saw a trio of blackbirds pecking at my overcooked fillets and the unburnt piglet pieces in the cold ashes. I checked my pack lying next to me, and nothing seemed missing or disturbed. My weapons also seemed untouched.

"It appears they are not thieves. Nor murderers. They let me live, or perhaps something stopped their hands," I said, but only the birds heard me. I was glad to be alive, but their words stung like burning flames.

Does nothing really matter? Is all of life meaningless? Does the Yett Sorr really exist? Does He exist but not care? Were my mentors wrong? Is it all just a false hope?

The pair haunted my lingering dreams. I shuddered again. They had pushed Zebah out of my mind, at least, replacing temptations with doubt. The other presence still lingered out of sight in the dreams, however.

I looked at my fish. "So much for fresh trout," I lamented. To live in the wild, you need to be less picky, so I salvaged any fish I could for a cold breakfast and left the rest to the birds. "All yours. Enjoy."

The birds eyed me, transfixed, but kept their distance. I double-checked my weapons and packed up my stuff, warming up as I moved. Last night's encounter, along with my dreams, had me on edge, so I carried my bow in my hand for comfort. The monk's challenges tormented my mind.

Everything returns to the ground...all is meaningless...was I foolish in believing in something more? In trying to make a differ-ence? Doing good never seemed wrong but took lots of effort. *Was I sacrificing my life for nothing?*

Such thoughts troubled my travels and hurried me along, making my strides long and quick. The road stayed along the river, its presence giving some peace to my uncertain mind. Cow and sheep pastures broke up the fields of wheat and barley that stretched off beyond the horizon on the west side of the road. Blackbirds sat on the wooden fences, and field hawks drifted overhead, looking for rodents. On the east side of the road, maples, oaks, and other hardwoods shaded both banks of the river, the woods stretching out of sight. I spotted an occasional deer under the canopy or crossing over into the fields. Similar travelers still used the roads, but in lesser numbers.

Despite keeping a steady pace, it still took me to almost nightfall to reach the ferry, most of the way uphill now that I reached the foothills of the Towering Peaks.

The smell of smoke tinged the air.

"Are you heading to White Cliff? Or answering the call for men?" the ferryman asked. He stared at my ears with one eye half closed, but added no insults.

The kingdom of HaerenVale bordered Wynchell, so they must be more familiar with elfin here. "First time this far north. Hoping for news. I heard eshkin came down from the mountains."

"Aye. Raiding the homesteads. Burning them, too," he answered, sniffing the air and rubbing the hairs on his chin. It appeared as if he tried to grow a beard without success, instead producing colorless stubble and fuzz. A simple round wool cap covered his head, gray curls coming out on all sides. "The Duke sent troops to the lumber camps. Callin' for men and arms. Lost contact with the dwarfin, I heard. Worst raids we've seen in a century, at least. But we've been protecting this corner of the kingdom for centuries. A few eshkin won't chase us off."

He tugged at the rusty mail hanging off his scrawny torso. His skin looked weathered from spending too much time in the sun, and I guessed the man had seen a few raids over the years.

"May the men of Wynchell stand strong," I responded. "How much to cross?"

"I can take you now, but I have to charge you full price. I don't go at night if I don't need to. Save you some money if you come at first light. Others will come and go by then."

"Cheap place to stay in town? Best place for a meal?"

He directed me to a small inn off the main road inside the town's walls. A hot meal and bed sounded good after a few days of traveling, not to mention missing last night's meal. Hopefully, I would get a quiet night.

The town of Farrin's Crossing rested in a crook in the river another mile up the road. Vertical logs, bound together, formed a wall around the town. Multiple roads and paths came out of the town proper, making for multiple gates of various sizes.

Squared logs chinked with limed mud dominated the architecture of the town, creating horizontal lines of white and brown. Down the main road, I passed several specialty craft stores closed for the night. Between the dwarfin smiths and human woodworkers, Wynchell had a reputation for quality art, like the goblets of horn used at the Duke's banquet in Erian. That brought traveling merchants looking for wares to sell.

Among the stores, I noticed a sign for a vek handler.

Good to know. I owed Devarim some updates.

The town seemed bigger than the village of Stonecrest back home, but smaller than Travailin. Locals filled many of the seats inside the inn, but there was still plenty of room. I found an empty table along the wall so I could watch and listen. A few stared upon my entering, and I heard "half-elfin" whispered here and there, but then they ignored me. Better than "half-breed" or other terms they could have used.

I felt the strain of the road drain away.

Most of the folks in the inn had either red or blonde hair, though I saw a few with light brown, but nothing darker. All of them, both men and women, had wavy hair with curls at the end. Even the beards ended with round locks on their chests. They seemed akin to the rest of Lageheim, yet a little unique, too.

I noticed that most wore a simple working tunic of earth tones accompanied by a round woolen cap covering the tops of their ears. A few had arming swords strapped to their belts, with left hands resting on the pommels and right hands holding mugs of mead. Some, however, wore more refined tunics with brighter colors, and kept clean shaven. I assumed these men owned the shops down the main corridor.

A tall blonde maid came around to check on me after a few minutes. She flung back a heavy braid over her shoulder to keep it from touching the table as she wiped it with a damp rag. Pushing up the white sleeves of her stained under-tunic, she limited my choice to mutton stew with a slice of sourdough.

At least it is hot, and I do not have to cook.

My order arrived within minutes, and I washed it down with a watered mead made locally. The latest gossip comprised eshkin raids to the north, the burning of farms, the duke's call for men, and a traveling brown-robed monk. The last perked up my pointed ears the most. It sounded like he had been here stirring up trouble before I encountered him. No one mentioned the name Derleik. They all just referred to him as the 'Wandering Eye', but I knew it was the same. A few arguments broke out about him questioning the Lage. I guessed he would find that amusing.

The innkeeper stepped from behind the counter over to the men getting rowdy. He was a big man, plump at the belly but had thick arms. A wavy brown beard covered his entire neck. The dirty apron did not take away from his fearsome scowl. "Now look here! We are all kin, even if there are a few generations of separation. There is enough trouble with the raids over there, between the waters!" His thumb pointed over his heavy shoulder towards the east. "Don't be starting more! We honor the Lage here, and if you don't like that, find another place to drink!"

The troublemakers grumbled but then grew quiet without fists being thrown. Two men gulped down their mead and stomped out. As the innkeeper nodded in satisfaction, a stressed woman entered the inn and glanced around. Unable to find what she was looking for, she dashed to one of the serving maids.

"Friedl, have ya seen Lief? Has he been here? He left this

morning and has not returned. My heart fears that I shall not see him again."

When Friedl shook her head, the woman asked around the inn, but everyone said no.

"Hilda, we'll watch for him and send him home when we find him," the innkeeper stated. "Many a-missing, with the eshkin raids and all."

"Eshkin still fear coming so close to town," Friedl said, trying to comfort her. "No raids happening here, are there? Just between the waters."

Hilda sat at a table with Friedl's arm around her. Tears escaped despite her best efforts.

"Are the youngens coping?" the innkeeper asked. When she nodded, he added, "Friedl, we're not too busy. Take her home. We will watch for him. Don't like the youngens being home alone."

The women both nodded and left.

Others in the inn muttered as they went back to their drinks and plates. "Changing times. Sheep have been disappearing. Even a few dogs. The reeve assumes eshkin, but nobody's seen them this side of the river. Just between the waters. Strange times we're living."

Some grumbled about the two troublemakers who had left earlier, questioning what they may have to do with any of the recent troubles, like missing livestock.

I didn't like two young women walking home alone in the dark with trouble about, so I slipped outside. With just stars and no moon, it was too dark for humans to see anything, even with the lanterns shining out of windows, but I had my elfin night sight.

I spotted Hilda and Friedl as they turned a corner. I followed, reaching the corner to find a narrower side road heading north out of town. One or two men-at-arms patrolled in town, but the duke's knight had taken most of the others to deal with the raids, according to the gossip in the inn.

I debated on approaching them with an offer to escort, but I figured I would just spook them. I knew how to avoid being noticed. Fortunately, it was only a mile's walk to Hilda's home outside the town's wall. She lived in a small cabin of squared logs with a workshop behind it built of matching logs. It was not a ranch, so Lief had to be a craftsman of some kind.

Finding a large tree in a dark corner, I sat down with my back against the trunk, watching the place. Friedl stayed for a while with Hilda and the children, but then left, hurrying towards the inn while looking over her shoulder. My eyes followed her as far as I could see to be sure she had no trouble, but also to be sure she did not return. I wanted to look around the property.

Hilda's lamp burned out, but I never saw Lief return.

I circled the property and decided Hilda and the children were safe at present. I headed up to my room at the inn, first checking to be sure Friedl made it back, too.

The following morning, I had a nice breakfast but was still curious about Lief's whereabouts. I traveled back toward his home. Though the road was little more than a wide path, enough traveled this way to confuse all the footprints.

To my surprise, however, just past the first corner where I had followed Hilda and Friedl, a beggar sat.

"Excuse me, sir, can you spare a copper for a poor fellow?" The man didn't look at me but stared at my boots. Dried mud covered his bare feet. A scraggly reddish-brown beard covered his face, and his clothes hung loose, looking two sizes too big.

I dug in my pouch and tossed him a daily. "You don't look like a local. Are you from around here?"

He studied the coin in his hand. "A half silver! Very generous, my lord."

His stare moved up a little farther but avoided my face. They seemed to focus on my weapons. "Me? Just a homeless wanderer, hoping for a safe place to rest." His accent didn't exactly match the locality, but there was nothing distinguishable about it either.

"Why have you set up here? Seems you would not see many folks passing by."

"Folks don't like ones such as me around their pretty shops. Out of everyone's way, here."

"Were you here yesterday? Did you see a leather worker pass by? A craftsman?"

"Don't recall faces, sir, begging your pardon. I can watch if you like. Maybe, if I see something, perhaps, if not too much trouble, ask for another copper as a reward."

My mind calculated my leftover funds. They were dwindling fast, but I could not deny him. "I may agree with that. If you see the leatherworker, named Lief, let me know or leave a message at the inn for Galieb. You will get some reward."

"Thank you, sir. Galieb, thank you!"

"What is your name?"

"Just call me...Otto, my lord."

Pleased with the pact, I proceeded along my way to Lief's house. Just past the walled edge of town, before Hilda's place, I spotted a discolored patch on some rocks. Closer inspection revealed dried drops of blood. I found nothing that indicated eshkin.

Could be just someone with a nosebleed or who cut themselves on a thorn.

I looked around to study the terrain. A small plot of trees—that could easily hide a predator—piled up against the town's wall. The road also dipped right where I stood by the bloodstain, the crests on either side high enough to reduce my view in either direction. Someone could ambush a victim in the dark without being seen. I knew it was time to check on Hilda before sending my report back to Devarim.

A ten-year-old boy was heading towards the house with a full bucket of water from the local well when I arrived. A mop of blonde hair covered his head, while some dirt spotted his cheeks. His short-sleeved tunic was dirty, but not ragged.

"Good morning," I said as friendly as I could, hands open.

"Ma, there is a strange man here. He's armed. And has pointy ears!" The boy called to the house.

They always notice the ears. Maybe I need to use my hood. No, too hot for summer. Perhaps a cap? Just accept your life, Galieb.

Hilda stood in the door, spear in hand, her long sleeve sliding back to her elbow to reveal a slender but strong forearm. Brown eyes looked out of a pretty, yet determined countenance, unafraid. A boy and a girl peaked around her aproned skirts, each a little younger than the water boy. The way she stood, she resembled a symbol of the enduring women of Lageheim.

"Hans! Inside, now." Her eyes never left me. "What are you? An elfin?"

"My name's Galieb. My mother is elfin," I stated, leaving the rest of my past unsaid. "I mean no harm. I was eating at the inn when you came in and Friedl took you home. Any word on your husband's return?"

"I know you not and you are not a Lageheimer. What business is that of yours?"

"My order trained me to help others, like the knights. I just want to help to find your husband and make sure you are all safe. I know eshkin are raiding close to here, and livestock have disappeared. May I look around the area?"

She brushed individual strands of blonde from her face before she spoke, while the rest of her hair remained piled up out of the way.

"We've endured much and will continue to endure. Times are always hard on the edge of the wild. But every woman's wary when her husband's away and other men know of it. If your words be true, they found a dead sheep dog just a few paces north of here. Near the river. All torn up. Some sheep and calves are missing, too. Don't expect a reward."

Sounded like permission. "I am not looking for any reward, my lady. Just want to help. Hopefully, we can find your husband." Hilda's hand never left the spear.

Out of respect, I gave the house a wide berth as I followed the road, which became nothing more than a narrow path leading north into the green. Waving grasslands decorated the low, rolling hills. These were not the woods of home with its hemlocks and hardwoods, but it was beautiful enough in its own way.

I came upon a shepherd who was guarding his flock with a spear, a short sword, and a sling, who complained of missing sheep. A large dog stayed close, growling at me.

Must be the ears.

Neither seemed pleased to see me at first, but I won them over once I told him I was investigating the missing sheep and heard about the dead guard dog. He pointed out where I could find a rock cairn closer to the river. He buried his beloved canine just where he had found him.

I found the cairn with little trouble. It was obvious the man had made the monument with care. Not much sign remained of whatever had killed the dog, but there was also no sign of any eshkin about. Eshkin tended to be destructive and lived for plunder. Perhaps a wild animal chased out of the mountains by the eshkin raiders found livestock to be easy prey.

I scanned the horizon, and sniffed the air for clues, the prevailing breeze coming out of the northwest. Dark gray smoke clung to the mountains to the north and east. My instincts told me to try the river for any tracks in mud or sand. Or maybe it was the voices of my mentors in my head.

The muddy banks kept no secrets from those who searched. I found paw prints of great size. Vollyr, the aged centaur, had trained me in tracking, but I had seen nothing like this before. It seemed to be a cross between a decent-sized wild cat and an oversized wolf, yet was neither. And it was way too big. The tracks measured more like the size of a bear print, but with canine claws.

The creature had an odd walking pattern to the tracks as well. I did not know what to make of it. I found a few drops of blood, too. Whatever it was, I guessed it swam the river with its prize. Not an easy feat in the strong current.

I backtracked and then discerned that the creature came from the south. Not fresh, but these tracks seemed too recent to be the ones coming from the sheep or the cairn. I assessed them to be a day or so old. I didn't get far before I lost the trail in the grasses, my experience being of the forest, and not grass-lands. The tracks seemed to come from near the town or Hilda's place.

I did not like my conclusions.

The town's reeve will want to know what's going on.

Heading back towards town, I stayed along the riverbank, following it south as it flowed downstream, just to see if I could find more clues.

Sure enough, I found some more of the beast's prints. Fresher. This morning even. I could see the walled village in the distance now, as the founders had established it right by a bend in the river. Boot and human footprints mixed with the beast's, cluttering the tracks. Whatever crossed the water this morning, it had moved close to town.

I pulled my bow out and checked my weapons as I followed the general direction I suspected it had headed. I switched between scanning the environment around me and checking the grass for signs. The open landscape rolled in small, wavy hills, limiting my vision. Clumps of trees dotted the river's banks occasionally, also restricting my view.

As I moved up a small incline, my eyes caught something out of place. Not thirty paces in front of me, brown and red ochre fur poked just above the hill crest. A savage-looking canine head came into view as I moved closer. The creature's short-snouted face focused forward in complete concentration on a female villager not five paces in front of it.

She stood as still as a statue, staring into the monster's eyes.

CHAPTER 11
SMOKE AND FIRE

I went from calm to full heart-pounding action in an instant. I yelled as I whipped out an arrow, then rushed up the incline for a better shot, releasing the broad-headed missile.

The beast remained transfixed on his victim until the shaft sank into his left bicep.

The creature howled in pain, and then shifted its eyes in my direction as it hunched down, dropping its head below the hill out of my field of vision. The villager collapsed, dropping out of my range of sight.

I scrambled up over the hill, pulling another arrow, fearing the beast would grab her and flee.

It did not.

Catching me by complete surprise, I plunged right into my enemy head-on as it rushed towards me. All I saw was a wall of spotted fur and teeth while oversized clawed hands reached towards me on extra-long arms.

I released the second arrow, but it flew over its shoulder. I dropped my bow and had just enough time to yank out my ax and dagger, sweeping my left foot back to dodge, not having the time to avoid its assault.

Canine jaws aimed for my throat, but my twist caused it to sink its teeth into my shoulder instead.

It knocked me over and clawed at my belly with its hind leg like a cat, and then grappled me with its two oversized hands, the claws on its fingers digging into my flesh. The only thing that kept me from being torn apart was my armor, though it ripped open my trousers and raked my left thigh.

I stabbed and hacked with both weapons, hoping to beat it away if not kill it. It used its arms for defense to keep me from landing a solid cut into its thick hide.

The creature released its jaws and turned its head towards town, listening while saliva dripping from yellow-stained teeth onto my torso.

It leapt away and fled as I swung at it a few last times.

The woman lay sprawled unconscious on the ground, but looked unharmed and breathing, so I took chase once I found my bow. The beast ran with great speed, making large strides with its two canine hind legs.

I watched it rip my arrow out of its arm and toss it aside without flinching or even slowing down. The rolling terrain kept me from getting off another shot. It plunged into the river, swimming across in mere minutes despite the current.

The beast stopped at the far bank, looking back with its large round eyes, rounded ears, and powerful canine jaws, still dripping saliva.

Before I could launch another arrow, it sped over the hills and disappeared.

"No way to catch it now," I grumbled to myself. If my life depended on it, I could probably swim across, but I would not try it today. I felt annoyed it got away, but also thankful that my armor had kept me from being torn to pieces.

I watched for a few minutes to make sure it did not return. I then hurried back to its intended victim to find several villagers assisting her. The men eyed me as they gripped their weapons. They all saw my ears but made no comments.

"Is she alright?" I asked.

"What happened here? And who are you?" questioned a man with salt and pepper hair. Several hands reached for knives and swords, though no one drew anything yet.

"Galieb. A ranger. I saw some monster about to attack her. I gave chase, but it got away." My still pumping blood added excitement to my tone.

The villagers looked me over for a moment with unreadable expressions, taking in my mangled brigandine armor and my torn trousers. I realized blood trickled down my leg.

"Looks like it got the better of ya'," the same man answered, rubbing his beardless chin as he looked me over. I guessed he was the leader by the way the others waited for his reactions. His clothes matched the others, but seemed a little finer.

"Aye," I answered.

"I am Ballard. The town reeve," the leader said, introducing himself.

The hands of the other men relaxed, letting go of their weapons.

The woman woke up and moaned softly. She gasped, eyes wide at first to find so many hovering over her until she recognized their faces.

They questioned her, but she remembered nothing since leaving her house.

I updated the reeve on my findings. When they asked the woman about the creature, she shuttered in fear, but did not know anything about it.

"She stared right into its eyes. Some kind of trance perhaps?" I suggested.

Ballard just nodded, but did not offer an opinion.

"Ranger you say? Can you track it? Over there?" the reeve asked, pointing across the river.

"I think so. I will try."

"If you find its den, let us or Sir Bastian know, and we'll round up men to stop it. I'll pay you if you bring me the hide."

"Sounds like a deal. I recommend you have men patrol around here. Focus along the river. It has been coming across. Maybe that is what happened to Lief."

"Ya, I heard Lief's missing. If this beast got him, I pity him." The reeve shook his head. "The duke is calling for armed men up at the lumber camps between the waters. Some are heading up in the morning. You can cross with them. Meet at the ferry at first light. Let Sir Bastian know about the beast. He may hire you for scouting, too."

A pair of men knew this woman's husband was a fisherman and that they lived next to the river. The men agreed to escort her home.

Every male villager strapped swords and slings on their belts from that day on. Most of the women did, too. Some of the folks also carried bows.

Heading back to town, I passed near Hilda's place. Her children saw me and rushed over. Hans now had an arming sword on his hip, too, but it looked too big for him.

"Did you find anything?" they asked with excitement. "Kill any eshkin?"

"No eshkin. But there's another beast about. Don't go out alone anymore. Make sure your mother knows about the beast."

"Any sign of our da?" asked the little girl, Delana.

"No. I am sorry. But I spoke with the reeve. Everyone's

looking." She looked very sad. They all did. She just nodded. I feared far worse but could not say.

"The duke's calling for men to fight eshkin. Maybe he went up there," said Albert, the middle boy.

"Maybe. Don't forget to tell your mother and neighbors about the beast. Do not go out at night and be alert all the time. Stay close to the house," I warned.

"Mom has a spear da made. We got slings and da's sword. See." The boys showed me the sword and their slings made of woven river reeds and wool, just like the one I saw on the shepherd's belt.

"Practice every day. And protect your sister and mother."

"We will! Just find our da!" Hans said. The others nodded as they all ran off.

My heart felt for Lief's family. Circumstance reminded me that the wandering monk, Derleik, was wrong. Life had meaning. Helping others had its worth. And if there was more to life than the rising of the sun, then something greater existed. Justice. Goodness. A universal moral law. And a Law Giver.

I went looking for the beggar, Otto, but didn't see him, so I continued onto the vek handler and sent an update to Devarim. I watched the vek slither off into the sky, its wings fluttering too fast to see, heading south with a pouch strapped to its back. Few knew of our abbey, and we kept it that way by telling no one. Because of this, getting a message back home took some planning. I sent my message to the vek handler in Travailin. From there, they would pass it onto the Inn. The innkeeper, Erdan, would see it got to Devarim.

The message would probably reach him before I arrived at the camps 'between the waters', as the locals said.

~

EARLY THE NEXT MORNING, I walked the mile back down to the ferry, which was nothing more than a large flat barge with a railing all around and a heavy hemp rope stretched across the Gaderon River. There was plenty of room for the six of us crossing that morning. The river slowed down at this area, but widened quite a bit. The ferryman had a man for each bank to work the cranks that moved the boat back and forth.

I warned the ferryman about the monstrous beast I had fought as we moved across the calm waters. He showed me his longbow, signal horn, and arming sword, his eyes confident but not cocky.

"He jumped me in a flash, even after I stuck an arrow in him," I warned. "The only thing that saved me was my armor."

Even through the under tunic, the small steel platelets of the brigandine irritated my shoulder where the monster had crunched it with his powerful jaws. I feared an eshkin javelin might force its way through the compromised section. The night before, I used a rock to flatten out the damaged platelets, but it really needed a skilled armorer. Not that I could afford that. Being out in the world was getting expensive.

I wanted to take it back to Stakhiljan, the artisan who reforged my sword. I imagined him muttering dwarfin blessings as he worked at his forge in Stonecrest. Alas, I was now too far away. My armor should still do its job, but now without the shine. Maybe that was a sign I was no longer an inexperienced acolyte.

As for my trousers, I had done my best sewing them together myself, squinting in the candlelight last night after working on my brigandine. They looked it, too.

A few healing berries this morning closed up the deep scratch on my thigh and also served as breakfast.

Once the boat touched the eastern bank, the rest of the men slung their round shields and packs onto their backs and headed for Sir Bastian's camp on the road heading east. I traveled upriver looking for tracks. It did not take me long to find where the monster crossed. Blood dotted the rocks and a few partial prints left impressions in the sandy soil. This is where it crossed when I chased it yesterday.

I marked the spot with a pile of rocks and continued up the shoreline for other telltale signs. I spotted the dog cairn on the far west bank and found some older tracks in the sand on my side. The trail headed southeast.

This second trail had faded more, so I went back to the first set and followed them. They headed east across the pastures in the general direction of the lumber camps. About half a mile from the river, the trail led to a small rock shelf jutting out of a hill, surrounded by a cluster of trees. Under the shelf, I found human remains and other bones. I also discovered a hole punch and a curved lip blade honed to a razor sharpness. Leather worker tools. It didn't look good for Lief.

The trail continued east, so I followed it after I collected the tools.

The creature had avoided the square logged houses and barns, but passed very close to some farmsteads. I spoke to anyone I saw, but none reported seeing the creature. Most of the folk on this side of the river were ranchers, breeding beef cattle or sheep. The men all sported thick beards curled on the ends, and were dressed in heavier work tunics and trousers. None of the clean-shaven shop keeper types here. All the men worked with swords on their hips and with other weapons close by. The women, too, kept spears or bows handy. The eshkin raids had them all on edge. However, very few of the folks in this area actually left their homesteads, despite the danger.

I passed burned and looted ranches, too. Lingering smoke kept the sky gray.

I lost the trail just before sunset, so I looked for a good place to camp for the night.

A new line of gray smoke now billowed on the eastern horizon, interrupting my search. The flames remained hidden behind the hills of the rolling grassland, except for a tinge of orange at the base of the darkening cloud of smoke.

Must be another raid on a farmstead.

I readied my bow and prepared myself for another fight. "Guess I am not getting any sleep tonight," I muttered as I headed towards the glow at a paced run. I could not let more people suffer without trying, if it truly was an eshkin raid.

I steeled myself for the potential battle ahead, not letting fear get a hold in my mind. Once again, I may be required to kill. It was becoming a bad habit.

As I neared the area, I scurried to a small knoll so I could scout out the situation before rushing in. This proved wise. A chaotic scene enfolded below me. Several broad-shouldered eshkin waved their arms and chased after panicked cattle and a few horses. If a cow got too close, they poked it with their javelins, trying to move them towards a large enclosed corral at the west end of the property. Another of the bald warriors set fire to the hay inside a wooden barn in the center of the property, as two other warriors threw out pitchforks and other tools. Several small wooden buildings burned to the north, releasing the heavy smoke that drew me here.

My gaze fell on what concerned me the most: a few of the eshkin had surrounded the house southeast of the barn, where it appeared the family had barricaded themselves within. Two warriors stood in front of the cabin built of squared logs, and two moved around to the back.

A dozen gray-skinned warriors were a bit much to take on alone, but they had spread themselves out.

Maybe I can divide and conquer, I thought. Plans formulated into my mind.

I hoped the duke's men had noticed the flames as well, but I could not count on that. I knew I was on my own, and no matter what, I could not abandon this family to a fiery death.

Cover seemed scant, the cattle having grazed the grasses low and trampled all the brush, but I had the element of surprise.

"Those two behind the house will never see the light of day," I whispered with determination.

The sun had already dipped below the horizon, with the last light fading fast in the smoky sky. My elfin vision would soon change from color to intricate shades of gray, reducing my bow accuracy to sixty paces at most. The closest warrior stood at one hundred paces. I regulated my breathing as I aimed. Releasing my breath and the arrow at the same time, the missile slammed into the left shoulder blade of the closest eshkin behind the house, piercing hides and thick leather armor.

He screamed, arching his back. Hands reached behind for the bolt, but never got past the top of the shoulder. The raider turned, staying low, scanning for his hidden enemy. The other raider behind the house glanced at him, but took no notice of his plight, focusing all his attention on the cabin. He also yelled in response, but only in battle lust, not pain. The two in front of the cabin still knew nothing of my presence.

I slipped forward down the slope of the hill. The darkness had all but taken over by now. Even with my elfin vision, one hundred paces was now too far for another arrow without moving closer. I assumed their night vision matched mine for distance, so I used that to my advantage, keeping to the shadows. The other eshkin warriors also became hard to see, except for those near the fires, whose silhouettes reflected an orange glow.

My second shaft hit the wounded eshkin below the right pectoral, killing him with little more than a grunt as his companion watched him fall. The second eshkin reacted with alarm and attempted to duck behind a tree. He was not quick enough, for my third arrow caught him in the hip.

As I rushed forward to get a better angle to finish my opponent, a burning torch flipped through the air to land on the cabin's roof. It slid down the steep slope in front, out of sight.

Now they are burning the cabin. Time to get the family out of there!

The wounded eshkin tossed a javelin at me as I came into his sight, so I twisted and it missed, but I failed to reciprocate.

At that moment, the family burst out the back door. Leading the charge was a bearded man brandishing an arming sword and a round shield. Behind him came his teenage son with a spear and wearing a metal cap, followed by a barking cattle dog.

A woman and a teenage girl bolted for the dark pastures beyond with a stumbling elderly woman held between them.

The father saw the wounded eshkin with the arrow in its hip by the tree and rushed forward to attack him. But another raider, one that had been looting the barn, came around the far corner of the house at the same time behind the man.

The boy defended his dad's flank by thrusting a spear at the newly arrived warrior. The eshkin parried and swung his sword, cuffing the boy on the helm, causing the youth to stagger. If not for their dog nipping at the raider's heels, the boy would not have survived. The eshkin kicked at the barking dog with booted feet, but never landed a blow. Enraged at seeing his boy stumble, the man turned back to defend his son. The father cut their enemy down, and the boy sunk his spear tip into the body to finish him.

My wounded quarry swung his head about, trying to watch the bearded man and me as he leaned on the tree, my arrow still protruding from his hip. He held a second javelin in one hand, his great axe in the other.

I put an arrow deep into his torso. He slid down the tree with his final breath.

Flames appeared on the roof.

More eshkin raced around the house, alerted by the barking dog.

I planted another arrow in the gut of the first to come around on the north side, and he collapsed. Another eshkin charged past him while one more came around the south side of the cabin.

"Let's get out of here!" I screamed. "Protect your family!"

Surprise crossed their faces, as if they just realized I was there, but their countenance changed to thankfulness.

We had no time to run.

The two newest eshkin raiders came right at us, tossing javelins. The father caught a javelin on his shield and moved into sword range with his son next to him.

I dodged the javelin coming at me, but my enemy followed with a heavy falchion cut. The tip scraped across my brigandine as I leapt back, drawing my sword. I parried the next cut and answered with a riposte, thrusting my point into his shoulder. He growled, spittle flying. His cuirass of hardened leather lined with fur stopped it from going too deep, but I knew the tip penetrated the torso.

We both created distance to assess each other.

I threw my bow to the side and slid out my axe as we circled. I slashed with my sword, following it up with a hooking technique with the axe, but he parried and cut. Both of us proved unsuccessful. A few more clashes left several cuts on his thigh and forearms, my longer blade proving the advantage.

We both heard his companion cry out in death throes behind me, so he turned to run. I threw my axe, hitting him square in the back. He crumbled to the ground, so I burst forward to finish him with a thrust to the heart.

I checked on the father and son. Their opponent lay dead at their feet. They both looked wide-eyed from the fight, but uninjured. The man patted his son's shoulder with pride. He nodded to me and pulled the javelin out of his shield, preparing for the next fight. We all stood, catching our breath, watching for more warriors to come around the home when we heard the sound of horns blowing.

CHAPTER 12
SHELTER IN A STORM

Out of the darkness rode a knight in full armor mounted on a large sorrel charger, followed by twenty men on horseback. Armed with spears, round shields, and swords, the men of Wynchell swept in between the now fully blazing barn and the smoldering home and assembled in the open field southwest of the barn.

At the sound of the horns, the remaining eshkin fled, scattering the cattle they had just corralled. The knight, barking orders, sent a dozen men after them.

The homesteader, seeing the raiders flee, dashed off into the night after his family. The youth followed.

What men remained dismounted and worked to save the cabin. Grabbing two buckets by a spring house south of the cabin, they soon had a line passing buckets back and forth from the spring to the cabin roof. A few other men soaked woolen blankets thrown out of the barn by the eshkin and beat on the fire. I hurried to join them. The barn was too far gone, so we let it burn. As we splashed bucket after bucket on the roof of the home, a burning chunk of the roof fell in.

Seemingly out of nowhere, the homesteader returned and snatched one of the buckets. The front door remained barricaded from inside, so he rushed around back to get in. A soldier followed him with a blanket. They smothered the burning shingles on the floor of the cabin while we did what we could outside.

I scrambled onto the edge of the roof, using wet rags to smother the burning shingles. The men shouldered a bucket up to me as others climbed up with blankets. Together, we worked until only steam and white smoke remained.

We all just watched the barn burn, making sure it didn't spread as we wet everything close by.

I now noticed the rest of the family standing to the side, hugging each other, watching the men work, having returned from the pastures with the father. The knight removed his helmet and approached them. I heard him inquire about any injuries and offered them comfort. Once satisfied they were all safe, he continued to command his men, making sure the fires did not spread, and ordered some to guard our flanks.

The rest of the soldiers returned with bloodied spears just as the barn collapsed in on itself, the flames reaching dozens of feet into the air.

After receiving the report from his returning men that all the fleeing eshkin were dead, the knight turned to me. "I am Sir Bastian of Langbard, knight of Wynchell. Who are you?"

Sir Bastian stood straight and lean, half a head taller than me. His wavy red hair and curled beard looked well groomed, but matted from sweat.

"Galieb Half-elfin of the Qoholet, at your service."

"Heard of the Qoholet. Scouts, or perhaps 'ranger', is a better term?" He studied me, his olive eyes drifting to my ears, which he noticed even in the minimal light of the fires. "You represented your Order well this night, despite your youth.

Thank you for your assistance. I understand you saved this family."

"Glad they are all safe. Just doing what they taught me to do: help others in need."

"Never met a half-elfin before. What brings you to this remote part of the kingdom?"

"A few weeks ago, I encountered a quad of eshkin while on my patrols. My Order sent me here, thinking more may have come down out of the mountains. And to assist in any way I can."

"There are plenty of eshkin, as you can see. More than I have ever seen in my lifetime. Half of Wynchell is burning or already burnt. It will take years for these families to recover. Devastating." The knight sighed as his eyes focused on the barn. "We could use a scout. The ones I sent out have yet to return. If they are not at the camp by the time I get back, I must assume they have perished." He watched me to see my reaction.

The job did not scare me. Folami and the others had trained me well. Maybe I should be scared. Maybe I just had youthful bravado. "Sorry to hear that. What do you need?"

"Where are the eshkin base camps? How big are these camps? How many eshkin are we facing? Which mountain pass are they using to enter Wynchell?"

"What is the status of the dwarfin of Sarengeld? I sent men with messages to their halls, but never heard back. We have received no contact from them. No veks are available to us here. We need more information. Can you help? The duke will pay you well—if you prove valuable."

"I will do my best, sir."

"It will take your best, young man. This is a dangerous assignment. Like I said, the others have not returned."

"I will not take unnecessary risks. Sir Bastian, there is

something else you should know." I paused, looked him in the eye to be sure he was listening. "Another monster roams your land." And I told him all I knew about the upright beast. Guilt and frustration weighed on me for not being able to track it.

"Dragon's breath! This is the first I have heard of the creature. We don't need another problem." His brow wrinkled in thought. "I will pass the word."

He stared off in thought. "Sounds like the reeve is doing what he can. He must believe you to be very capable. And you demonstrated that here. I will stand by Ballard's promise if you kill this monster. However, my need is greater. We need to gain control of this invasion before I can send him help. My mission takes priority."

We all camped at the homestead for the night, which gave the family comfort. I didn't mind having all the extra swords around me, either. Sir Bastian stated he had sent multiple patrols across western Wynchell checking on the homesteads. He planned to clear all the eshkin among the homesteads west of the lumber road before going after the raider's larger camps farther north.

"You need to gather your family and follow us back to my tents. I have men fortifying the lumber camps as we speak," the knight said to the father of the rescued family. "All my patrols have the same orders: bring everyone to safety."

The landowner argued, stating he had to gather up livestock and rebuild his home. He agreed to send his family with the knight, however. The youth begged his da to let him stay and help.

The folk of Wynchell were hardy, surviving many hardships. Just like this man, a large portion of them refused to abandon their livelihoods and all they sacrificed to carve out a home here.

~

"I CAN SEND a few men with you," the knight said to me at breakfast. Our morning meal consisted of fresh steak strips, fried apples, bread, and eggs, courtesy of the knight's cook and the family.

"Unless they can match a ranger's skill, I prefer to travel alone," I replied.

The knight studied me, sizing up my youth to see if I was just boasting.

"As you wish. The road from Farrin's Crossing travels due east to the lumber camps. That is where I set up our base. Both settlements sit at the crossroads where the pastures end at the edge of the woods. We call this forest between the waters 'Wood Harvest'. Our people have been harvesting lumber here since the Tyrian chieftains ruled. Even before Lageheim and King Walferd the Just.

"From there, the other road continues due north along the edge of the canopy. It leads directly to the dwarfin halls of Sarengeld. If it is easier, follow our tracks east and you will cross that road eventually, but you will be north of our base. However, I fear the eshkin control the road to the north of the camps, so use caution. It's a two-day march from the cross-roads to the halls under normal circumstances."

"I don't plan to use the roads," I said.

"Use your best judgement. As long as you complete the job safely. And in a timely manner. It is dangerous no matter which way you go, either through the open pasture lands west of the road or through the forest to the east of it. There seems to be more eshkin hiding in Wood Harvest now that we are chasing them off the homesteads. Be wise."

I set off immediately after that, heading northeast. Eshkin prefer the night, so I hoped to get as far as I could before they moved about after sunset. Still, they are not like goblins who despise the sun, and I could never be sure.

The land seemed open at first glance, but wooded lots and hedgerows divided some pastures. Trees and brush filled the draws between the rolling hills and broke up the view. I kept to the edges of the pastures and stayed below the skyline as much as I could.

I had to be wary of what may be hiding amongst the brush in the draws, but timid rabbits and annoyed birds were all I encountered. The occasional lost livestock gathered under any trees they found for safety. Empty but intact farms mixed with burnt shells of log buildings in other places. Smoke hung in the air, irritating the lungs.

I found horse tracks at a creek crossing from one of the knight's patrols, so I felt safe the first day. I never saw more signs of the upright beast, though I watched for it. It hid its tracks well or had circled back across the river. Hopefully, the citizens of Farrin's Crossing remained prepared.

I came across a small homestead as a summer storm rolled in, causing the daylight to end early. The place appeared recently abandoned. The owners must have left with Sir Bastian's men, or the eshkin had chased them off. I found no corpses, so chances were they just left.

Watching the low black clouds roll towards me made the hay-filled barn an inviting place to settle in for the night. Entering the cabin felt invasive, so I didn't. That was a family's home. A spring house sat near the cabin with the water flowing out under the south wall, forming into a small stream as it headed to the Gaderon River.

Inside the tiny log structure, I guzzled my fill before filling my waterskin. Nothing tastes better than water bubbling out of the ground!

When I came back out, a small, domesticated goat greeted

me at the door with a bleat. Mostly black with small horns, the creature appeared young. I couldn't imagine someone leaving it behind, so I assumed it was a stray, drawn to the water and shelter. Predators would get her if the eshkin did not, but I couldn't do anything about that. She seemed leery of me yet wanting my company, so I talked to her as I searched the place. She hovered close. Finding some grain, I fed her a few handfuls before I settled in for the night.

The low clouds blocked out the mountains as heavy rain dumped down. I, or should I say we, sat watching the rain come down in hypnotic sheets until it eventually slowed to a lighter pattern.

After peering over my shoulder for the last two days, the entire experience calmed my soul. I so enjoyed watching a good rain, as long as I was not getting drenched by it.

The clouds lifted higher but remained. The rain and wind helped to clear the air. I now noticed the glow of fires reflecting off the night sky somewhere in the far distance. Eshkin drums blended with the noise of the raindrops on the roof, destroying the tranquility. Ranger Horten taught us that eshkin chant and dance around the fires for hours before beginning their raids after sunset. The group I encountered last night must have started early.

I debated setting traps before curling up in one of the stalls, but looking down at the goat, I suspected she would get tangled in them before any eshkin arrived. In the end, she settled down in the hay with me after I closed the doors, leaving one open just a crack.

"I don't blame you for staying close, little one. It is scary out there right now."

She responded with a pleading bleat.

"Just be quiet. We don't want to draw any enemies in here looking for a snack."

After a few hours of sleep, the goat woke me with a frightened cry. All I could hear was the drizzling rain tapping on the roof.

"Better be ready to flee, Lil," I whispered to my new companion. "Shh." I grabbed my pack and strapped my weapons on. 'Lil' I called her, short for 'little goat.'

"Hey Muck, maybe humans here still," came a loud voice in the eshkin tongue.

"Look around. If someone's here, we'll find 'em."

The goat and I remained well-hidden in the barn, but I remembered what happened to the last barn. They had no reason to burn it down, but that did not mean they wouldn't. The rain had soaked everything, but the hay inside was dry.

I glanced at Lil, hoping she would cooperate. "You shouldn't have named her," I scolded myself.

The door stood open a crack, allowing for a peak to the north. I could see several armed figures moving about. I tiptoed to the east wall of the barn and peaked out a hole in the boards. A bunch more rummaged the property. I estimated at least a dozen, probably more like two dozen total, surrounding me.

The eshkin poked around the property for a while, looking for anything of value, including weapons, food, tools, even blankets. Eshkin produced little on their own. They mostly scavenged from their raids.

They filled their water skins at the spring house. Afterwards, they fouled the waters with their waste.

One walked over to the barn door to inspect the structure. I hid in the corner, but I could see the eshkin through the boards of the stall. His right earlobe had two iron rings, while the left one sported two bones. Leather and sheepskin covered the eshkin's broad shoulders and a round torso. Tusks jutted above his upper lip, one twice as long as the other. His round dome sported no hair, just dry gray skin and old scars.

Seeing him triggered flashbacks to Dolf and the rest of that patrol. This one seemed taller than those three, but perhaps my memory was off.

Lil paced around the back of the barn, bleating. She could sense my nerves on edge, which added to her pacing. I squatted down with my sword and axe drawn. Part of me pitied the creature, but the rest of me knew Lil was drawing my foe right to me.

"Looks like we'll have roasted goat tonight," laughed the eshkin as he approached the goat while he pulled his axe off his shoulder. Lil panicked even more, bleating and running back and forth, not sure where to go.

As he moved to end Lil's life with his axe, the corner of his eye caught sight of me crouched down beside him. For just a split second, my blues encountered his black orbs.

CHAPTER 13
KEEP RUNNING

I exploded forward, ramming my sword tip deep into his gut, up under the hardened leather armor, surprise still on his face. He tried to swing his axe around, but it was too tight, the handle bumping against my left vambrace instead.

He howled, spitting up blood across the hay as he stumbled back.

The spike of my axe passed through the cuirass and sank into his chest, his legs collapsing under him. The falling body pulled at my blades, still deep within the cavity, but I kept a firm grip.

I knew the warrior's dying shriek had alerted the entire patrol. Outside, eshkin bellowed and scrambled towards the barn.

I bolted out the door, hoping to make it to some brush or get out of sight fast, my blood-covered blades still in hand.

Lil bleated with fear as she ran right beside my heels, kicking up mud. The eshkin hooted in laughter at the sport, clacking their jaws together before giving chase.

"Come on, Lil! Let's get out of here! Stay close!" I said, as if she understood every word.

One eshkin almost collided with me, but I dodged him and his falchion and kept running, my legs soaked by the wet grass.

Javelins landed all around.

I looked down to see that Lil no longer ran beside me. Dread hit my gut as I slowed to look back. I could see her behind, still bleating as she tried to catch up to my long strides.

I ducked a thrown javelin.

Scowling, I sheathed my axe and sword as I sprinted over to her. I scooped her up and threw her over my shoulder, still grumbling as mud splattered on my face, a few drops getting on my tongue.

Her bleating increased. One eshkin closed in. I drew my sword again.

I parried his cut and performed a wild slash, causing him to stumble back, slip on the wet grass, and tumble over a bush.

Sword in one hand and goat on my shoulder, I sprinted off again.

"You're a fool, Galieb!" I scolded out loud.

But I couldn't leave my new friend to those butchers. She weighed more than she looked, but the adrenaline kept me going. At least she was small for her breed. Her fur rubbed my cheek and beard, and she smelled of wet fur and manure.

The drizzling rain got into my eyes. Mud covered both of us and the grass soaked my trousers. We zigzagged across the pasture and crested a hill.

They didn't need torches, but the overcast sky limited their night vision. Mine, too, for that matter. I just needed to stay far enough ahead.

My only actual plan seemed to be not to die.

But I even questioned that motive as the goat bounced on

my shoulder. Thankfully, she stopped bleating. Javelins still landed close, some very close, but I couldn't afford to look back. I just hoped nothing hit either of us.

I ducked into a ravine, using the soggy, thicker brush to my advantage. Sparing a glance back the way I came, I couldn't see them. I dropped Lil next to me.

"What would a rabbit do?" I muttered to myself as I crawled my way up the water filled ravine and caught my breath. Lil hugged my hip but didn't make any noise.

The rain stopped.

Or a deer? A deer would flee until it felt safe. A rabbit would dart into the brush or find a hole to hide in. Someplace out of reach if possible. Well, I ran for a while. Both darting and fleeing.

I did some breathing exercises to calm down. *I doubt eshkin stamina can match mine, even carrying my newfound friend. Keep running for now. I can hide later.*

I did not know if that was reasonable or not in my excited state, but I went with it.

Stop comparing yourself to a rabbit! What about a cat? Even a lion would flee if surrounded by a pack. I am no lion. Knights are more like lions. Rangers are more like panthers. Or owls. Stalking silently. Not an option here.

Flee it is.

I considered finding high ground to use my war bow. With the right spot, I could pick them off one by one before they reached me. Perhaps without being seen.

That seemed to work at the barn burning yesterday. Until the family came out.

But I feared using all my arrows. I had lost a few since leaving home, but I should still have enough to deter this small patrol. Sure, I'd probably retrieve most of them, but maybe not. Either way, I would need more for this excursion. I had no doubt of that. I still had plenty of miles ahead. Perhaps the duke or maybe the dwarfin could help me resupply. At least my bow was an option.

Lil added another unknown factor to any plan I came up with.

I listened but heard nothing but water dripping off the bushes. I peeked out of the brush. No enemies about. I crept out of the brush to the edge of the ravine and looked across open pastures and grasslands. No eshkin in my sight, but the darkness and the hills hid much.

We started moving again, using the hilly landscape to my advantage. Bushes cluttered the ravines between the hills and an occasional maple grew here and there. The eshkin and I caught glimpses of each other, but each time, I gained on my pursuers. They no longer tossed javelins.

Eventually, they gave up, so I changed course and headed north before drifting northeast to put more land between us.

After seeing no signs of their pursuit for another hour, I crawled under another sopping bush to get a few more hours of sleep. Lil stayed right by my side.

In the morning, I stretched to work the kinks out of my sore, wet body. Looking down at myself, I realized I was a muddy mess. Mud covered my trousers from the knees down and was also across my left shoulder and upper arm. My weapons needed tending, too. I did not clean them properly after the fight, and they could use a good sharpening. Rust was another concern with all the rain. Too many rough nights since leaving home.

Was that just a few weeks ago?

Lil had risen before me and grazed close by. I took that as a good sign. The sky had cleared, and the sun peaked over the green rolling pastures, revealing the great Towering Peaks to the north. A beautiful morning, but I could already taste the humidity as I prepped for the day.

Sir Bastian said it was a two-day journey, so I estimated I had traveled half the distance the first day. I hoped to reach the dwarfin halls by nightfall. Of course, I had a new ward now. Risking my life last night for this little creature, I couldn't just abandon her.

Part of me thought it was foolish to make such an effort for a goat. I had planned to leave her to her fate, but when the time came, I could not do it.

Why did I go back for her? I was risking not only myself, but my mission. Why? Because she was innocent. A vulnerable creature before the hands of brutal destroyers.

Someday, even if a loving family takes her as their own, at the right time, they would slaughter her for food. But that was acceptable and probably quick. I saw a purpose in that.

I cared more for Lil than the eshkin that was about to kill her. And the same for the assassin back in Travailin.

Death had its place in this world, such as punishment for heinous crimes, yet seemed out of place much of the time. Tragic in many circumstances, but most would say 'just' in certain others.

What about risking the mission and perhaps other lives in Wynchell?

I did not see myself sacrificing people's lives for the goat as a standard practice. A wicked person, perhaps, as I understood wicked.

Am I wise enough for such judgments?

I knew the answer to that was 'no,' yet I did not feel my choices were wrong, either. I had to do what I felt was right until I learned otherwise.

For now, I figured the right thing to do was to see it through and get her somewhere safe. I didn't know if she would slow me down or give me away. Funny how I refused Sir Bastian's help for those same reasons.

I feel like I am still solving Qoholet puzzles or being put through one of their tests. And not for the first time since leaving home.

The eshkin, Lady Zebah, the assassins, Derleik the Wandering Eye, tracking the beast—they all felt like trials or tests of some kinds.

But this is real life now. Lives are at stake. I do not know if I am failing these challenges or not.

One thing I could not deny: I felt the hand of providence drawing me forward. Someone, the Creator perhaps, the being the Qoholet called the 'Yett Sorr,' must want me to have this companion.

I also know one of those javelins should have found me or Lil as we fled the barn, but not one of them did.

I had been drifting northeast since leaving Sir Bastian. Here, the homesteads seemed more spread out, and I did not see as many. The raiders burned to the ground every one I saw, along with much of the surrounding landscape. Smoke lingered in the air and a few trees still smoldered despite the previous rain. Dead bodies lay among buildings, both human and livestock. The eshkin had tied one man to a post and stabbed him to death with javelins. Seeing such evil actions boiled my blood. I did not stop at any of the places.

Soon after sunup, I encountered the road north to the dwarfin halls. Just as the knight stated, the grasslands ended at the dirt road. Wide enough for two wagons to pass, it ran along the edge of a forest that stretched out of sight east, north, and south. I wondered if these woods were part of the VenKeth, but quickly dismissed that idea. Lumbermen harvested this area in the past, unlike that mysterious forest, which few dared to enter.

Slinking behind some bushes, I watched the road before crossing. Lil munched fresh grasses on the slope behind me, unconcerned. I didn't have to cross the road to follow it north, but being in the trees was preferable to the open pastures on this side.

Everything appeared quiet, so I tiptoed out into the open and knelt beside the road. The rising summer sun was quickly drying everything out, but the road remained muddy with small pools of water in the low spots. Lil drifted over to see what I was doing. She never wandered too far away.

I checked for prints and found tracks in the mud. During the night, after the rain slowed, eshkin must have crossed the road heading southwest.

I snagged a branch and blurred our steps as best I could behind me before darting under the leafy canopy on the other side.

The tracks moved out from an abandoned camp. Some firepits still smoldered. The brush all around lay crushed, and the trees bore marks of abuse. It appeared as if they had tried to burn the forest, but the rain put it out.

I scowled.

Hopefully, Sir Bastian and his crew will deal with them. I found nothing more worthwhile, so we continued north.

Sir Bastian had told me that lumbermen had been harvesting trees between the rivers for generations. This section comprised older trees and must not have been harvested for decades. That made traveling swift with less undergrowth, but that also meant more open visibility.

I stayed close to the road but remained under the trees as I sped north with bow in hand.

I passed more sections of burnt forest, including some areas that still had flames crawling across the landscape, somehow surviving the rain. There was little I could do by myself. Inside, I wept at all the destruction I had seen since crossing the river.

Near the end of the day, I stopped to look ahead. I knew I

must be getting close, for the landscape sloped upward as I moved into the foothills. Deciduous trees gave way to evergreens, which now spread out from both sides of the road, the grasslands disappearing a few miles back. Glimpses of the road winding up the bare slopes gave me an idea of where to find my final destination. The mountains now loomed above me and over the trees, casting long shadows in the bright rays of the late afternoon sun. Colors reflected off the slopes as the cool afternoon breeze brought fresh alpine scents and some relief from the muggy day.

I heard a melodious rushing stream coming out of the high crags, so I moved forward until I found its mossy green banks. I sat down to rest and eat some jerky and cheese next to its cold pools. Lil seemed alert, but drank her fill and munched leaves off the bushes. Goats will eat anything.

While we relaxed, faint sounds of clatter came to my ears. I shoved the rest of my food in my mouth and listened. Getting low to the ground, I crept from tree to tree towards the noise. Not too far from my resting spot, I spotted a sentry pacing back and forth in a watchful manner, his hard boots crunching over the forest floor. A falchion remained sheathed at his belt and several javelins hung in a quiver. I heard more activity beyond —much more.

Between me and the dwarfin halls stood a very large camp of eshkin.

CHAPTER 14

AT THE DOORS
OF SARENGELD

T hankfully, the sentry did not see me.

Unseen movement was one of my best skills. Almost winning at the Qoholet Spring Games is not the same as being out here, however. There, I missed out on a ribbon because my mentors sabotaged my efforts as part of my final tests. Character means more to the Qoholet than a prize. And from where I was hiding now, it meant life or death. Not just to me, but possibly to others as well.

Lil rattled the bushes and my nerves, bringing me back to the present.

Of course, the Qoholet never trained me with a goat tagging along.

The sentry looked our way. I froze in place. Lil munched a mouthful of leaves with her back to the camp, uninterested. The chomping of her teeth sounded like a mischievous boy clacking rocks together in my ears. Just as the thought crossed my mind, drums started beating, drowning out all else. The eshkin day began.

The sentry stared back towards the camp for a minute, then continued his pacing.

I crawled over to a fallen pine tree where I could rise up and see better, yet remain hidden. I checked on Lil, but she did not follow. Another guard came into view to my left. He stopped and leaned on a rock. The first paced to my right. I gauged the distance between the two. I was confident I could slip between unnoticed.

Galieb, your job is to get a message to the dwarfin, not play tag, I reminded myself. *Do you want another run dodging javelins? What about Lil?*

Thankfully, I listened to myself and just observed for a while, studying the camp. The trees ended near where the sentries stood, the camp grounds being cleared of all brush and most of the trees, leaving just hacked stumps. Patches of burnt forest marked the eastern edge of the camp. Whether burnt from carelessness or on purpose, I could not tell. A corral of grunting pigs was not too far from me, and a few cows stood tied next to it, sorrowfully lowing. A dead ram lay on the ground in its own blood, untouched except for the flies. Dozens of domed yurts of stretched pigskin sat among long triangular structures. Sod roofs formed peaks in the middle of the buildings, but reached to the ground at steep angles. Cut stone covered the fronts, with steps leading down to wooden doors halfway below ground level. Most were just a little taller than me, but the one in the center of camp stood twice as high and thirty paces long.

What could they be? They do not look like eshkin constructions, but must have been sitting there for centuries.

Soon the sentries changed, and activity increased across the camp as more warriors moved about. Eshkin came out of domed yurts of pigskin and began lighting fires in shallow dug pits. Some sharpened and repaired weapons. All total, I estimated five score warriors.

After the drumming finally stopped, I noticed a group of eshkin working their way up the hill, fully armed, following the road. Night had now fallen, limiting my vision of the camp.

My brain told me to give the camp as wide a berth as possible. But the landscape seemed to limit that option as two elevated arms of rugged terrain reached down the mountain on either side of the road, forming a small valley. The eshkin camp stretched across its mouth, with the road and creek both meandering right through its middle.

How can I get past the camp? Perhaps I could use the trees and yurts as cover and slip through the edge as I remove any sentries in the way? One well-placed arrow could drop this sentry, but he may cry out before giving up the ghost, or another could happen by at just the wrong moment.

With all the stars now bright in the sky and the activity drowning out my movements, I backed off, taking the goat's small horn in my hand so she had to follow.

We worked our way west in a wide arc around the camp until I reached the tip of the rocky outcropping forming the valley wall. Eshkin yurts dotted the mouth of the valley, with a few scattered ones butting up against the ridge. The eshkin were all moving about now, so I figured sunrise may be a better time to reach the halls.

As I planned my next move, Lil started climbing up the steeper ridge, finding a trail only she could see. I scowled at first, but soon realized it was a smart move and followed. She hopped right up while I struggled over the steep, rocky terrain. Pebbles cascaded down as I scrambled. I paused, fearing I had alerted the entire camp, but I heard no pursuit.

We reached a spot that leveled off with a rocky overhang, creating something like a small cave. It faced southwest, keeping us out of sight from the camp. I peered around the corner of the overhang, looking down on the camp. The camp lay sprawled sixty feet below amongst the stumps and grass-covered mounds.

The stars above, along with the faint sounds of the stream cascading down the valley and in through the camp, gave me a false feeling of peace. Looking at the triangular structures from here, I realized this place appeared to be some type of settlement, but not one of the lumber camps of Wynchell and not of eshkin. All the buildings in Wynchell were of squared logs. Here I could see that all the triangular structures faced due south in parallel lines. Dwarfin stonemasons built the Qoholet Abbey and White Stag Inn, but I never heard of dwarfin building structures above ground for themselves. I assumed they all lived in underground halls, but that seemed the most reasonable explanation.

Scores of eshkin milled among the yurts, or sat cooking over fires. Smoke drifted up to my nostrils. An eshkin jogged into camp and went into a yurt. He came out again and jogged off east.

A messenger? Were there more camps farther east? I pondered as I scanned the eastern horizon, but the ridges limited my view.

I settled back into the cave and pulled out my cloak. My bedroll would be more comfortable, but I may need to flee fast. The cloak would keep me warm enough, even in these cooler hills.

Once I settled in, Lil came back from her foraging to check on me.

"Good job finding this spot, Lil. Anywhere else would have left us vulnerable." Lil bleated at me in response. "Shh. It's not *that* safe."

After a few bites of dried fruit and hard biscuits, I closed my eyes. Lil plopped down on top of my hips and legs, worming around to get comfortable. She dropped asleep, not interested in my comfort at all.

I woke to find Lil grazing contently on tuffs of grass nearby. She bleated upon seeing me wake. It was not quite sunrise, but the sky showed the first colors of light. A cool, light breeze ruffled my cloak. I crawled over to the edge of the ridge, looking down on the yurts once more. A patrol of eshkin worked their way back to their camp from the mountain road with picks and hammers in hand.

"Well, Lil. Now may be a better time to try for the dwarfin halls. Are you coming?"

Lil bleated a yes. At least, that's how I interpreted it.

We continued north up the ridge line, heading towards the looming mountains and paralleling the valley below. Large boulders formed the crest of the ridge, jutting up above the rest of the hill. These formations forced me along the eastern side of the ridgeline, with the angle of the slope getting steeper. In order to continue, I had to shimmy along the slope above the valley, exposed to the camp.

Warriors still milled about but seemed to settle down, preferring the darkness as their day ended at sunrise. Vulnerable as I was, all it would take to notice me was for one to look up.

The slope remained steep, but not such an incline that I had to cling like a spider. Pebbles fell as my feet sought sturdy footholds. My left hand felt for handholds as backup.

Lil pranced on ahead of me, stopping to nibble tuffs of grass as she went. She seemed quite at home. My heart pounded.

I am glad you're having fun, I muttered to myself, hoping none of the eshkin noticed me.

I was thankful the rangers had taught me how to blend in

and had provided cloaks of grayish green. Even my brigandine and trousers were of soft browns, so as not to draw the eye. Natural tones complimented to our skills of unseen movement.

After an hour of inching my way north, I passed out of sight of the camp with a sigh of relief. After continuing far enough to feel safer, I worked my way down to the valley floor among a cluster of aspen. Sweat covered my body, and my muscles shook from the stress.

After a brief rest, I scanned up and down the valley to be sure all remained clear of eshkin or any other danger. Lil joined me by leaping off a rock and kicking her hind legs. She seemed delighted by the fresher grass here, too.

I rolled my eyes. "Come on, let's go."

Overall, the valley was open with just a small clump of aspen or spruce here and there, making me feel exposed. Here, it would be hard to hide or move unseen. I did not feel happy with that, but the only way forward was to travel in the open.

I used the road as the faster option, hoping all the eshkin had returned to camp for the day. The rushing stream blocked out much of the other morning sounds. A few birds fluttering in the trees told me that nothing dangerous was nearby. I tried to move fast, but Lil slowed me a bit. She did not like rushing, but did not want to be left behind, either. She bleated her protests.

The sides of the valley closed in as I gained elevation, and the trees disappeared. The walls of the mountains loomed above me. I crested over a small ridge and the ground leveled before me. A long open valley, cleared of all rocks, trees and bushes, stretched between the two walls of the mountain ridges. Only the stream spilling down off the eastern ridge, flowing down along the canyon wall on the eastern side, broke up the plain.

At the far end, built into the side of the mountain, stood

the twin stone doors of the dwarfin Halls of Sarengeld. Rich carvings of overlapping weaves arched the doors. Chiseled on either side of the doors were depictions of dwarfin standing guard and looking down upon all who neared.

The doors appeared sealed shut.

I jogged forward across the field to get a better look, continuing right up to the doors. The dwarfin figures towered over me at three times my height. Deep gouges marred the lower parts, showing the attempts of someone trying to dig their way in through the thick doors.

The eshkin carrying picks.

"So, Lil, how does someone knock on stone dwarfin doors? Is there a bell of some kind?"

Lil ignored me, grazing on the short grasses as I looked for some way to communicate. I hated shouting. I never enjoyed drawing attention to myself. That's why being a ranger suited me in so many ways. Having scores of eshkin nearby added to the discomfort.

I saw no other way. I looked around to be sure no one else was listening, and then I gave a shout. "Hark! Dwarfin of Sarengeld! I bring a message from Sir Bastian of Wynchell! Does anyone hear me? They seek your welfare!"

I waited, but nothing happened except for the cawing of a few crows, disturbed by my yelling, as they flew off the west ridge. They circled over me as if to protest my presence before landing again farther down the slope.

Now what?

I walked back and forth along the cliff face, about sixty paces across, seeking any clues. I did not like being at the end of the valley. It made me feel cornered, but I guess that is how the dwarfin designed it.

Time to get out of here.

Lil felt cornered and vulnerable, too, and started bleating

and pacing back and forth, hiding behind me. As we moved towards the eastern wall, she bolted ahead, zigzagging up the wall, climbing her way up about three times my height onto a small ledge.

"I am glad that was easy for you," I said to myself.

I started back across the valley to find a safe place to sit and figure out my next move, when the crows started cawing again. I looked over at them, but they focused their attention on the end of the valley.

A full patrol of eshkin came up the hill over the crest.

"Dragon's breath!" I cursed and grabbed my bow. "I'll empty my quiver before I kill all of them!"

CHAPTER 15
GATHERING ESHKIN

My head swiveled side to side, looking for some place to flee, but nothing became obvious.

The eshkin spotted me now!

They started howling. A few started running towards me.

"If you can hear me, dwarfin, I could use some help!" I yelled.

My first arrow dropped the front warrior, striking his throat at a hundred paces. The second bolt hit another one square in the chest, sinking through the hardened leather.

That caused the other twenty to pause.

Lil bleated at me from above. The ridge was steeper here than the other had been farther down, but it was not sheer. I hung my bow on my quiver and scrambled up the cliff wall to join her on the small ledge.

The eshkin charged forward again. The first few warriors came within javelin range by the time I got up to the ledge. One bounced off the rock next to me, and one stuck into my backpack.

Lil climbed up out of sight, bleating loudly in fear.

My skills do not match those of the goat, so I dared no farther. Balancing on a ledge on the side of a cliff wall seemed precarious, but it was better than being surrounded by blood-thirsty warriors.

I dropped the pack next to me with the thrown lance still stuck in it and readied my bow. My toes hung over the edge and my elbow hit the wall, limiting my ability to release well.

Another javelin stuck next to me and clattered to the ground, but its owner also fell to the ground with an arrow shaft in his heart.

The tusked warriors continued forward towards me. Several more fell in rapid succession to my arrows.

Seeing death on the faces of their companions, most retreated while a few continued their charge. Eshkin lay dead or wounded, scattered across the valley.

Two brave souls now stood right below me, and more than a dozen hid behind the far crest at the end of the field, their heads poking over the top to watch.

One raider below me threw a javelin. I deflected it with my bow.

He hooted with admiration and frustration, clacking his teeth. Both raiders wanted the glory of killing the ranger.

I planted an arrow in his skull in response as the other took his shot.

I twisted in place, but had little room to dodge. The point stuck in my brigandine, the tip nicking my rib on my left side. A cry escaped my lips. The arrow in my hand dropped to the ground.

He pulled out another javelin as I reached for the next arrow, each racing to be first. The javelin in my rib stuck out at a downward angle, and I almost tangled my bow in it.

As he prepared to finish me, I shot first, just pulling the

string halfway. It was enough. The bolt planted into his face. He collapsed next to his companion.

No elfin ears hanging from belts today. At least not for you.

I yanked the javelin out of my armor and dropped it. Blood covered the very tip.

None of the remaining raiders dared brave my bow, but gathered at the far end of the valley.

Instead, they just lapsed into hooting at me and clacking their teeth in rhythm. The sound put me on edge, which I assume was its purpose. Their numbers increased as more gathered on the edge of the crest, coming up from the camp below.

I leaned back against the cliff and checked my wound, then my quiver. The wound was nothing serious, but it hurt and still bled. My quiver only had a dozen arrows left.

Not enough to kill them all, even if you did not count the rest of the camp, most of which must be rushing up here by now.

I also had my prized silver arrow, but I did not want to use that until it was the right time. My right hand clenched and unclenched unconsciously at the memory of the vow and of my hand print permanently etched into the shaft.

A noise brought me back to the present.

The continued scraping of rock on rock came from behind me. I turned to see the stone doors opening inward.

The eshkin lost interest in me as all eyes focused on the dark tunnel beyond the open doors. All was silent.

Then the faint sounds of boots stomping on rock echoed from the shadows.

Out came a lone, grim-faced dwarfin with a war hammer in his hand. He moved to stand on the east side of the door, nearer to me. An opened faced, crested helm covered his head, and steel armor covered a coat of mail. A full black beard reached to his belt, and thick braids dropped out the back of the helm. He stood a head taller than my gnomin mentor, Lilke, but the crest of his helmet would only reach my throat.

Behind him, more dwarfin soldiers came forth, four abreast, and each fully bearded, holding full length rectangular shields and spears pointed skyward. The sun gleamed off the matching crested helmets.

The first dwarfin pointed and shouted orders in the gruff dwarfin language, his war hammer resting on his shoulder. Twenty paces past the doors, the four stopped, kneeling down to plant their shields against the ground. Shields clanked as they jostled together, working to form an interlocking wall.

Behind them, more soldiers jogged forth in the same manner. The first dwarfin, the apparent leader, pointed to the right of the first quad as he barked again. The second quad followed his hand and joined the line to the right, the bottom edges of their shields striking the ground in line with the warrior beside them, then shifting to overlap. More marched out, commanded to the left in a like manner. So it continued, four shielded dwarfin at a time: right, then left.

When the marching stopped, sixty dwarfin stretched the width of the valley. The warriors shifted, and some spears dipped, removing the illusion of perfect proficiency. In the end, however, the wall seemed solid. The commander nodded as he stood behind the line on the east side near me and tucked the tip of his beard in his belt.

Behind them, one more strode forth, a war hammer in his hand like the first. His beard was more gray than black and grew longer than the rest of his companions. It remained tucked in his belt. He moved to the west side of the door, staying behind the shield wall. Taking over the command, he growled out new dwarfin orders. Spear tips dropped forward, the butt ends braced into the solid ground.

At the far end of the valley, the gathering eshkin watched the dwarfin formation with gusto. Scores of the invaders now brandished unsheathed steel in challenge to the dwarfin. Jaws clacked in ever-increasing volume as more joined in the harmonized ritual. Soon drums took over the beat, adding to the nerve-jarring noise.

The whole eshkin camp must be up here, I thought.

A lanky eshkin stepped forward, robed in mail to his knees and crowned with a tall helm of steel. Both hands held his great axe over his head as he challenged his enemies with a roar.

The dwarfin's response was silence.

Everyone ignored me.

Pointing with his axe head, the eshkin leader grunted out orders and a third of the warriors ran forward. Javelins rained down upon the dwarfin line with heavy thuds.

The first wave of javelin throwers stopped and fell back as another third raced forward to do the same.

A third wave followed in disciplined unison until every tusked warrior launched his lance.

Over a hundred missiles clattered among the shield wall, each dwarfin huddling beneath shield and helm. But the assault proved useless against dwarfin armor, bouncing off all. The two dwarfin commanders called out encouragement as the javelins pelted down before them.

Eshkin curses followed the missiles, but all to no avail. The chief turned and stirred his raiders into a frenzy.

Drums beat faster and louder as the eshkin leader paced before his warriors, waving his axe. The last stomp of his dance was in unison with the last beat.

Clacking his jaws, he swung to face us with a dramatic swoop, pointing his axe with a roaring bellow.

But it would be his last, for just as he turned, my silver

arrow sunk into his chest, piercing mail and flesh as it planted into the corrupted heart. With a silent gasp, he collapsed before the line of eshkin. Shocked silence swept through the ranks as all became still.

Disbelief soon turned to rage as the entire horde of eshkin raced forward, their screams filling the valley.

As the raging mass of wild-eyed warriors barreled forward upon the shield wall, a long horn blast echoed off the walls, drowning all other sounds.

There stood the first dwarfin commander to come out, a gleaming silver trumpet raised to his lips, his bearded cheeks puffed with exertion.

At the sound of his call, a score of armed crossbows appeared along the top of the ridges on both sides of the valley. As one, the dwarfin archers pummeled destruction from above.

A dozen eshkin fell to the bolts.

The dwarfin warriors below braced for the assault.

By the time the charging raiders reached the shield wall, four of my arrows hit their mark.

The dwarfin soldiers grunted and almost faltered, but then stood firm, spears piercing the thick hides and furs acting as eshkin armor. Some of my dwarfin allies fell, but the line closed in and held.

Spears tangled on the mangled bodies of the most determined eshkin as more clambered over their comrades, causing the dwarfin to abandon the spears for handheld war hammers.

Falchions and great axes struck steel as war hammers shattered bones in grueling hand to hand battle.

The eshkin fell by the dozen, frustrated by the effectiveness of dwarfin shields and armor.

Soon the frenzy died, and fear moved among the eshkin raiders as their companions crumpled beside them. Dwarfin grit matched the strength of their famed steel.

A few eshkin turned and fled. Then more and more, until all soon followed.

Bolts released with a jolting grunt as the crossbows once more brought death to the fleeing raiders from the ridges above.

The dwarfin trumpet sounded a second time, calling the shielded warriors to give chase.

Down the valley, the remaining eshkin fled.

Down the valley, the dwarfin followed.

I slid off my ledge and hurried after as dwarfin healers rushed out of the stone halls to assist the fallen.

Below at the yurts, the eshkin regrouped for a last stand, not easily giving up what they claimed, even though they no longer outnumbered the dwarfin.

The armored warriors hit them like rocks in an avalanche, hammers lifting and falling as the eshkin parried and cut with desperate ferocity.

In the end, the eshkin line crumpled. Those remaining fled east into the forest.

No dwarfin gave chase. The trumpet sounded once again, but this time in victory.

I stopped on the slope just above the camp, my bow still in hand, watching the eshkin run. Satisfied, I sighed with relief. What a pleasure to see them flee.

But it was short lasting.

With little warning, I found myself with an armored warrior in front and one behind, weapons drawn.

"A half elfin with a dwarfin crafted blade. An odd site indeed!" stated the dwarfin horn blower with suspicion, his cold black eyes peeking out from below a crested helm. "How did you come by that sword? And what are your intentions?"

CHAPTER 16
WITHIN THE DWARFIN HALLS

Time for your best diplomacy, Galieb, if you don't want to end up in a dwarfin prison.

"Hail, victorious warriors of Sarengeld!" I smiled, keeping my hands visible, my bow still in my left hand. "Galieb of the Qoholet at your service. The good knight, Sir Bastian, sends word. The Duke of Wynchell feared for your status and promises aid. Even now, knights and warriors gather at Wood Harvest awaiting word from your halls. Valiant men prepare to sweep eshkin out of the protectorate."

Nothing happened for a full minute. They just continued staring at me. I feared my words were poorly chosen.

Finally, the commander spoke. "And the sword? What is the story there?"

"A gift from my mentors. A human blade reforged by the Artisan Stakhiljan, a son of Norir." I knew not if those names would mean anything to them.

"That is a valuable gift. I am Vigglod, second of the Saren Guards." He waved off the warrior behind me. I could now see that streaks of gray touched the dwarfin's braids in back and

149

his beard in front, which he tucked back into his belt. His faced looked almost peach in color against the black strands. Steel pauldrons covered his shoulders, which were broad compared to his height. His arms bulged underneath his mail coat and steel vambraces.

"May your beard ever grow, Vigglod," I answered, remembering the proper response. "I consider Stakhiljan not just one of my mentors, but a friend."

Vigglod gestured to the blood on my brigandine. "I see you received a wound. We can get you some assistance."

"Just a prick. Nothing serious. I have ways of healing. Please care for your own first. So, what is this place here? It looks to be more than an eshkin camp."

"Dellinfett, we named it." He rubbed his broad nose and stroked his beard. "Centuries ago, a son of Norir named Delling discovered a hunk of iron ore here. It was of such fine quality, he built a furnace and created the steel we are renown for. A few weeks ago, the eshkin overwhelmed the iron masters working down here before forcing us all back into the Halls. May all their blades rust!" he added with a raised fist.

"They fled your hammers this day, Vigglod," I encouraged.

"Aye. I am one of the few who is a guard by profession. Gold brings with it the need for guards, but for too long we did not have a need for soldiers, our halls being within the boundaries of Lageheim. Most here are miners or people of craft. Now we are training with spear and shield out of necessity. I fear this is a precursor to changing times."

Most of the dwarfin stayed to clean up the camp and prepare for more assaults. Soon, axes bit into trees and picks dug into dirt. I stood amazed at how quickly fortifications grew. A berm formed around the former eshkin camp and the triangular buildings. Spiked logs, half buried in the berm, poked out like brown horns on a dragon. I pitched in as I could, though I could not match the strength or stamina of the dwarfin. I noticed among the eshkin yurts a stone altar, just like the one I saw along the road. A replica spear leaned against it. On top lay the burnt remains of some poor creature.

Once satisfied with the progress, Vigglod took me back up the slope to the Halls. On the way back, I salvaged what arrows I could, for I only had a few left in my quiver. More dwarfin moved in and out of the large stone doors and set about pilfering the dead eshkin and diligently cleaning up the scene. The crows hopped among them, getting what morsels they could.

At the edge of the slope, we encountered the dead eshkin chieftain with my prized silver arrow still in his torso. The arrow slipped out of his body with ease, completely unscathed.

"See this, Galieb," Vigglod pointed to the eshkin chief. "His helmet is all one piece except for the crest." The dwarfin used his finger to indicate the various features. Putting the helmet aside, he took the great axe laying close by. "Here, the axe, too. Dwarfin steel, this is. Not to the quality of your sword, nor even our war hammers, but not the usual crude eshkin craft. Where did this low-ranked chieftain get it?"

"Eshkin have a reputation for raids and scavenging," I stated.

"Yes, but what other dwarfin settlements did they raid? There are no other dwarfin in these mountains. The closest kin to us are at the UnderHalls of Volberg, far to the south."

"Maybe they killed a merchant dealing in dwarfin weapons or a dwarfin mercenary?" I suggested.

"I fear slavery, though most dwarfin would refuse, even under threat of torture or death."

Lines in Vigglod's face became more apparent at the thought, but we turned our attention to the needs at hand. After taking a few healing pearls for myself, I passed out the rest and assisted with the wounded as best I could, using the skills my mother taught me.

A dwarfin crossbowman accosted me about Lil, stating he stumbled over her on the bulwarks as they prepared for battle, pointing to the eastern ridge above the valley. I stood confused and apologetic. So Vigglod explained to me that on either ridge above the valley, the dwarfin had cut channels into the crest of the ridges so that crossbowman can quickly race to the end of the killing field. This allowed them to rain down bolts on the eshkin warriors. The dwarfin called them the 'bulwarks.'

The crossbowman grumbled, but apparently now was feeding and caring for Lil. My heart felt relief at her safety after all we went through to get here together.

From there, Vigglod took me through the mighty doors. A long, narrow tunnel stretched for fifty paces before widening.

"Only another dwarfin could get through those doors when closed, except maybe a stone giant," Vigglod stated with a gleam in his eye. "Once through those doors, invaders become surrounded by murder holes in this first part of the tunnel, with crossbowman ready to cut them down from either side and hot oil from above."

Once beyond the tunnel, a great cavern opened up, the top twenty times my height. Carved pillars ran down in two rows on either side of me. Thick veins of gold laced the walls and roof like the stripes of a tiger. Tall, narrow windows high above the doors allowed shafts of light to illuminate the gold and highlighted the massive carvings of dwarfin statues within the great hall. I could not help but gaze up in wonder at its beauty.

"Iron upon the hills, gold in these mountains and streams. 'Sarengeld' translates to 'iron and gold' in the common tongue," Vigglod explained to me.

"I am impressed, Vigglod."

"Our halls are beautiful but seem simple compared to the Volberg and other halls. We are just a small place."

"I can only imagine," I said, my neck craning to see it all.

Vigglod stopped me and tucked his beard back in his belt, as it kept coming out as he walked. "As is the custom of the dwarfin, we must present you to Ivar. He is our Appointed, the ruler of Sarengeld. He will make the final decision about your status here. Give your message to him."

"Status? What do you mean?" I asked with apprehension.

"Most likely he will treat you as an honored guest since you aided us in battle." He stroked his beard again. "But there are other possibilities."

"Good ones, I hope." My apprehension grew.

"Prison is always a possibility. We are all on edge since the eshkin attack. Present yourself as you did to me and I see no trouble."

Do I have a choice? I did not see myself fighting my way out if his ruling went against me.

"Why do they call him 'the Appointed?'" I asked, to change the subject.

"All dwarfin trace their ancestry back to the Five Fathers," Vigglod explained. "You mentioned the Artisan Stakhiljan, calling him 'a son of Norir.' Do you understand what that means?"

"Norir was his ancestor, but that is all I know."

"Yes, Norir is one of the Five Fathers. At our beginning, many centuries ago, each father went in a different direction. Norir came northwest. We here at Sarengeld are descended from Norir. So are the dwarfin of Volberg to the south of Lageheim. We are all kin and have one ruler, Torir, the most direct descendant of Norir. He is the appointed father of our time. Torir resides and leads from Volberg. Torir decided that Ivar is the leader here and has the title of 'Appointed.'"

By the time Vigglod explained it all, we reached the seat of the Appointed at the end of the cavern, set in the center of a half round cove carved out of the back wall. Ivar sat on an ornate chair of black iron, and gold, set on a raised rectangular dais. Golden rings covered each finger. The end of his beard lay spread across his thighs in long stripes of deep brown, and white. He looked imposing, seated there, looking down on me. Vigglod introduced us, but did not bow and no one asked me to do so.

"Never before has a half-elfin entered these halls. And one wearing a weapon of dwarfin mastery. Interesting times indeed. What brings such a ranger to our home during a time of peril?" Ivar inquired in a guttural dwarfin voice that did not match his glamor.

"The Duke of Wynchell sends word, concerned about your safety," I said, not sure of dwarfin customs. "Eshkin warriors have not only wreaked havoc at the doors of Sarengeld, but across much of Wynchell. Many fires burn in the land between the rivers. The knight, Sir Bastian, gathers men to push the raiders back into the mountains, including those at your doors."

"They no longer peck at our doors, thankfully. May we keep them from doing it again," Ivar growled. "I hear you played a part in that."

"A small part. Your warriors, along with Vigglod, earned the victory." I nodded to my companion.

"Let us hope you are truly our ally and not some deceptive infiltrator. Or a thief come to steal our gold." He watched my reaction, but I had none, for I was neither. "You appear to be a messenger and friend, but the possession of that sword raises questions for us. Hand it to me. Tell us its story."

I saw no choice but to do so. I removed the sword from my belt without unsheathing it, scabbard and all. Vigglod took it from my hand as the other dwarfin of the courts moved closer. Vigglod wanted to inspect it, but dutifully handed it to Ivar, who slid it out of its sheath.

His eyes changed from stern to excited as he admired it. "True!" Ivar said. "True!"

He handed it back to Vigglod, who grasped it, then squinted as he studied every inch. Other dwarfin bristled with impatience, so he passed it on to another, who passed it onto others in the court. Each dwarfin, including Vigglod, said the same: "True, true!"

"What does that mean?" I asked Vigglod.

"We do not know your friend, Stakhiljan, but we see his mark on the blade and the dwarfin blessings. You said he is an artisan. But he is more than that. He is a *true* artisan. True artisans no longer learn by regular means, because they know all that another can teach them. Instead, they discover. Few dwarfin reach the honor of a true artisan. No one here has yet reached it, and I know of only a few that are alive today. Yet none of us knew who Stakhiljan was until now. We will not forget!"

"Stakhiljan is very humble," I said. "I knew only that he is highly skilled. He serves my order, the Qoholet. He reforged this sword from my father's Kianovan blade."

"Treasure this gift, young half-elfin. You won't find a finer sword," Ivar said.

After each one studied it, they gave it back to me.

"May it bring you more victories," Ivar said. "Today is a significant victory to us, though small compared to many others throughout history. Yet worthy of celebration. Please join us for a feast this evening, Ranger Galieb, Half-elfin."

I bowed at the waist. It sounded like I would not rot in prison. "I would be honored."

"Welcome to Sarengeld. Stay as long as you need. You and your...pet."

After meeting the Appointed, they found a room for me so I could rest and prepare for the feast. They also took my brigandine to be repaired, criticizing the human craftsmanship.

"Human's finest, but not dwarfin quality," was the observation.

I told them I could not afford their skills, but they scoffed and thanked me for fighting alongside them.

Not all the dwarfin seemed pleased to have me in their halls. A few residents treated me with suspicion, not liking humans or elfin, and distrusting half-elfin. They mumbled accusations that I must have stolen the sword, claiming I was too young to own it.

While they repaired my armor, I went to look for Lil. A dwarfin guided me through many winding tunnels of smoothed stone lit by glowing lamps and window slits, climbing up the inside of the mountain. Gold veins streaked across the ceilings. At the end of one tunnel was a small stone door where my guide left me.

I went outside and found Lil high above the main gates along a stream and amongst the gold mines. Small flocks of sheep also wandered among the green pastures that dotted the slopes, watched over by dwarfin shepherds. She seemed happy to see me, but soon went back to frolic with her new friends.

The sun faded in the west, leaving a red sheen across the mountain slopes and distant clouds. I settled down to enjoy the grand and peaceful view, looking across the Wood Harvest below. In the distance, I could just make out the last rays of light reflecting off the towers of White Cliff and thought I found the Woodsman Camp where Sir Bastian now prepared for battle. Faint gray smoke lines showed the exhausted fires of the destroyed fields and pastures to the west. Farrin's Crossing looked untouched from here, at least. Fresh black smoke rose from fires still burning to the east and south.

Smaller ridges stretched out from the main peaks above us, looking like fingers grasping the Wynchell landscape. Over these finger ridges, and at the base of the mountain walls, another group of thin smoke lines rose.

A nearby shepherd pointed at the smoke. "Over there to the east is an even larger eshkin camp than the one that was at our gates."

Once the light faded so that only the fires illuminated the night, I headed back. Lil followed me all the way back to the small door on the side of the mountain. After a quick scratch behind the ears, she ran back off to the greener patches.

Before the feast, I found great delight in a sauna bath. Water poured down out of the heights in through a cavern before it rushed out to meet the creek in the valley. The dwarfin diverted a stream through a chamber and turned it into a sauna. I had to share it with a few hairy dwarfin, but I felt refreshed. It was the first bath since the Duke of Erian's banquet. All I had to wear was my undertunic and poorly sown trousers, but no one seemed offended.

Presentable once again, I joined the dwarfin in celebration of their victory. Massive decorative lamps now lit the Cathedral, the name of the main great hall I had walked across upon my arrival, the glow dancing upon the golden veins. Massive platters of wild boar served as the main dish, but local beef and mutton also delighted the tongue. Large loaves of sourdough bread and mugs of mead passed freely.

Vigglod told me during supper that they found a few human prisoners in the eshkin camp. "They are in awful shape. Abused for sure. They appear to be Wynchell farmers. Lost everything."

"What will happen to them?"

157

"We will care for them until they are strong enough to go back to any family they have left," Vigglod said before he ripped wild boar meat off a bone with his teeth.

"Maybe they can take Lil. She can't come with me. I need to get back to Sir Bastian."

"Where is the little grass chewer now?"

"Still prancing about on the green pastures near the mines."

Vigglod laughed. "I will mention her to them. We can spare some things to help the folks as well."

Soon the joy of the dwarfin victory, along with the free flow of mead, led to a burst of song:

Shield and spear, steel and stone!
Dwarfin warriors defend our home!
Eshkin raiders flee and fall!
None can enter our golden Hall!

CHAPTER 17

THE LOST PATROL

When I met the freed slaves the following morning, it wrenched my heart. A mother and her young daughter had survived an eshkin raid on their farm, only to be taken as slaves. They watched their farm burn to the ground and witnessed their family cut down in front of their eyes. I learned eshkin usually killed all they encountered, but sometimes they took a few slaves for menial tasks or to abuse.

Black and blue bruises covered the slaves' bodies, and they looked gaunt as if half starved. But I also saw jaws that were set and a will to overcome the trauma they had been through.

Lil accepted them, and the girl promised she would take great care of the goat. The dwarfin assured them that the two could stay in their halls until they recovered and it was safe to travel again.

More determined to stop the raids, I set off.

My brigandine fit as comfortable as ever, looking clean and new. Dwarfin craftsmanship is unmatched. As for my quiver, it did not hold as many as it could, even though I retrieved a few arrows from eshkin torsos. The dwarfin didn't have any arrows for me, for they only used crossbows, but they gave me twenty bodkin arrow points, promising a Wynchell fletcher could get me quality shafts and make the arrows I needed.

Traveling went much faster without a goat trotting behind me. The road south seemed deserted and eerily quiet compared to the trip north just a few days earlier. Perhaps between the dwarfin battle and Sir Bastian's patrols, the eshkin had pulled back.

After a full day of walking, I camped in the woods that night, crawling into a pit made by a fallen tree, the impressive root mass making a pleasant shelter. I dared no fires.

The next day went just as fast until I came upon another camp. Circling vultures above and on the ground alerted me to the place. Rotting flesh baking in the summer heat assaulted my nostrils. I almost wretched as I drew closer.

This camp, however, was not eshkin. What remained of men and horses lay scattered under the trees, some still in their bedrolls. Pouches lay looted. I counted twenty men. None survived.

The eshkin must have surprised them in the night, I deduced with a heavy heart. *A few days ago, at least.*

Lying discarded in the dirt, I found the banner of the Duke of Wynchell, two gold rivers forming a 'V' on a green field. I brushed it off as best I could and then rolled it up and tucked it carefully into a pouch before heading south once again.

I reached the lumber camp not long after that. It surprised me how many people milled about. Dozens of hardworking lumberjacks, armed with swords on their hips, still worked at sawing and loading logs for transport to the mills at White Cliff. Hundreds of others prepared for battle.

Sir Bastian had established a fortified position at the top of the slope across the road from the lumberyard. Professional men-at-arms wearing tabards with the Duke's colors mingled with homesteaders and townsmen from Farrin's Crossing. Everyone moved about armed with swords, spears, and shields. Longbowmen stood among them, too, prepping quivers full of arrows.

The families of the farmers camped near the center of Sir Bastian's fortified camp, most being women, children, and livestock displaced by the eshkin raids. Most did not have tents, but created makeshift shelters out of blankets, wagons, and lumber scraps. The duke's men-at-arms all had small tents which they established in rows surrounding the farmers' area in the center. Ten paces of open space surrounded the tents of the duke's men, creating a path for movement around the camp. Surrounding everything was a large square fence made of spiked logs nailed together into free standing X's.

Sir Bastian and his squires established their tents near the east side of the fortified camp. Poles as tall as a war horse's rump encircled a small section of the camp. Green woolen panels like bland tapestries stretched between the poles, forming a woolen wall around their large tents. This wall formed a small court, and a corral for their horses, separating the knight and his squires from the rest of the camp.

As a soldier led me to the tent of Sir Bastian, I stopped in my tracks.

Two ferocious creatures stood next to the entrance of the knight's outer court. As big as draft horses, the beasts eyed us suspiciously. Their eagle-like beaks tore at the freshly slaughtered heifer held down by their fierce front claws. Large silvery gray feathers flowed back to form crests on the heads. More white feathers, dotted with rose and indigo, covered the neck, chest, front legs, and their massive wings. The rest of their form resembled warhorses, chestnut fur covering the rump and back legs. White feathering adorned the back hooves.

The knight's squires chuckled at me. "Fearsome creatures, aren't they? Called hippogriffs."

"They come from Aeryie," a second squire added. "Duke LeMont raises them himself. Trains a company of hippogriff riders to patrol the Towering Peaks across the northern border."

"Aye. Five things uphold the might of Lageheim: the wisdom of the Law, the covenant with the dragon, the prowess of the knights, the strength of our bows, and the patrol of the hippogriff," stated the first squire with pride. "Those creatures are one reason no other kingdom dares to attack us."

"Their riders assure everyone the beasts won't harm us, but they still scare the hide off me," whispered the soldier leading me.

Inside Sir Bastian's tent, two men stood facing the knight, but glanced at me when I walked in, interrupting their conversation. One frowned, but neither said anything. They stood dressed in gambesons that reached down to the knees and split at the waist for riding. Short recurve bows sat in bow quivers that hung on their belts. Each sported trimmed beards common in the kingdom.

"Ranger, you have returned!" Sir Bastian exclaimed. "I am glad you are well. I am sad to say the other scouts never returned. What news do you bring, uh, half-elfin?" Apparently, he had forgotten my name.

"Greetings, Sir Bastian, and good sirs," I said to the other men standing there, since Sir Bastian did not introduce us. "I apologize for interrupting. Galieb at your service."

The knight muttered an apology for poor manners and introduced us all to each other. "This is Jarman and Kean. Duke LeMont of Aeryie was kind enough to send us two hippogriff riders to assist us in stopping the raids."

They nodded back, hands resting on their sword hilts.

I turned back to Sir Bastian. "The dwarfin send their greetings and thanks. They defeated the eshkin pounding at their doors. However, a larger camp gathers to their east. The dwarfin believe that is the main camp, and that canyon is where they are coming out of the mountains."

"That is good news about the dwarfin. And Jarman and Kean spotted that big camp two days ago," the knight said. "We are waiting for our last patrol to return and for the duke's battle-mage to arrive with reinforcements. Then we will see about finding this camp and chasing them all back into the hills."

"Sir, your last patrol may not return. I found some of your men slaughtered just a few hours north of here. Next to the road. Ambushed in the dark. Here is the banner," I said as I pulled it out of my pouch.

The knight took the banner from my hands. He said nothing for a few minutes as he gently unrolled it. "I am sorry to hear that. Good men, each one." He sighed. "Would you mind leading one of my squires back there to confirm it is the missing patrol?"

"I can. Make sure they come prepared. It is eerily quiet out there."

After leaving Sir Bastian, I went to find arrows. I did not like having a half-full quiver. The squires told me where to find the fletcher, so I trudged through the camp until I found her.

"A bearded elfin! I heard you were here in camp," said the fletcher, a weathered, old woman. "Some say us folks here in Wynchell have elfin ancestors. It's our olive eyes and red hair. And living so near the VenKeth." She winked.

I doubted it, but said nothing.

After a lengthy discussion about the craft of arrow making, we decided the arrows used by the longbowmen of Lageheim would suit me fine.

"I served the duke making arrows for almost two score years," the gray-haired woman stated. "Seen many bows in my time. My late husband made plenty, too. But never seen a centaur-styled bow before."

She stood up, looking as thin and wrinkled as an old sow. She waddled on stiff legs over to grab a bundle of arrows, her back heavily arched from years of craftwork. The bundle filled up my quiver, but she also gave me a second full quiver with a flat bottom that could sit upright on the ground. Made of plain cow's hide, it looked battered from past battles.

"I have little to pay with, just some dwarfin made arrow points and a few coins."

"Are you in the service of the Duke?" the woman asked.

"Yes, Sir Bastian hired me as a scout."

"I'll take these arrow tips to use on the next set, but the arrows are complimentary for your service. That's why the duke taxes us. Dragon's breath! Seeing the centaur bow was worth the arrows."

"One more thing. Are you from Ferrin Crossing?" I asked.

"Lived there all these years."

"Any news of the beast attacking people?"

"I heard a few things. The reeve established patrols along the river, but no one has seen it since the ranger chased it across the river. No attacks that I heard. Was that you? You the ranger?"

"Aye. Thanks. Good to know."

"You are full of surprises," the woman added. She spit and smiled at me. "Not bad looking either. I like them ears."

My stomach growled after that encounter. Evening had fallen behind me as we finished the conversation. Finding the grub tent, they filled up a plate for me. Not as good as the dwarfin feast, but better than my trail food.

As I waited for my plate, I saw a scrawny little man scrubbing a pot.

"Otto? Is that you? What are you doing in this camp?"

The beggar from Farrin's Crossing still wore the tunic two sizes too big, but now had old boots on his feet. They looked like they would fall off at any time.

"Aye, good sir. I remember you. Don't forget the elfin-man." Like last time, he refused to look at me, but stared at the ground. "No one likes a beggar, no, sir. That big shiny knight put me to work cutting vegetables and cleaning pots. I hate it."

"At least you eat better."

"Yes sir, that I do." He cackled. "Don't worry about me."

"I found the man I asked you to watch for. On this side of the river. That beast killed him."

"Aye, eat him, too. Now they took up arms against the gnoll, they did."

"Gnoll? You know what it is?" I asked, my eyebrows shooting up.

"Uh, beggars such as me hear the talk of others. Good listener, I am," Otto responded quickly.

"Well, here is the copper I promised, for your troubles."

"Thank you, sir. Very generous," he said as he took it, still avoiding eye contact.

"Stay safe."

As I walked away, I heard him whisper, "Can't forget the elfin-man."

AT DAWN, a squire with flaming red hair, named Aidan, organized twenty mounted men-at-arms to follow me back north to find the camp. Riding was a pleasant change, but I felt exposed on the road next to the thick forest. Mounted soldiers did not worry about noise either, but chattered as they rode, their weapons clanking against each other. I kept my pointed ears alert.

We arrived at the site. It angered all the men to see that most of their comrades had been butchered in their sleep. We all dreaded handling the decomposing bodies, but it had to be done. Being late morning, I did not expect too much trouble, but stood as a lookout, bow in hand. They lay the bodies in a mass shallow grave on the west side of the road with the feet of each one pointing east. They could not tell me why, except that it was tradition.

One soldier carefully dug up a sapling and replanted it by the grave as a marker, watering it from his own waterskin.

Squire Aidan spoke a few words as we all gathered around the sapling and grave. "These men served their duke, their king, and our people with honor. May the Lag Giefan, the true Law Giver, grant them mercy and grace in the next life." And that finished the service.

The burial wore out the men, so most sat to rest. Some ate, but many could not after the grim work.

After the men settled down, my eyes caught glimpses of gray movement in the bushes. Maybe just sparrows flittering among the branches?

I slinked down to get a better angle, every footstep placed with care, my eyes never leaving the brush. A branch rustled. Patches of gray and brown. The glint of steel.

Eshkin scouts!

I put an arrow in one, dropping him where he squatted, but the other fled.

Yelling a warning to the men, I bolted after him, heading northeast farther into the forest. I rushed through the trees, watching for an opportunity to stop him with my bow before he alerted someone else. I finally gained on him, stopped and released an arrow, hitting him in the kidney.

He shrieked and stumbled.

Not dead like I hoped.

He crawled forward, grunting.

I moved forward ready to finish him, but three armed eshkin rushed out of the trees and reached him first.

They saw the arrow in his back, looked around, and finally spotted me. The three warriors yelled at me as they drew weapons.

I could now hear more eshkin yelling beyond the trees, and I could see movement through the branches from the same direction that the three warriors came. I could see yurts, too. The yurts sat among the trees in numbers that went beyond my field of vision. It seemed a very large camp.

An alarm went up. Drums started beating so loud it felt as if they were right next to me. More warriors came out of the yurts and into my view with weapons drawn.

Dragon's breath! This was not just a raiding party. Those eshkin scouts were part of a small army.

I turned and fled back to Squire Aidan and his men-at-arms. "Run! There are about five hundred eshkin behind me!"

CHAPTER 18
THE BATTLE OF WOOD HARVEST

I leaped onto my horse as Squire Aidan barked orders to mount and retreat, but I was already doing that.

Javelins dropped around us, severely wounding one man. The men-at-arms remained disciplined, retreating in an orderly manner as they dragged their injured companion onto his horse.

Eshkin burst out of the trees, screaming war cries. Some came out onto the road in front of us. The men cut them down from horseback as we galloped away, Squire Aidan bravely holding back to bring up the rear.

An eshkin rushed up to me, but I kicked the raider away as we rode off.

It didn't take long to put some distance between them and us, so we slowed to a canter. A force of that size planned more than just raids. They came to destroy Sir Bastian's entire company.

Squire Aidan and his men rounded up the lumberjacks from their tree cutting as I raced up to the fortified camp to give warning.

At first, all just looked at us in confusion, but soon I heard the clear ring of horns calling all to arms.

Lumbermen rushed with swords in hand up toward the fortified settlement as the squire and his men guarded their flank. Women scrambled to gather up children and livestock into the center of the camp.

The squire got everyone within the spiked fencing just as the first eshkin came rushing south down the road, and throwing javelins as they charged up the slope.

My pounding heart matched the intense panting of my steed.

"Calm yourself. Controlled breaths," I told myself as I patted my horse, talking to him as well.

My heart settled, but my horse remained skittish. I assured the animal using elfin tricks my mother taught me, whispering calming elfin words.

With both of us under control again, I stayed in the saddle for a better view of the battlefield and to move wherever needed.

Arming my bow, several of my arrows found their targets as the eshkin closed in on the eastern side of the camp. Other longbowmen released arrows from within the camp, dropping as many foes as they could as the raging mass closed in on the thinly manned spiked fence that served as the only fortifications.

The first eshkin soon swarmed our position as men-at-arms in mail and spears dashed forward to intercept. Homesteaders with shields and swords rallied to their sides.

The cluttered mass of hand-to-hand combat made it too risky to continue with arrows, so I pulled out my sword.

I saw a farmer fall down beneath an eshkin attack, so kicking my steed to a gallop, I swept down upon them. The force of impact pushed the point of my sword clean through the enemy.

As the raider collapsed, my sword yanked right out of my hand, wrenching my thumb as it remained stuck in his torso.

I had trained in mounted archery, but only touched on mounted swordsmanship.

The fallen farmer stood up and saluted me with his blade as I dismounted to retrieve my weapon, the both of us watching each other's back through the chaos. I threw my axe at a charging warrior as I worked my sword blade loose.

I yanked it out just in time as another eshkin came at me swinging a falchion. I parried and cut, but missed. He hacked at me with his blade, but I kept him at bay.

With a quick parry and dodge, I sliced the tip of my blade across his throat.

The farmer cut down the brute coming up behind me. I nodded my thanks.

As I looked for my axe, two nerve-shattering screams tore through the air.

The hippogriffs each pounced on an eshkin, their claws digging deep as they took to the air. The flying steeds swooped across the field, their riders now picking off enemies with their bows as the fierce steeds dropped their bloody victims amongst their fellow eshkin. A few tried to toss javelins at the flying beasts, only to fall short with the weapons landing amongst their own kin.

Sir Bastian emerged from his tent in full armor, standing as an invincible foe. No blade breached his armor as the knight swung his battleaxe, taking out each eshkin who dared come against him.

But more of the gray-skinned warriors surged past the spiked logs, pushing into the camp. I feared we may not stop them.

The knight mounted his barrel-chested war steed and gathered his armored squires around him, a dozen mighty men in all. The mounted force charged forth from Sir Bastian's court, then turned right to pass across the front of the damaged spiked log barricade.

Eshkin fled before the sharp points of the lances and thundering hooves.

At the far south end of the field, I lost sight of Sir Bastian and his company. Some eshkin, however, cried in rage, preparing themselves for the mounted company to return.

The increasing clamor of galloping war steeds reached my ears as the knight and his men swept back across the front of the spiked fence again, but this time north towards me. Eshkin toppled before them as they did in the first charge, until a few fearless raiders leaped onto the horses' backs.

Some clawed at their armored enemies before falling, trampled under heavy hoof. Others held on, pulling down a few squires, their horses' legs kicking wildly in the air.

Men, steeds, and eshkin all screamed. The mounted charge slowed to a halt as the enemies tangled.

Two brutes clung to Sir Bastian's saddle, trying to drag him off, but he cut them down with his sword. His sorrel war steed slashed and kicked with hooves, keeping any other eshkin at bay. Eshkin surrounded the squires and Sir Bastian. Clouds of dust engulfed the mass of men, warhorses, and eshkin warriors as I watched Sir Bastian's sword lift and fall. The squires fought just as hard. More eshkin scrambled forward, disappearing into the dust cloud. None of us could see what was happening.

Fear gripped me as I raced forward, but they remained too far away.

I heard another set of rushing hooves behind me that did not belong to Sir Bastian or the squires. A new unknown paladin charged onto the field, sweeping across the front of the spiked barricades. He wore full armor similar to a knight, and a horse's head decorated his heater shield.

His lance pierced through a tusked raider, and his white war steed trampled more under his hooves. He dropped his impaled spear and pulled his sword, the shape blade biting deep into gray flesh.

The dust parted as he came to fight beside Sir Bastian. Together they slew one after another, for none could stand before them, nor pierce their guard.

Soon, I too joined the fray. I cut one eshkin, then another, standing over the squires who had fallen. The men who remained mounted formed a wall with their steeds, keeping those injured and lying on the ground from getting slaughtered.

The horse charges had done their job, cutting off the eshkin within the fencing of spiked logs from those outside. The soldiers and farmers, emboldened by the courage of Sir Bastian and the unknown new arrival, surged forward, slaying the eshkin warriors that had breached the spike barricade. Others rushed to attack those still surrounding the horsemen. Quickly, the men-at-arms reformed the line along the spiked barricade to protect the camp behind them.

The hippogriffs continued their passes, bringing death from above.

Seeing the tide turning, the eshkin abandoned their attack and fled back to the cover of the woods as others took cover within the abandoned lumber camp next to the woods. Those eshkin still arriving from the north took a stand along the road and the tree line and threw javelins to cover their comrade's retreat.

Some farmers wanted to give chase, but Sir Bastian called them back.

A horn sounded, calling all to firm up the front line. Sir Bastian, the armored newcomer, and the uninjured squires assisted those who had fallen, helping them back behind the barricades and into the camp.

Many onlookers came forward, desiring to know who this new paladin could be, but I knew him by his steed. He wore not the colors of the Duke of Wynchell but showed the blue and gold of the Defenders of the Lage. The tall man dismounted and removed his helmet, revealing thick black hair.

"Did the Lady of the Lakes give you permission to leave her side, good Erik?" I called out.

"My friend, Lady Zebah now has a new title as Countess of Theomund, wife of Lord Archibald, son of the Duke," Erik Blackmane replied. "Third in line to be queen. She has more pressing matters on her mind than this humble servant. Galieb, I am glad you are faring well."

"Ranger Galieb, you will show this brave paladin proper respect and address him according to his rank. Good Sir, I am Sir Bastian of Langbard, a knight of the Duke of Wynchell. Your appearance was timely!"

"Sir Bastian, an honor to fight by your side." Erik bowed to his superior. "You must forgive my friend. Last time we met, I corrected him on my rank. Squire Erik Blackmane at your service."

"Of the respectable Blackmane family," Sir Bastian said. "I cannot yet afford one of your fine horses. May I express how pleased I am to have you join us? I would knight you right now if the Defenders allowed such things."

"Ranger Galieb is the one who first reported to us about the eshkin raids. I hurried here as soon as my duties allowed. My poor steed is tired and needs rest."

"My squires will help you get settled." Sir Bastian waved to the armored man beside him removing his helmet. Blond hair fell around his shoulders as he scratched at his dark beard. "Squire Colten, please see to all of Squire Erik's needs. Now I must see to my defenses and men. The eshkin will attack again. Join me for dinner in my tent. Everything we have is at your disposal."

"The honor is mine, my lord." Erik bowed again.

Sir Bastian turned and walked off with the rest of his squires.

Erik would not let others care for his horse, so the two of us followed the other squire back to the stable area. Blackmane brushed the stallion down and watered and fed the steed himself, making sure all was just right.

"The people of Theomund all adored the Lady Zebah," Erik explained, "and the marriage turned into a grand celebration. Even King Reinhart and Queen Adeline attended, bringing the little heir, Wilhelm, with them." After the wedding, Erik heard more about the raids taking place here and desired to come immediately, concerned about the farmsteads being burned. "Sir Lucian was kind enough to let me come," he added. "He knew the news tore at my heart."

We spent the rest of the day tending the wounded and preparing for the next attack, which all expected to come after darkness fell. The men dug hasty trenches and created berms along with the spiked logs to increase the fortifications around the camp.

While the men strengthened our defenses around the camp, Sir Bastian called some of us to a counsel over supper.

I met with Erik and we entered the tent together as the sun dropped low over the grasslands. Jarman and Kean, the hippogriff riders, already sat at the table in the center of the canvas tent. The nine uninjured squires soon trickled in behind us. Three injured squires remained under the care of the healing cleric and her female assistants.

It was a little crowded with all of us seated around the rectangular table. A gray haired cook in a forest green tunic and a white apron scooted around us as he served a simple meal of beef stew in maple wood bowls. Several platters of sourdough bread accompanied the soup. He filled our wooden goblets with wine or mead as we requested before leaving us.

"We need to guard our flanks," Sir Bastian counseled us as we sat and ate. "Groups of warriors may move around and attack us from the sides or rear. How many did you see, Galieb?"

"I did not see the entire camp, but I estimate they outnumber us two to one, sir," I responded.

"Guarding our flanks will thin the front line," the red-haired squire named Aidan admitted. All the squires remained dressed in full armor, except for their helmets and gauntlets.

"But it must be done," Sir Bastian replied, also wearing most of his armor. "We will station men at the back and sides, with the dominant force in front. Horns will sound to warn us of where they attack."

"Eshkin are brutal and terrifying, each skilled in battle," stated Colten, the squire with blonde hair but a dark beard, who assisted Erik. "Half of our men are farmers, herdsmen. Brave and hardy folks of the borderlands, but not trained fighters. Most are still weary from the intense day."

"We have the advantage of the slope and fortifications," Erik said, "not to mention horses. All of us here are strong in our armor. We can defeat them."

"And the hippogriffs," added Jarman, only wearing his gambeson. His bow and other weapons sat by the door of the tent.

"We can hope the reinforcements arrive soon with the battle mage. Then we will chase them across the mountains,"

Sir Bastian explained. He spoke many more words of encouragement before letting us go get what rest we could.

Erik first went to check on his steed.

I followed. "Checking on him again? You care more for that horse than for anyone else. And I know how much you care about others."

"'The righteous care for the needs of their animals,' the Lage teaches us," Erik responded. "And Stedgyr deserves all the attention I give him. I cannot rest until I know he is well."

WITH THE DARKNESS came the beating of drums as they reverberated from the trees and the lumber camp below. We could see some activity among the abandoned lumber equipment and wagons, but most of eshkin's new camp remained hidden in the woods. Images played across my mind of them dancing about their fires, clacking their jaws, and vowing our deaths to their gods. Maybe they slaughtered sacrifices on makeshift altars, as I had seen in the other camp.

The drums continued for hours, the nerves of all strained.

After the intense battle and laborious preparations, the dreadful beating kept us from any needed rest during the night.

We did not know when the attack would come, only that it would come. The moon would not rise for hours yet, the darkness giving the eshkin a considerable advantage. Even my elfin eyes could not see too much beyond the barricades despite straining my eyes.

Sir Bastian stationed his squires around the outside of the camp, two on each side, with Squire Aidan staying next to the knight. Sir Bastian assigned each farmer under the leadership of a squire. They could rest until called, but were to remain armed. Half of the men-at-arms also took a rest, while the other half kept watch around the perimeter. Erik stayed on the east side, facing trees where the earlier attack took place. He knelt while leaning on his halberd, either meditating or praying.

Midnight came and went before they attacked. The drums never stopped.

They gave no warning cry. The eshkin just rushed up the slope in silence except for the sounds of boots hitting the ground. Javelins rained down on us on the south flank first. Followed by more on our north. Horns called from both.

Then a large barrage of javelins came from the front, needle points racing down, piercing a thigh here, an exposed hand there. Every wound one too many. Men raised shields hurriedly, but for many it was too late, for we could not see the javelins coming.

Farmers raced out of their tents to join the men-at-arms who now gathered up behind the spike berm.

Our longbowmen answered, shooting blindly in the half moonlight, watching for glints of steel to reveal a charging enemy. Front line soldiers planted the butt of their spears along the barricades as the first wave of bodies collided with substantial force.

Establishing myself in a prominent central location behind the men-at-arms, I launched arrow after arrow, marking my targets with care, making every arrow count.

Erik stationed himself towards the north end of the eastern side as Sir Bastian planted himself towards the south. Each hung back, watching for breeches in the lines and shouting encouragements to the men.

The other squires, being better armored than the regular troops in a combination of mail and plate, fought side by side with the soldiers and the farmers at the spiked berm.

The eshkin pressed the line, screaming taunts and striking heavy blows with falchion and axe. More waves of raiders shifted north and south, even going around the west side, seeking for weak spots in our flanks.

As my arrows became less effective, and the masses clashed together, I leapt into the fray to strengthen the lines. With sword and axe, I cut and stabbed to keep the eshkin at bay. The longbowmen followed my lead, now wielding arming swords with round shields. Every man that could wield a weapon fought hand-to-hand to keep an eshkin from entering the camp.

For hours we held the line, all praying for the dawn in our exhaustion. But the sunrise delayed in coming and the eshkin did not tire. The spears of the men-at-arms tangled and broke as the eshkin pressed in. Swords left their sheaths to parry axe and falchion as each side cut and hacked to get the advantage.

Overwhelmed and weary, the men-at-arms failed.

Eshkin warriors broke through the line near Sir Bastian. Striving forward to fill the gap, the armored knight swung his halberd with great power, fearless in his might, emboldening to all his men.

The gray-skinned warriors pressed in, now surging inside the barricade. The eshkin tasted victory.

Another breach occurred to the left. Men scattered before a deadly axe and the huge eshkin who wielded it. An iron cap sat on his head, and a coat of mail reached to his knees. On his stretched earlobe hung five rings, marking him as a chieftain.

The battle-hard chieftain swung his axe in great arcs, defying all before him. With mighty strokes, severed heads fell from tumbling bodies.

The brute fixed his eyes on Erik, who strode forward without fear, halberd in hand to stop this terror from his destruction.

One fighter struck and then the other, but neither gave quarter. Blow after blow followed as the rest of the battle raged around them.

As the fight intensified, it seemed all others slowed, every eye watching this outcome as if the entire battle rested on its victor.

The chieftain swung a heavy blow, catching Erik across the helm.

The paladin staggered, and we each held our breath.

But Erik did not fall. The five-ringed eshkin raged forward with a second assault, but Erik stood his ground, blocking and striking with his halberd. The Defender of the Lage increased his blows, each one mightier than the last, as the chieftain gave way under the assault, halberd clashing against axe.

My ears perked as I heard Erik's voice rise above the rage of battle and the clanging of steel. He sang as he fought, his voice growing stronger, now belting out hymns of praise and supplication.

The knight gave a final blow, smiting his enemy to the ground. As Erik Blackmane cleaved the head off the great chieftain, the first rays of dawn streaked across the battlefield.

CHAPTER 19

NEW ALLIES

With the rising sun and the death of their chieftain, the resolve of the eshkin wavered, but they fought on.

Sir Bastian rallied his men and pushed the eshkin back, once again closing the breaches in the line. Squire Aidan guarded his flank.

Now the hippogriffs, which had torn with beak and claw any eshkin which passed the barricades, took to the air as their rider rained missiles on the faltering invaders.

One by one, the eshkin turned to flee. It was not long before their hearts failed, and they all raced from the battlefield. The longbowmen sheathed their swords to take up their bows and send a few feathered arrows after the fleeing enemy.

"Men of Wynchell! Squire Erik! To steeds! Let us ride them down!" called Sir Bastian. All who had horses mounted as others opened a gap in the damaged barricade.

"Galieb! A horse! Come!" yelled Blackmane.

I sheathed my weapons and leaped onto the proffered mount.

With the blast of horns, the knights led the charge down the slope with me by their side. We added to the victory, slaying the eshkin as they raced towards the cover of the trees.

My sword swung left and right, having learned not to lodge it in a body.

The remaining warriors scurried through the lumber camp and darted into the woods, disappearing under the canopy.

Sir Bastian ordered us all to dismount, for it was too hazardous to ride through the trees. We prepared our weapons and strode on foot through the lumber camp. A few of the tusks warriors hid among the destroyed wagons and large saws, ambushing us as we searched the camp. A few men fell victim, but we killed them all before entering the woods.

Beyond the lumber camp and the tree line, we stalked into the eshkin camp among scores of yurts, fire pits, and corrals of grunting pigs. Warriors rushed us from every side, popping out of yurts and from behind trees, determined to turn defeat into victory.

We, too, fought on, despite the heaviness of our arms, knowing we could not fail.

Erik's song once again drifted across the battle, meandering around the trunks and caressing our ears. Our spirits revived at hearing the hymn, and our arms once again found strength to carry on.

We knew victory waited before us. The eshkin knew it, too, and soon our enemies scattered deeper into the woods, abandoning their camp.

"Victory is ours!" Sir Bastian called out. The men gave a hearty yet winded cheer.

"Sir, the men are exhausted," I reminded him.

"Yes, but we can't rest yet. We need to check the wounded. And rebuild the barricades. They may try to return and catch us unawares. After a rest, we must find their main camp up north and send them back into the mountains." He turned to the men. "A great victory, brave soldiers! Just a little more work before we can rest. Any spoils are yours. Destroy the camp."

I searched around to see what I could learn. Eshkin destructiveness was evident around us with butchered trunks, fecal matter piled near yurts, and lumber equipment rendered useless. Small fires threatened to grow into blazes.

There was no sign of my other quarry among the eshkin, this gnoll beast, as Otto called him. It seemed to have disappeared or gone into hiding since crossing the river. We found altars as in the other camps, stacked stone with a model spear. This time, however, it looked like the eshkin had sacrificed one of their own.

Seeing the altars brought frowns to the knight and his squires, but for Erik, it brought a deep anger. He pulled apart every stone. Prayers could be heard under his breath. Once we destroyed the raider's camp, we all returned to Sir Bastian's fortified establishment.

We spent the rest of the day caring for the wounded and refortifying. Sir Bastian estimated his casualties to be about one hundred able-bodied men, or one third of his troops, either injured or killed. Erik had some magical healing ability, more than I, but it did little for so many. One cleric healer moved among the wounded, focusing on the neediest, and many of the women helped as they could.

Wails of sorrow over lost husbands, brothers, and fathers drifted across the camp.

"The eshkin loss seems twice of ours, but we know not how many still wander the land," Erik said to Sir Bastian.

"Though weary, all remain resolved to rid the country of them, no matter what it takes to do so," Sir Bastian answered.

"The men of Wynchell have fortitude," I agreed with a sense of respect for the locals.

"And their women," added Erik with admiration.

~

THE WORK CONTINUED in shifts until nightfall. Just about that time, a new horn sounded. A small company of reinforcements arrived, lifting all our spirits.

"I am Cuthbert. We total twenty men-at-arms," explained a cleric, leaning on an oak staff. "Accompanying us is one of the duke's battle mages, and I have two companions of the order. Plus supplies."

The man smelled of herbs, which is what I guessed he carried in the large pouch draped off his shoulder. The embroidery decorating his cuffs and neck indicated his rank, for the robes of the other monks were plain. His clerical 'brothers' stood behind him in matching sienna robes and staffs. All three had shaved both their heads and faces to discourage vain thoughts.

Behind the clerics, rode the battle mage and the twenty men-at-arms, armed with spear, shield, and sword.

Just like the clerical orders, the magic-user guilds specialized in certain skills. Battle-mages trained in the arts of magical warfare, and every noble who could afford it kept at least one at his court.

This man had the wavy beard of the locals, but kept it precisely trimmed, rounded at the base, and it was a more reddish brown than most. A black gambeson with offset buttons down the front stretched to his knees, under which the man wore black trousers and black leather boots. On his belt hung multiple pouches of hard leather. On his shoulders hung a dark linen cape, clasped with a flame-shaped pin. His olive eyes darted about under a wide-brimmed hat, taking in everything in around him. He spoke very little.

The clerics went to work at once to heal those in need. The battle-mage walked throughout the camp, but did not speak or assist.

The following morning, I rose early, feeling refreshed and ready to go. I found Erik in full armor, tending to his stallion, waiting for the orders to move out. Every face I looked into showed the same expression—we wanted to take the fight to the eshkin.

Leaving only a small band to watch over the camp, Sir Bastian ordered the bulk of his troops north through the woods, following the tracks of the fleeing eshkin. The hippogriff riders flew ahead, but only caught glimpses of raiders running under the forest canopy. The clerics and battle mage followed behind.

Sir Bastian asked me to scout ahead since I had actually seen the main camp from afar. Tracking groups of fleeing eshkin seemed easy enough, even on horseback. Wide trails meandered through the Wood Harvest from centuries of cutting lumber, allowing the company to make good time the first day.

I kept myself a few miles ahead of the main body. I was glad to separate from the crowd.

Erik traveled with me for the first few miles, but soon picked up on my irritation and eventually fell back with the rest. As much as I enjoyed his company, he made too much noise for scouting. It felt good to be alone for a while after all that interaction with people. Rangers need their alone time.

Late in the afternoon, I came across a stream tumbling southeast towards the Kwit River. I dismounted to inspect the mud for tracks and to water my horse. Plenty of eshkin had either rested here or crossed within the last day. A few unusual moss-covered rocks grabbed my attention. Upon closer inspection, I realized these were all that remained of some ancient ruins. Something had been here long ago. I knew of no local lore that would shed light on these remains. The trees seemed thinner here and with the stream, it may make a good campsite for a few hundred men-at-arms.

As I sat to ponder my next move, I felt something making its way upstream towards me. Every sense focused in that direction. The presence was too discreet for eshkin, which usually tromped forward with an arrogance of destruction. I checked my horse, which looked up and pointed his ears in the same direction. He did not spook, at least.

Quietly, I readied my bow and notched an arrow as I shifted my weight from one foot onto the other until I was behind the thicker brush. I heard nothing but the pounding of my heart, but my horse still watched the creek.

Whatever it was, it knew how to move with stealth. My horse gave a nervous neigh, much to my annoyance, but I didn't move. I just kept scanning to the southeast.

I thought I heard something here and there, but nothing ever presented itself. Nothing I could pinpoint.

My nerves remained on edge. How long should I wait until I was sure it had moved on? It didn't seem to be a deer or some animal.

Perhaps it was the gnoll beast? It seemed cunning and intelligent.

I strained for any noise behind me, fearing I missed it flanking me. Sweat trickled down my back. It felt like hours, but only a few minutes passed.

"Don't shoot, Galieb! I am coming out," said a voice I recognized immediately. A tall, bearded man stepped out of the brush, far closer than I would have guessed.

"Devarim! I am glad to see you! What are you doing here?" I jumped up to greet him.

"Same as you. Tracking eshkin." My mentor smiled and

greeted me like an equal. "Our training must have worked. You are still alive!"

He jested, but I could see the relief in his face. He worried about me more than he spoke.

"Plenty of things are trying to change that!"

We sat by the stream and took a few minutes to share stories and listen to the water burble by. Apparently, eshkin had set up another large camp along the Kwit River to the south. Not only did they raid within sight of White Cliff, they started raiding the elfin kingdom, and Lord Faeranduil had had enough. With Devarim's help, the elfin destroyed that camp. The remaining eshkin fled north with the elfin in pursuit.

"The elfin are right behind me," Devarim said as we sat watching the minnows dance in the small pools. "They should be here shortly. We know about your entourage. They are not so quiet."

"I better let Sir Bastian know about you, then. We can camp here together."

Returning to the creek with Sir Bastian's company, we found the elfin troops already there, setting up camp on the far side of the stream. The elfin camp seemed to blend into the woods. The elfin moved about with grace, orderly, with hardly a noise. Those not guarding the perimeter reclined with watered wine and fine delicacies as they observed the clumsy humans with some reserve. They all had long, thick, straight hair, whether red or gold, jet black or ivory white. Some added delicate braids to the sides or down the back. They had full eyes of bright green, sapphire blue, or honey brown. Large, pointed ears similar to mine framed ageless faces with smooth skin.

The men of Wynchell, in comparison, spread out with much impact and banter. They stomped and chopped and built fires. Though it seemed random at first, the camp ordered itself for defense, forming several parallel circles with the tents mingled among the trees and brush. They corralled the horses and livestock in the very center. The men cleared the brush around the perimeter for two paces to prevent an ambush.

Soon, new aromas wafted across the forest as support staff prepared supper. Overall, the citizens of Wynchell were men of the wilderness and felt at home under the trees, and worked with similar efficiency to the elfin, even if the extra clatter was slightly annoying to their new allies. In return, the humans also watched the elfin with uncertainty.

After Sir Bastian gave his orders, I brought the knight, the high cleric, and Erik to Devarim and the elfin king. I recognized the elfin royal whom I had met years ago as a young boy when my mother took us to live with them for a short time. He stood just a hint shorter than the other elfin, who were on average shorter and leaner than most humans, but his ageless countenance spoke of a being of both power and authority. Like Devarim, the king left an impression on all who met him.

"Sirs, may I introduce Lord Faeranduil, King of Haeran-Vale," I spoke, knowing to honor the elfin lord first.

Faeranduil dressed in a long-sleeved high collared robe of emerald green, trimmed in a bright white with a deep maroon leather accent, woven of silk and fine wool with elfin skill. On his belt hung the paired saber and dagger of the elfin known as *lase n eck,* named after their own martial art. His left hand gripped a carved staff marked with elfin letters. Low on his brow rested a silver circlet styled after deer antlers that wrapped his long, straight, white hair. Faeranduil had a reputation as a learned arch-mage of great wisdom and magical ability, and he looked the part.

The three men bowed to the elfin.

"And Wise Protector Devarim of the Qoholet, my mentor."

Devarim stood tall in his simple brigandine and ranger's

cloak, exuding strength and wisdom. The silver gray in his beard and dark hair only added to the impression. His eyes betrayed intelligence and sophistication beyond his rugged exterior. Two elfin sabers adored his belt, and an intricate war bow rested on his back next to his quiver.

After I introduced them, Faeranduil and Devarim nodded greetings to the men of Lageheim. As impressive as the leaders appeared to the average man, they paled next to the king and ranger lord. I felt small among them all.

After exchanging pleasantries, the elfin king turned to me. "Young ranger, are you not the only son of Edhelwen?"

"Yes, sire. Galieb N'ethilion at your service. We met before, when I was just a boy. I am honored you remember."

"I cannot forget the circumstance that brought your mother with a small boy to us. Now you have grown. To me, that was but a passing decade. I forget that the half-elfin sprout like a spring flower, more in the ways of men than our people. Are you now among the Qoholet or still an acolyte?"

"Galieb spoke the oaths this summer, Lord Faeranduil," Devarim answered. "The counsel has great hopes for this young man." His tone carried a touch of pride, which stirred my heart.

"My blessings upon him to fulfill all those hopes. Your mother is well?"

"Yes, sire, last I saw her," I answered. "She still enjoys her gardens."

"Sire, she is a member of the Council at the Abbey, adding to our blessings," Devarim said.

"That is wise, Devarim, in my eyes. I would do the same if she had remained in HaerenVale. Well, I am sure she worries about her son being here among our enemies. When you see her, give her greetings from my lady and myself."

"Most certainly, my lord." I bowed.

"Now, good men, we must discuss battle plans. I understand there is another magic-user in the camp? Maybe he should join us as well?"

"A battle mage named Grimwald. I will retrieve him, sire," I offered.

"Yes, please do so. Galieb, I want you here as well."

The elfin king called for food, and we all ate the best we had in weeks. Even better than the dwarfin feast.

THE MORNING STARTED EARLY, but slow. Several servants had gone missing over the last week, and now another deserted our company, or so it appeared. Otto, too, was not a reliable worker, disappearing periodically, but that did not surprise me. Ambition did not seem part of his character, but I knew he would continue to linger with the company, even if I could not locate him this morning.

While waiting for breakfast, my predawn explorations lead to the discovery of tracks. Gnoll tracks. The beast must be following our company. Servants and cooks made easy targets. Too many boots had trampled over the clawed marks, so once again, I failed in tracking the beast.

I immediately found Devarim and updated him on the situation.

"Hmmm. Well done, Galieb," Devarim said, looking over the prints. "You always excelled at tracking. Stealth and archery, too."

"Maybe, but I can't seem to find the beast. I don't feel very successful."

Devarim smiled. "There is one key component you are missing. It is why I cannot track him either, besides all the contamination by the men-at-arms."

"A key component? What am I missing?" I asked, frustrated. I suddenly felt young and inexperienced.

"His tracks—and I believe it is male—change and blend with the others. The beast you saw is a shape shifter of some kind. A lycanthrope or a doppelgänger. Perhaps even a minor demon. The beast you are hunting is hiding among us. It could be anyone."

A shape shifter! No wonder I kept losing him! If he changed form, his footprints would change. But everyone wore boots. Wouldn't all his prints be barefoot? I remembered finding barefoot tracks back at Farrin's Crossing. I needed to be more alert next time.

"Sir Bastian is a knight of quality but is merely an experienced warrior with a code of honor and expensive armor. Your friend, Erik, is a Defender of the Lage. Defenders are more than knights. They are paladins. Paladins have special abilities. Just as the Qoholet are more than scouts or fighters. We are elite rangers. Defenders, such as Erik, have the ability to detect the unholy by magic. Make him aware of the monster if you have not done so already. Perhaps he could sense something."

"Yes," I said, thoughtfully. "He sang as we fought, and it lifted all our spirits. Strengthening us when we were exhausted."

We spoke to Erik at breakfast, and he agreed to remain alert for any signs of wickedness.

"Detection is not an exact skill," Erik stated. "Defining what is or may be 'evil' or 'wicked' is very nuanced. After all, everyone breaks the law, so we are all lawbreakers and wicked in some sense. I am just a squire and have not taken the oaths, so I have very limited skills. However, I will remain alert and prayerful."

As the rest of the men and elfin packed up to leave, Erik and I wandered about, meandering between all the tents and around all the areas of the camp. Erik drew on the little magic he knew, hoping to discover the hidden danger, but he sensed nothing. We spoke with one wagon driver who claimed he saw someone or something with a large bundle over its shoulder, but that was all we could learn. It added to my belief that the creature now followed our camp or was nearby, but I could not find it.

Not being able to solve the mystery, we went about doing our jobs. Devarim and I scouted ahead as Sir Bastian's troops prepared to march. Tanyl, the elfin king's Master of Scouts, joined us. Sir Bastian found extra horses for them both to use.

Devarim seemed pleased as the three of us worked our way through the brush. I knew not the reason. Perhaps he enjoyed the simple pleasures of nature as he paused from performing heavy responsibilities, but I could not help but suspect he delighted in my company, like a father with his son. And I enjoyed his presence as well. I also felt humbled beside these two masters, watching and learning, hoping not to irritate them as Erik did me.

All elfin excelled at wood lore compared to most men, but Tanyl reached the highest levels of tracking and hunting to be named the Master of Scouts by the king. Elfin seem timeless, but he was middle-aged, making him a few hundred years old. He dressed in the silken tunics common among his folk, his being a decorative pattern of olive and rust. An elfin war bow rested on his back and he wore the *lase n eck* blades crafted by his people. Of his thick blonde hair, he stated, "I keep it long, for it enhances my senses." Indeed, it went all the way down his back.

As we tracked ahead through the trees of Wood Harvest, the men of Wynchell travelled close behind, followed by the company of elfin.

After moving north for several hours, the looming mountains drew closer, reminding us we were now approaching our destination.

The woods ended suddenly as live trees gave way to burnt ruins. Blackened trunks and charred brush were all that remained of the once beautiful evergreen canyon. Smoke lingered in the air. Eshkin found pleasure in destroying and stealing property not their own. This time, however, they also did it for defense. We could not approach their main camp without being noticed.

Tanyl called us to a halt as we moved among the burned trees. Dismounting, we soon heard the movement of an eshkin patrol. Cover was scarce, but we squatted among the charred sticks, leaving the horses behind tied to a pair of untouched trees, branches still green.

We sat in silence, as still as rocks, as the patrol moved closer. We counted four unhappy warriors walking directly towards us.

"Don't know how we got the unlucky draw," said the first.

"Yep. What's the point of patrolling? We know them round ears are out there. And that blue skin had to kick the elfin hornet nest, too," added a second.

"End up with an arrow in the back, if we ain't careful," the third said.

"I don't think things are going like the blue skin planned. But they don't tell us nothin'," the first added.

"All of you, just shut up," grumbled the fourth and last in line. "I don't like it either, but maybe we can get some extra grub tonight. Remember, we serve the Forsaken first. Not the blue skin." The four drew closer, but didn't see us.

"More likely, the best meat will be gone by the time we get back," stated number three. "The Forsaken is the one that put blue skin in charge."

"Better do what he says, then. So shut it!" The fourth

paused and looked around. "Them elfin are too close! I can feel it! Too close to the trees here. I don't like it. Let's turn that way."

"Hey, what's tha...ugh!" Tanyl's arrow protruding from his throat prevented the front one from finishing his comment. He perished without another word. The third one in line dropped dead as Devarim planted a shaft in his chest.

"Blood and Bones! Let's get outta here!" shouted the last in line.

The remaining two turned to flee, but I put an arrow in the buttocks of one of them, causing him to stumble with a scream. I berated myself for not ending him with my arrow. I rushed forward to finish him with my axe, but Tanyl reached the wounded eshkin before I did and dispatched him.

Devarim went after the last.

The remaining raider zigged and zagged, using the tall burnt stumps as shields. Devarim raced after, closing the gap.

We lost sight of both as we hurried to pursue. Following behind for several hundred paces, we all rushed into the mouth of the wide open canyon, the mountain peaks staring down at us under the white clouds. Dead trees gave way to a valley cleared of all trees and brush.

There, Devarim stood over the corpse of the last warrior.

Far up the slope, stretched between the canyon walls, a long rocky berm filled with spiked logs marked the edge of the fortified eshkin camp.

The sound of drums rolled down towards us. They knew we were here.

CHAPTER 20

TRAITORS AMONG US

As we stood over the bodies of our fallen foes, studying the eshkin stronghold, the rest of the company caught up to us. Sir Bastian rode out from the burnt sticks onto the edge of the open valley. The knight sat straight in the saddle, lance pointed to the sky, staring up at the enemy who had terrorized the citizens of Wynchell. Erik sat mounted on Stedgyr beside him on one side, the high cleric Cuthbert astride a horse on the other, staff across his knees. We strode down to join them as the squires established their men-at-arms in a line at the edge of the open field, ready for battle. Archers positioned themselves behind them among the burnt trees, long bows standing tall in a row. Wynchell banners of gold V's on green fields stirred in the mountain breeze.

Sir Bastian finally broke his silence. "They await us. After burning our homes, let us give them such a rout that they do not dare return for another century."

King Faeranduil soon arrived with his warriors, slipping into place on either side of the human array, guarding their flanks.

"The sun will set soon," Devarium reminded the knight. "Darkness works to the eshkin advantage. Best to wait until first light."

"Hopefully, the eshkin are agreeable to that and do not attack," Sir Bastian responded.

"The elfin will keep watch," Faeranduil assured everyone. "We need not the heavy slumbers of men."

"My gracious thanks, sire." Sir Bastian nodded. "We will all sleep well knowing that."

Dead trees fell to axes as berms and trenches came into existence. The fortified berm stretched east to west across the edge of the cleared canyon, curving back into the burnt area at the ends. A shallow trench paralleled the berm in front of its entire length to further hinder any charging attackers. Narrow channels between the spiked berms allowed for the charging of horses.

The sun dropped below the horizon as we secured our position. Sir Bastian set a few men along the berm in shifts, both farmers and men-at-arms, while the others rested, despite the elfin king's offer. Faeranduil did the same.

A summer storm rolled in to hasten the evening and block out the light of the three-quarter moon. The dry slope before us quickly turned to mud with rivulets forming throughout the camp, washing away the blackened topsoil. This was not ideal for mounted or any other form of combat. Some of the spiked barricades had to be reset, too, for the running water gathered in the trenches and softened the berm.

The drumming continued uninterrupted by the storm, but none of us saw any sign of an imminent attack, so I crawled into the tent they provided me to get out of the heavy rain and manage some sleep.

~

Blasting horns and yelling men brought me out of my deep slumber around midnight. As I rushed out of my tent, bow in hand, cool damp air hit my skin. Darkness reigned under the heavy clouds, limiting my elfin vision to precise shades of gray.

A man-at-arms stumbled past me, coughing and retching. He collapsed in his own vomit. I checked for a pulse but found none.

Utter chaos reigned as I moved towards the front line behind the berm.

The sound of snapping branches and a thud startled me. Similar sounds followed, like heavy raindrops. Not rain, but eshkin javelins. One struck nearby. I grabbed a helmet off a dead man struck by a javelin and hid behind a tall burnt stub of a tree.

A putrid stench touched my nostrils. *Toxic cloud!* flashed in my mind as I yanked my cloak across my face. An unnatural rush of air bowled me forward as it pushed up the slope, rattling the dead tree stumps. The downpour of javelins stopped, and the toxic cloud dispersed.

I continued forward, looking for Devarim and Erik. At the edge of my vision, many of the eshkin lay scattered on the open ground above us from the rebuffed toxic cloud. Out of the clouds, a small bolt of lightning flashed down, lighting up the open field as it struck a raider and turned him into a charred ruin. The blast knocked down those around him.

A second bolt pierced the night, striking another enemy and scattering more. Two thunderous booms echoed across the battlefield.

As my eyes readjusted, a wild-eyed horse galloped right past me from out of the darkness. Ignoring the horse, I established my position and took aim with my bow, launching a few arrows at tusked warriors still within my sight.

Without warning, a large fireball arced across the sky. I

watched in fascination and helplessness. Time slowed as the fireball crashed down with a whooshing sound east of me, flames spreading on impact behind our fortified front line. Many men screamed in terror as they burned alive.

As the fire consumed all within its range, the drums echoing down the slope suddenly changed. Eshkin turned to run back up the hill.

A man in full armor charged past the barricades, encouraging his steed as he led a small force of mounted warriors after the retreating eshkin. In the dark, I could not tell who led the counter assault.

I saved the rest of my arrows. Feeling a little useless, I continued my search for Devarim and to see what else I could do to help. I found the ranger standing by the barricade, his bow, *Blesfyr*, in hand.

The elfin king stood beside him, the light from the fires reflecting off both of their features.

"Galieb! Good to see you safe!" called Devarim.

"Aye. I didn't know eshkin could wield such powerful magic! I thought they were just raiders?"

"Historically, they have always been just raiders and opportunistic thieves," Devarim answered, his face grim. "But we have seen organized military attacks. Now magic. Someone is commanding them. Large forces such as this are unknown."

"Eshkin worship Eshek," Faeranduil said. "Petty clerics and warlocks who wield some magic are not unknown. But fireballs and poison clouds are beyond their ability. We face an arch mage."

Devarim frowned, his jaw tight. "They accomplished what they planned. Dozens wounded and killed. No rest for most this night. The third watch will end before we all settle down again."

Within minutes, the group of mounted men returned, confirming the end of the skirmish.

Erik dismounted from Stedgyr and joined us. "A fell night, I must say," he lamented. "There is more to them than we anticipated. 'May the Lawgiver rescue me from my strong enemy, for they are too mighty for me.'"

Anticipating no more attacks this night, we all returned to camp to see what could be done. The clerics moved among the wounded, healing many with their effective skills, both magical and mundane. The uninjured cleaned up the damage as the moon slowly peaked out from behind the clouds, aiding us in our work.

I assisted a man with a javelin wound, while Erik stood nearby, healing those he could with the magical skills he possessed.

A man-at-arms in full mail and helmet came to us with a message. "Sir Bastian requests your presence at his tent," the man stated. "Squire Erik, the knight requires you as well."

We found Sir Bastian standing outside his tent in a gambeson and helm, his long sword strapped to his hip. Several squires stood by him. At his feet knelt a man in chains. The prisoner appeared to be one of the duke's men-at-arms.

The knight's face appeared rigid as he frowned, his hard eyes peering into the darkness.

Soon, Devarim and King Faeranduil joined us.

"I called you all here to be witnesses to this man's trial," Sir Bastian stated, his voice betraying his weariness. Surprise crossed our faces. We all looked at the man on the ground. "Squire Colten, tell us all what you witnessed."

The blond squire, standing apart from the others, cleared his throat and gathered his thoughts.

"Sir Bastian, my lords." Squire Colten nodded at each of us. "What I tell you is true, as I witnessed it happen." He cleared his throat again. "When the attack started, you, my lord, Sir Bastian, ordered that I should go to the corral and prepare our steeds for a charge. As I approached, I noticed how agitated they seemed, some neighing and calling out." He paused. "My first thought was that maybe some raiders had somehow slipped past the elfin watch."

"Very unlikely," Devarim stated, and Faeranduil agreed.

"Yes, I quickly dismissed the idea," the squire said. "Then I wondered about javelins falling among them, but the camp is too far back for them to reach."

Squire Colten then pointed to the chained man.

"Once I was close enough in the dark, I realized what was happening. This man here was in the corral. The gate was open, and he was scattering the horses across the camp. I commanded him to stop. I first thought he was just foolish, confused by the attack. But then I saw the stableman. He lay dead outside the corral."

My eyebrows raised at the realization, as did Erik's. Devarim and the king just listened without expression. Years of experience left few surprises.

Squire Colten continued. "This man then attacked me when confronted, but I subdued him. By this time, most of the horses ran off into the dark."

I thought of the panicked horse that ran past me earlier.

Sir Bastian still frowned, but he spoke calmly. "What do you have to say? What is your defense? You know me to be a fair man. These here, your jury, are all just men...people."

"Aye, tis true. I will not deny it," the prisoner stated, looking at the ground.

"Did you kill the stableman?"

He said nothing for a moment before giving a quiet answer. "Aye."

"Killing your brother in arms. Scattering horses. Attacking

my squire. How could you contemplate such things? These are treasonous acts during war. Are you willing to answer why?"

"I serve the Forsaken," the man said flatly.

Sir Erik blustered. "What is this blasphemy? The Lage rules here. We serve the Lawgiver. Do you wish to add blasphemy to treason and murder?"

The prisoner looked over at the paladin with eagerness. "I saw him. He approached me in the street."

We all must have looked baffled.

Erik spoke up. "Who? You saw who? What do you mean?"

"One of the old gods! He calls himself Forsaken, but that was not his name before. I saw him!" The man swore an oath that it was true.

"Just a charlatan! You are throwing your life away for a trickster." Erik almost begged him to see his foolishness.

"He had power. Incredible power. Promised riches to the faithful, and life in paradise to those who proved their loyalty."

"What of righteousness? What did he say of that?" Devarim asked.

The prisoner had no response.

Sir Bastian spoke up. "According to the Lage, the punishment for treason, murder, and blasphemy is death. On the field of battle, we cannot spare men to send him back to White Cliff. What do the witnesses say?"

"Do you recant or repent?" Devarim asked.

"No. I am loyal to my god." He shook his head but refused eye contact.

"Loyalty?" Sir Bastian asked. "What of your oaths to the duke? You would die for someone that used you and now abandons you?"

The prisoner said nothing more, but only stared at the ground.

"If you have nothing more to say, we will make a judgment," Sir Bastian stated.

"It must be death by execution, though it saddens me to say so," Erik responded. "That is the law."

"He has shown himself to be untrustworthy," Faeranduil said. "Execution it must be. Do you wish one of my warriors to do it?"

"No. I will do it myself. It is my duty." Sir Bastian sighed. "Thank you all. Let us meet again in an hour to make plans for the assault on the eshkin. Morning will come soon enough."

Sir Bastian got his halberd from his tent.

Erik said a prayer before the knight beheaded the traitor.

It shook me to see the execution. It was not the blood, nor was it the hard judgment of the Lage. What shook me was the failure of us all. Even the presence of the elfin king and such men as Devarim did not sway this traitor.

"Galieb, your face betrays you," Devarim said to me as I stood staring off into nothing. "Many thoughts cloud your mind. Do you wish to share them?"

I gave a sad smile. Wise Protector Devarim could slay a dozen eshkin at once and still watch over those who trusted in him. "Is my countenance so readable to my mentor? This is what troubles me: Lageheim remained a prosperous land, and most lived comfortable lives. The king and the rulers all seemed to treat their people well, allowing for many opportunities. Why betray that? What was in a man that he would do such a thing?"

"The man heard something that he took for truth with promises of wealth and power. And a happy paradise even in death. Many succumb to such desirable ideas."

201

I understood Devarim's answer, and it made sense, but I felt there had to be more. "Those reasons seemed so...petty. Shallow promises of power and wealth. Promises unsubstantiated. No call to righteousness. There was no requirement of doing good. Just loyalty. Loyalty is a good virtue, correct? Yet something seems wrong about it."

Devarim put his hand on my shoulder. "Wealth and power can be useful tools to those who are moral, but dangerous to all when in the wrong hands. Loyalty is a fine enough virtue, but loyalty to the wrong ideas or entities only attach you to evil. People loyal to the wrong things or people, can end up committing other great acts of evil in order to be faithful to the virtue of loyalty. You cannot sacrifice one virtue at the altar of another."

"Thank you, Wise Protector. That is helpful, but I see I still have much to learn. The Qoholet tenets say that evil and suffering are an inevitable part of this world. But seeing the cruelty of the eshkin and such betrayal in actuality is another matter." I did not like Derleik the Wandering Eye, nor Lekhash, his fox-like companion, but now I better understood his challenges.

"Do not give up hope, Galieb. There is more at work in the world than just evil. It is the duty of the Qoholet to discover what or who that is."

AT THE COUNCIL of the leaders in Sir Bastian's tent, all decided it would be best to wait for the morning light to attack. However, before sunrise, Devarim and the elfin scoutmaster Tanyl would lead a flanking mission to infiltrate the eshkin stronghold. That patrol would all be elfin except for me and Devarim.

We rested a couple of hours, then we set out a few hours

before sunrise. We hoped to scale the canyon walls of the valley and come into their camp from the east behind their spiked barricades.

As we prepared to leave our tents, Devarim guided me to a quiet spot among the burnt trees and told me it was time to learn new things. "You remember the Theory of Magic?" he asked.

"Yes, sir. All created things release an excess of energy named 'radiance'. Some objects, especially living beings, generate more than others. The manipulation of radiance is called magic."

"What magic do you know? What did your mother teach you?"

"Just healing spells," I answered. "Like the healing pearls using comfrey leaves."

"Good. They are simple, but effective and vital. Rangers specialize in certain spells. But you can't learn them all at once. Some are more advanced and take time to learn. I will share a few simple ones, like starting a fire. Precision at every step is key when it comes to magic, as well as concentration on what the radiance is doing. Right now, watch me closely as I 'enhance my senses.' The ability to see in the dark is not gifted to humans."

He muttered a few unique syllables and then placed an oregano leaf on his tongue before chewing. I sensed increased energy around him as the herb took effect. "All five senses improve," he said, "not just the eyesight. So be careful what you do, especially what you eat once it takes effect. Something with a bitter taste will be even stronger tasting. Like the leaf I just ate. Later, I will show you how to use magic to enhance your martial skills."

With everyone ready to face our enemy, Devarim led me and a dozen elfin eastward into the darkness. The drums had stopped, and all seemed quiet in both camps. Whoever commanded the eshkin knew the attack would start at dawn and had prepared a defense. Though we could not see their barricades in the dark, we assumed by the lack of activity that gray warriors waited with anticipation for an assault along the fortified berm.

We slipped across the burnt deadwood before reaching an untouched wooded area in the eastern foothills. There, we began the steep climb up the rocky ridges that reached down out of the higher peaks. Our movement slowed as we scrambled up the sheer slope.

By the time we crested the top of the ridge, the first hint of light showed itself beyond the distant haze. Clouds still lingered from the storm, but now a few morning stars poked through in the west. The peaks behind us looked purple in the starlight. As the land dried out, the summer humidity rose to meet us, promising to be a hot, humid day, even here at the base of the mountains.

Working our way down the other side of the canyon wall, we heard Sir Bastian's horns. All was ready. From our vantage, the entire battlefield filled our vision. Directly below us and to our west, we could see our enemies' camp. Eshkin warriors stood in long lines across the valley, poised for the attack behind the high spiked berm they had built. An armored chieftain moved among the ranks, waving a large spear, shouting orders and threats. Behind the defensive lines of warriors, hundreds of yurts clustered across the north end of the valley floor between the two walls.

Hundreds of paces to the south of the eshkin camp, across the cleared fields at the open end of the same valley, determined men and elfin prepared to assault the eshkin line. Out of the burnt trees and out in the open, they stretched in four lines across the base of the valley, with Sir Bastian and his mounted squires and other men-at-arms in the center, the elfin and the farmers on the flanks. The rear lines consisted of longbowmen with quivers of arrows. Faeranduil, a horse now provided for him by the knight, rode beside Sir Bastian. Grimwald, the battle mage, stayed at the very back with the clerics.

As soon as the horns blasted, two fireballs streaked from the hands of King Faeranduil and Grimwald, trailing smoke and ash as they exploded among the eshkin warriors lined up behind the spike berms.

Sir Bastian raised and pointed his sword at his enemy. Two hundred men and about fifty elfin advanced up the hill.

And so the battle began.

CHAPTER 21

THE BATTLE OF
BURNT CANYON

E shkin scrambled to dowse the fires with buckets of water from a stream running through the camp. Following the path of the fireballs, hundreds of heavy arrows rained down among the raiders. Eshkin crouched behind large, crude wooden shields, rendering most of the arrows useless.

Another larger fireball answered the first two, this one coming from the eshkin line and landing among the scattering longbowmen.

I searched for its source, but I could not see who cast it. More fireballs rolled across the sky from our allies at the bottom of the valley, hitting the eshkin defenses, trailing smoke and causing mayhem.

The raiders crouched behind the large shields, only aware of the enemies in front of them. With great speed, two hippogriffs swooped down the mountainside behind the eshkin ranks, the riders releasing arrows into the vulnerable backs of the gray-skinned warriors.

We, too, prepared to add our missiles to the attack on their left flank when an oversized head of matted hair appeared above the yurts. Wide shoulders led to long arms holding a long shaft like a small tree trunk.

"One of the cave giants out of the high hills has joined them," Tanyl observed.

"Two, it seems," Devarim corrected as another moved forward on the far side of the camp. "They could be brothers by their features."

"Notice the heavy leathers and furs draped down to their knees," Tanyl said. "Not just crude skins used for covering. Someone provided extra protection for them."

"Look at that!" I exclaimed.

Each giant placed rocks larger than a man's head into a socket carved into the end of each of the tree trunks. The giants then swung the trunks in a downward motion, catapulting the boulders down the slope. The rocks bounced through the ranks of our advancing allies. Men scattered to avoid their paths, but some were not fast enough. The rocks crushed chest cavities, shattered skulls, and snapped limbs as they tumbled down the slope.

"Focus on the giants!" Tanyl called as we began launching arrow after arrow from our bows.

The arrows struck the giants, but barely penetrated the furs. Grunts escaped from their bearded mouths, and they stood like pincushions, but it only slowed down the throwing of rocks.

Devarim stood, with the string of his bow, *Blesfyr*, stretched to the corner of his mouth, cloak pushed behind his shoulders. The heavy arrow raced across the distance, striking the exposed neck of the closest colossal.

The creature groaned, slapping at his neck as blood leaked

out. But before his hand even reached the shaft, a bolt of lightning cracked down out of the sky at the exact point of the arrow's contact.

The giant's entire body lifted off his feet to land on his back, his furs aflame. In a panic, the oversized creature rolled about, attempting to extinguish the flames, snapping the burning shafts stuck in his leather armor. The thrashing giant crushed any eshkin standing too close. Moments later, he lay still, smoke rising from his coat of fur.

I cheered at the victorious shot.

"Number three for today. That is all the charges I have for now," Devarim told Tanyl.

They both set about killing eshkin one by one with regular arrows.

Following their lead, we all rained death from above.

The eshkin now became aware of our presence on the wall above and behind them. This prompted a patrol of angered raiders to scramble up the canyon wall towards us.

Another volley of arrows from the Wynchell longbowmen below joined ours, landing among the disoriented raiders.

I tried for the face of the second giant, but he stood at the far end of my range, my shaft only hitting his lower torso as he continued tossing rocks among the men moving up the slope. One boulder struck Grimwald as he launched another fireball, crushing the battle mage's pelvis. A cleric rushed to his aid.

It seemed chaos ruled as the battle raged. Pausing to check my quiver, I watched in horror as a green toxic cloud formed in front of the barricade and drifted down the slope toward the troops. I felt helpless to cry out or somehow stop it.

But my fears turned to relief as I saw the long hair and green banners of the men-at-arms flying forward at the rushing of air. Only the elfin lord could have answered with a wall of wind, pushing the poison cloud back up the hill towards the eshkin.

The cloud dissipated without harm.

As for the hippogriff riders, they swooped down the slope behind the eshkin camp twice more, felling our enemies.

After the third pass, a thin figure with long white hair stepped forward from out of the eshkin yurts. Four long spears of flaming red energy streaked from his hands, two shafts at each flying beast.

One hippogriff, ridden by Jarman, swooped and maneuvered out of the way, the energy bolts just missing both steed and rider. The other pair of fiery flames fulfilled their purpose. Though Kean and his hippogriff dove and banked, to all of our horror, a flaming spear passed through his wing with a shriek. Kean and his steed tumbled down with wing alit, crash landing behind the advancing company as smoke trailed behind in a spiral.

Another horn sounded below. The armored men and elfin warriors ran forward, crossing the last steps of the field of battle to rush the barricade as the longbowmen paused their assault.

The eshkin clacked their jaws in anticipation, axes ready in hand. The thin white-haired mage gestured and shouted. Without warning, magical thorns sprung out of the trampled ground as the men of Wynchell reached the front of the barricades. Scores of men became entangled in the piercing net of briars.

Devarim took aim at the fellow with the thick white mane, but the arrow ricocheted off him as if hitting a rock.

"A magic shield surrounds the man," Devarim grumbled in frustration.

"A wizard for sure, but he is not human. Can you see his ice-blue skin in the morning light?" Tanyl asked.

Even from here you could tell he was lean, and shorter than the average man. An elfin for sure, but never like one I ever seen.

"One of the Fanalfin," Tanyl explained. "An elfin tribe banished for their study of dark arts and the rejection of our goddess, Amilye. No one has seen them beyond the northern ice before."

"I have never heard of them," Devarim stated. "But I would guess he is the one organizing the eshkin."

It surprised me that Devarim did not know about them. His knowledge always appeared vast. He had traveled much and studied more.

"Faeranduil will deal with him," Tanyl assured us.

That I believed. We all knew the king to be a wizard of the highest order.

Even as I listened to the exchange of words, the thorns shriveled, letting the now injured men to surge forward.

Just as the longbowmen below stopped their assault, we dared not risk targeting the eshkin as both armies clashed in hand-to-hand combat. We could hear the cries below and the striking of steel on steel. As we prepared to advance down the slope, eshkin warriors popped up over the edge and rushed us.

Devarim leaped forward, set on protecting those under his charge, his grim countenance hesitating the attacking foes. Unsheathing his sabers, he cut down two enemies at once before they could even strike.

Close behind, elfin blades swirled as they clashed with eshkin axes and falchions.

Sword and axe now in hand, I joined the fight. An eshkin charged at me. I dodged his falchion and stabbed my sword tip deep into his chest, watching the life leave his eyes. Another raider made a cut at me on my left. I blocked his falchion with my axe and parried the enemy's second cut with my sword after yanking it free from the falling corpse.

We blocked and swiped at each other, neither getting the upper hand.

I scored across the eshkin's forearm, causing blood to run down to his hand. With a clack of his jaws, he slashed across my chest, but it did not penetrate the steel plates of my brigandine.

I stumbled back, and he pressed in fiercely. Dodging a blow, I sliced his thigh open, severing the artery. He tumbled down the mountainside after his legs failed.

With no more eshkin to oppose us, Devarim leaped down the mountain to join the foray. The rest of us scrabbled behind at his heels.

We approached the camp at its flanks and weaved among the yurts, slaying any enemy who opposed us.

We could not trust the yurts to be empty, so we looked within each one, swords first. Several hid slaves and prisoners. We freed those we could with promises to return once all was safe. A few able-bodied men grabbed weapons and joined us.

A small clan of eshkin sat in one of the yurts. I raised my weapons, ready for an onslaught, but it never came. To my shock, females and young sat among the males. I had never heard of anyone speak of females or young before when mentioning the eshkin.

"Do not strike, half-blood. We not enemies," a large eshkin male warned as he stood up, struggling with the Common Tongue. "But we defend family."

Showing his empty hands, they brandished no weapons nor showed any aggression. Other males stood with him, along with a few females.

"Who are you?" I asked.

"Others enslave us. Call me Craven. Wear name proud. Braver to stand, then to follow. They do not see."

"You do not fight?"

"We did not choose here. They force us. Blue skin and top shaman, Mukluk. Just like force lobeless like you. Make all slaves. Humans do not know. Some eshkin reject Eshek. Some eshkin reject new god. We few, but live. We want to raise our herds. Left alone."

Was this some trap? I called to Devarim, and Tanyl joined us, too.

"Who is this new god?" I asked, as Devarim and Tanyl entered the yurt.

"Call himself Forsaken," Craven answered. "Old man, but strong. Overcome Eshek. Only one eye. Use boar spear."

Tanyl spoke first. "There are rumors of peaceful eshkin among the elfin legends, but never have I seen one. This is the first I have ever seen females and youth. I know not how to counsel. King Farenduil should decide."

"If you slay us, we fight. We die proud. We not killers. Defend family with honor."

Devarim looked around the tent. The sounds of war raged about us. "What do you want? Decide quickly."

Craven scowled. "You no listen? Live in peace. Leave for mountains. Raise herds. Raise family. If no kill, we leave. Find new home."

Devarim rubbed his chin with the back of his hand before answering. "Go now, while the rest fight. If you come back or attack us, we will slay all of you."

Tanyl looked displeased but said nothing.

Craven gestured to his people. "We go now. Give warning first. Over mountains. Many enemies, like rocks on slope. Hairs on dwarfin head. Many eshkin, men, dwarfin, blue skins, beasts. Coming, like a raging river."

Then they left.

Outside the tent, the other elfin gathered with a few of the freed men who found weapons. They all looked shocked as the eshkin families came out and fled into the mountains.

As we eyed them suspiciously, another group of eshkin attacked us. Two dwarfin led them. Pale skinned with wiry dark beards. Not like any of the other dwarfin I had seen. Kin from another place. They brandished heavy forge hammers and wore scaled breast plates. Simple steel caps sat on their heads. They attacked fiercely, but we slew them all.

After overcoming the strange dwarfin, we stalked forward and struck the enemy's flank, eshkin dying on our swords, fear and shock forever planted on their faces. I struck down three eshkin before the tusked warriors turned to face us, yelling battle cries of hatred.

At the spiked trenches, eshkin, men, and elfin clashed with great intensity, the eshkin wild-eyed and savage, using falchion, axe, and even tusk. The armored chieftain no longer cursed at his troops from behind, but now stood at the front line beside the other gray-skinned warriors with spear and shield. The remaining giant, standing almost twice the height of men, stomped into the melee, swinging his trunk like a club, knocking men asunder. He stood at the far side of the field, but we were now too engaged to reach for our bows.

I could see the knight and the squires at the front of their army, fighting with vigor.

Sir Bastian swung his halberd and few stood against him, though his armor looked battered and worn. Erik fought with a long sword and heater shield, facing his enemies without fear. Songs reverberated from his lips.

Elfin warriors slashed with sabers and cut with daggers, the blades only blurs of cold steel. The eshkin army numbered twice ours, and despite the valor of our allies, the raiders held the men and elfin at the barricades.

As our scouting party weakened the east flank, the tide turned in our favor, the knight and squires pushing through.

But it would not last.

The giant suddenly went berserk, swinging his trunk in wide berths and crushing blows. None dared to come near, whether ally or enemy.

Scores of new eshkin coming to join the camp now raced down out of the mountains, filling in the thinning gaps and covering the area behind my company.

Devarim formed us into two lines, guarding each other's backs.

The battle raged.

The clear call of a silver horn sounded on the western slopes. I looked towards the sound, not knowing if it was friend or foe. There stood Vigglod, the sun's glare reflecting off the silver instrument. A score of dwarfin armed with spear and shield, helms on their heads and war hammers at their sides, rushed forward into battle, calling dwarfin war cries. My heart rejoiced at seeing our new allies come to our aid.

Without fear, they assaulted the half-mad giant, ducking under his swings to hamstring him from behind. His trunk-like body collapsed behind the mass of battle, his face twisted in shock as he fell.

Within minutes, the giant's head flew in an arch above the crowds to land among the yurts.

Hope blossomed in my chest, and I could see the light on the faces of my friends. In contrast, despair grew among the eshkin warriors. Still, they clacked their jaws and fought harder.

Without warning, the blue-skinned mage extended his arms, throwing a cone of frost at the elfin king and his allies, not caring whether it hurt friend or foe. I watched aghast as men, elfin, and eshkin all suffered from the blast. Fingers froze to frosted weapons. Many stumbled as their legs went numb, even in the summer heat.

I wanted to run to their aid, but too many stood between us.

Only Faeranduil and those about him seemed unaffected by the attack. Locking eyes on his foe, Faeranduil gestured with his staff. The ice-blue mage stood with a furrowed brow as he pushed helplessly against invisible walls. The elfin king had dropped a magical cage around his foe. Curses against the king reached my ears as the mystery mage struggled to break through the cage of force, but to no avail.

A raider attacked me, and I slew him, but when I looked again at the blue elfin, he was gone.

Another horn sounded in the forest, and up the slope rode seven knights in full armor. At the center of the charge led a knight with a gold crest on his helm, his green and gold banner flapping above him. The Duke of Wynchell himself had come.

By now, the barricades were in disarray, with gaps for the horses. The Duke charged through with his company, eshkin falling to hoof and lance.

Some raiders retreated, hope gone from their faces. But the eshkin chief, eight rings in his dangling lobe, roared in defiance. The warrior came against me first, as if determined to die a warrior's death and to take all his foes with him. He wielded a boar spear adored with feathers, and a large, square shield. Scale mail draped to his knees.

"Mukluk! Mukluk!" his companions called as they rallied beside him. Here was the eshkin shaman Craven mentioned. A servant of the Forsaken.

Devarim leaped between us, meeting the great chieftain, swords in hand. The chieftain grinned and clacked his jaws, thrusting with his spear and shield. Devarim moved in a blur, dodging the thrust of the spear as he shifted to the chieftain's left. Before the eshkin could bring the spear point back into play or turn his body or shield, the ranger lord sliced off his head with his saber, slaying him where he stood.

The remaining eshkin, after watching their leaders fall, turned and fled, scattering up into the mountains.

Tanyl called to his kin, and the elfin pursued them to the top of the canyon, cutting down those they caught.

I stood exhausted, looking at the surrounding death, stained sword and axe still in hand.

Devarim cleaned his blades, sheathed them, and then walked up to me. "Wynchell once again lives free of raiders," he said.

"Thank the Creator," I responded. "And thank you for killing the eshkin shaman. He may have been too much for me."

"Come, there is still work to be done. We may have survived unscathed, but many did not. The clerics will be over-whelmed. The freed slaves will need aid, too."

As Devarim spoke, Vigglod approached us, his war hammer stained with blood. He wore the same helm and armor as the last battle, and his silver horn hung from his belt.

"Vigglod, thank you for coming to our aid," I said. "Victory seemed within our grasp, but you saved lives. This is Wise Protector Devarim, chief of the Counsel of the Qoholet, and my favorite mentor. Devarim, this is Vigglod, Second Guard of the Halls of Sarengeld."

The two greeted each other.

"We heard the fierce battle, the sounds reaching our sentries upon the hills," the dwarfin guard said. "The dwarfin armor and weapons among the eshkin peaked our concerns as well."

"Dwarfin forgers attacked us," I said. "We had to slay them. They seemed different from you and others I have met."

"Aye, I saw them. Foirgyn," Vigglod responded. "The descendants of Foir, the Deep dwarfin men call them. Some say the Short Beards, or Blackbeards. The Tolerated races know of the Five Fathers that emerged after the War of the Giants, as I spoke to you when you stood in our halls, Galieb Half-elfin. We are all sons of the Five Fathers and serve Hamor Dammerik, the creator of the dwarfin. Only the dwarfin know there was a Sixth Father named Foir. Foir, in bitterness of the war, rejected Hamor and went into the Deep serving demons. It is rare to see Foirgyn above ground."

I sighed. "Blue-skinned elfin, Deep dwarfin, cult worshiping traitors among us—we are entering troubling times."

"You are right, Galieb," Devarim said. "There is much more afoot than just eshkin raids. We do not know what it all means. Have hope, young ranger, we also encountered peaceful eshkin."

"Peaceful eshkin?" Vigglod exclaimed. "Who has heard of such a thing? I must say I doubt your words, ranger."

"It is true, Vigglod," I answered, "though I would doubt it too if I had not experienced it myself."

Devarim spoke up. "It is no longer clear who is friend and who is foe. We must be wise in our dealings in the future. One has to be careful wherever we go so we know who are truly enemies and who are truly allies."

"What of these blue elfin, you mentioned?" asked Vigglod. "I never heard of the like."

"The idea is novel, even to us, Commander Vigglod," answered Devarim. "Just like the Foirgyn, our allies tell us some elfin turned against their kin, rejected the elfin god, Emilye, and served evil. They are the Fanalfin. The high elfin drove them out and many went north, into the regions of ice. Even the elfin had not seen them beyond the ice until this day."

Vigglod spat in response. "Troubling times, indeed!"

"Come, as the commander of the dwarfin, let me take you to the other leaders," Devarim said.

DEVARIM TOOK Vigglod to Sir Bastian and King Faerenduil, as I sought for Erik. I found the squire a little battered from the battle, but he moved among the wounded, healing and helping the freed slaves as he spoke words of comfort, quoting the Lage.

"What abuse they suffered! They left these slaves half-starved and parched." Erik scowled once he saw me. "The wickedness of eshkin astounds me."

"I have seen much evil since I took my vows. More than I ever expected. No wonder the abbey teaches us the way it does," I said, shaking my head.

I conjured up all the healing berries I could and passed them to the needy. It helped restore some vigor, but was not enough with so many. "Your healing powers exceed mine. I have done all I can do. I will see about getting proper food and water for them down at the supply tents."

Our camp sat among the unburnt trees far down the slope, so I jogged the distance down to the supply wagons. Behind the fortified berm and all the tents and corrals, the support staff had established the supply areas. Much of the food, extra arrows, and other supplies had come by pack mule, but three wagons had bounced over roots and rocks along the rugged lumber roads through the Wood Harvest to arrive here this morning. These three wagons now sat in a row at the very back of camp. The cooks, fletchers, and smiths set up here as well.

I hoped to find the supply master to organize getting the needed food to the makeshift hospital in the open battlefield. As I approached the supply area, I noticed a longbowman standing by a wagon, quiver half full. Perhaps he would know who to ask.

As I moved to within thirty or forty paces, I perceived the archer stood unmoving and staring straight forward, locking eyes with a civilian.

The first thought that sprang in my head was another traitor.

The civilian also stood motionless, his back arched forward as he stared back at the bowman. Farrin's Crossing and the female victim came to mind. The gnoll beast had paralyzed her with his eyes before attacking me.

As I realized the danger, the hunched man launched forward, crushing the archer's throat with his jaws as it transformed into the gnoll beast.

My jaw clenched in anger. "Otto!" I called, as I yanked my bow off my back. "It's over, false beggar!"

The gnoll raised his head to glare at me, blood dripping from his muzzle. "Die, elfin-man! I eat your flesh!" he barked.

I stood ready, releasing my arrow as he spoke. The missile sank deep into his flesh above the heart.

The gnoll screamed a gruesome howl that echoed across the supply area, causing all the nearby servants and cooks to flee. He grabbed at the shaft to pull the arrow out but released his grip with a curse as if it burned him.

For I did not use any ordinary bodkin arrow, but the silver arrow of my vow. The beast grabbed the dead archer, leaped over a wagon, and fled into the woods as the arrows spilled out of the victim's quiver.

I raced forward past the wagons, hoping to hit him again, but the trees did not allow for a clean shot at this distance. He already outpaced me, even carrying his prize. My quiver was almost empty from the battle, so I scooped up a handful of the spilled arrows off the ground and pursued.

Blood dripped across the ground as the gnoll ran, both his and his victim's, allowing for easy tracking. I would not lose him. I also now knew his tricks of shape changing. He would not fool me again.

Telling myself I may be in for a long chase, I raced into the wilderness after the creature.

CHAPTER 22
BLOOD IN THE CHAMBER

I t did not take long to lose sight of the gnoll, so I concentrated on the trail, staying alert for an ambush. The beast did not hide his tracks but fled in more or less a straight line due south—following the path the army used traveling north. Apparently, he had a specific place in mind.

It had been a long, exhausting day, and my adrenaline drained away within a few miles. I wished I had grabbed a horse, but I kept moving on foot until the daylight waned.

It seemed best to find a safe but comfortable place to sleep before darkness fell, even with a bright moon rising. I found a rocky shelf to sleep against and set some makeshift traps to wake me in case the beast came looking for me in the night. I was tempted to call this beast "Otto", but the name didn't fit the gnoll form.

I still had my pack, which I had taken to the battle, but most of the contents I had left at my tent. Thankfully, I had some dried fruit, cheese, and bread. It wasn't much, but it was better than nothing.

As I settled in, my mind raced. I needed to rest if I was to face this creature with full strength. And I would need my full strength. Perhaps I acted foolishly racing off and not getting Erik and Devarim to help in the pursuit, but I was the one who had failed to protect the monster's original victims. The Qoholet Council had sent me to Wynchell as a newly sworn ranger. They sent me to find out about the eshkin raids, but I knew there was more to it than that. I represented the abbey and made vows to fight evil and protect others. The reeve of Farrin's Crossing had hired me to track this monster. So far I had failed. How many had it killed? Too many. I needed to fulfill my agreement or die trying.

THE NIGHT PASSED WITHOUT INCIDENT. I woke refreshed and determined as the first light touched the dark sky. I knew that today, one of us would die.

I munched on the last of my food and then took a few moments to stretch and meditate. While darkness lessened and the light grew, I gathered my weapons and continued after the blood trail.

Within an hour, I found the body of the archer lying in the brush, his corpse partially eaten, the last of his arrows next to him. I guessed the man got too heavy for the gnoll. A large spot of blood stained the ground, but I could not tell whose.

Maybe the gnoll beast had lost too much blood and was slowly weakening. Maybe I would find it dead. Best not to get my hopes up.

There was no sign my arrow had weakened the creature. I had to consider it knew of a way to heal itself and that I would end up facing it at full strength.

After a few hours of tracking, I knew I had reached my destination when I saw the moss-covered ruins sticking out of the forest floor. I could hear the peaceful stream nearby. Here, just a few days ago, Devarim had sat beside me, asking about my adventures. More than a mentor, he was the closest thing to a father I knew. He loved me since the day I was born—even before I was born. The thought of him gave me courage and determination.

I looked up at the sun. It had just reached its zenith.

I continued forward. Drops of blood led me to the bottom of a small south-facing cliff. The open mouth of a small cave lay at the base. My silver arrow lay in front of the opening next to a spatter of dried blood.

This seemed to be the place the beast chose as its lair.

Near the entrance stood an altar of stacked stones, just like the others I had come across. Burnt human bones lay on top of it.

This gnoll beast must also be a servant of the 'Forsaken' god.

I looked back at my silver arrow.

Perhaps the beast left the arrow for me to find as bait in a trap.

I spun around to put my back to the cliff wall. I peered around me, not wanting to be ambushed.

All seemed quiet, so I stalked about with weapons in hand, not only to clear the area of any potential attacks, but to check for another access point into the lair. Most burrowing animals have more than one entrance and exit to their makeshift homes, but I found nothing, so I returned to the hole in the cliff.

The mouth of the cave was small.

Apparently, the monster did not plan to come out to me, but waited inside like a spider on its web. My mentors' voices all screamed in my head not to go in, but the time to finish this had come.

I could not fit into the hole with all my gear, so I dropped my pack, quiver, and bow. Most likely, I couldn't use them in there, anyway.

Even my sword may be too big, but who knows? Perhaps it opened into a vast cavern down below?

I removed my sheath and kept my sword in my hand. It would be a crawl on my belly into a dark hole. Even with elfin vision, I did not relish the idea. My death, in some form, waited for me in there.

It took all my will to squat down and crawl in, sword point in front, axe in my left.

I could barely raise my head as I pulled myself along with my elbows, my belt catching small stones on the smooth floor. The scraping of my sword and axe against the rock certainly gave me away. The path continued about fifty paces from the entrance where the light did not reach.

I trembled.

It would be madness to do this without elfin eyes. Perhaps I was mad already. Determination drew me forward, not to mention the suffocating pressure of the enclosed walls.

The tunnel appeared colorless to my eyes, but I could still see the narrow corridor open into a chamber in front of me. The far wall was maybe ten paces beyond the tunnel opening. I paused a few feet from the end, my senses all alert.

Nothing. No sound, no movement, just the musky smell of dead air.

Like a tomb. Perhaps the monster wasn't in here?

No, I knew it was waiting for me in there somewhere.

It had all the advantages. I could imagine it tearing me apart the minute I try to leave the crawl space.

I did not move, but lay still in the passage as long as possible, quieting my breathing, which seemed magnified by the stone.

The clacking of claws on rock caught my ears.

The creature moved across my field of vision with a low growl.

I continued to lie there, but I knew if I waited too long, my muscles would stiffen and I would go insane from the confined space.

The gnoll moved around the chamber with growling huffs, his claws scraping against the stone floor. He squatted and peered in at me, so I poked him with my sword tip, nipping his cheek. A deep snarl escaped his muzzle as he jumped back.

Time to face my enemy.

I needed a distraction to crawl my way out and get to my feet before he could pounce on me. But what? He walked by again, the remains of Otto's tattered clothes dangling almost to the floor.

That might do.

Devarim said that it should be a simple spell for me because of my elfin blood, but I had yet to try it. I concentrated all of my efforts, remembering what my mother had taught me about magic. Placing my sword down, I rubbed the tips of my thumb and forefinger together. I drew on the magical energy around me and focused on the edge of the rags the gnoll still wore.

At first, nothing happened, but I kept concentrating and rubbing my fingers. Fire sparked at the hem of the cloth.

It blazed, but quickly died, like a dry parchment.

The sudden burst of flame did no harm to the gnoll, but the shapeshifter shrieked and patted at it with his paws, dancing in small circles.

It worked! Go!

I grabbed my sword and used the distraction to scramble out of the crawlspace. The upper half of my body cleared the hole. It seemed too slow and awkward, so I pulled my knees to my chest to push on the walls with my feet and roll away.

Not fast enough!

Claws dug into my brigandine, and teeth crunched down

on my right vambrace, almost causing me to drop my sword. One massive hand grabbed my left arm as claws sunk deep into my biceps, rendering my axe temporarily useless. A hind foot raked the front of my torso.

I twisted my wrist and banged the sharp edge of my sword blade against his neck, drawing blood, but not cutting deep.

Both of us grunted in pain.

He tossed me across the chamber, using my left arm as leverage. I tumbled about ten paces against a far wall, dazed, my head saved from the solid wall by a pile of silver wares and dusty shreds of cloth.

I scrambled to my feet with my back against the wall, holding my weapons between us as blood ran down my left arm and dripped off my elbow. I kicked away the silver chalices and other debris around my feet for better footing.

The gnoll stepped towards me, but then hesitated as he looked at my sword point aimed at his chest.

The beast squatted with one hand on the ground, out of reach of my weapons. We stared at each other intently. This was the first time I really looked at him. Saliva dripped from his open mouth and short canine snout. Large rounded ears sat on the top of his head, both faced towards me. His arms seemed too long for his hunched torso. He had oversized hands with thick pointed nails on each finger, including his thumbs. His legs matched that of a canine, though he walked upright.

I noticed the wound from my silver arrow above his heart. Pulling it out had made the opening much worse. Blood still seeped from it and now it festered. His neck and jaw wounds also oozed red.

As we stood across from one another, I got a quick glance at my enclosed arena.

The chamber appeared larger than I expected, oval and maybe twenty paces across the narrow sides. The bones of his victims lay scattered about on the floor. Several bowls of coins and jewelry rested on the floor and in nooks of the wall. Unknown symbols and runes of ancient origins marked the walls in various hues of gray with my elfin vision.

Our eyes met during my scan. One cataract white, one bottomless black. Both pupilless. I could not tell if his eyes were truly those colors or if it was just the shades as they appeared to my elfin vision in the lightless chamber. I felt myself being drawn into the blankness of his orbs. Even in the pitch darkness, he tried to hypnotize me like he had done his other victims.

Madness stared back at me. Torment.

I wrenched my gaze away, releasing a held breath. The elfin's natural resistance to charm saved me. The lack of light seemed to lessen the power, too.

The monster leaped forward in a sudden attack, swiping with his long arms but keeping his distance. I stabbed at it with my blade, but I only nicked his forearm as he retreated.

It was a feint, testing my reaction, but I drew more blood. If I could keep him at bay, and keep adding to his cuts, he may bleed out before I did.

My left arm felt weak from where his claws dug into my bicep. I didn't know if I still had full use of it.

The gnoll made more feints, swiping with his overlong arms, trying to claw me. I managed another nick or two, and so did the beast. I now had parallel scratches across my face.

"Curse you, elfin-man!" it growled. "Forsaken curse you." It continued muttering in an unknown language. It started pacing on the other side of the chamber with a crazed look on its face. Its tongue came out in a pant like some rabid canine.

As I watched it, I realized it was not just madness that had overtaken this creature, but also fear.

This powerful monster feared me. It could see its end. The

mismatched eyes shifted to the opening, as if it considered fleeing. I rushed forward, slashing with both weapons, getting between it and the exit. It dodged my attacks, backing away from the entrance.

Until we finished, neither of us would leave. It would not kill again. One or both of us would die here.

CHAPTER 23
GIFT OF A GRIFFIN

The gnoll suddenly leaped on me, claws and muzzle first. Fear pushed it into suicide, taking me with it.

I jammed my sword blade deep into his chest as he crushed me against the wall, its teeth clamping down on the side of my body as I twisted to protect my throat. I sank my axe into its side. The axe came out and went in again.

For a full minute, every one of his muscles seemed taunt, his hands and jaw clamped on me. Then the monster sank, pulling me down the wall, its vise-like jaws loosening their grip on my neck, allowing more of my blood to escape to soak into my undertunic.

Thankfully, no blood squirted across the room, so it must have missed my jugular and arteries by just hairs.

Assuming it was more human than beast, I anticipated the changing of forms as it died, but nothing happened.

A gnoll was its true form.

I pushed the lifeless body off me and shifted to a sitting position against the wall. The first thing I did was clamp my right hand over my neck to stem the bleeding. The blood slowed but didn't stop.

I may die, too, but I fulfilled my promise. This beast would kill no longer.

With my weak left hand, I pulled out my last comfrey leaf. I struggled for breaths. Closing my eyes, I concentrated on creating the healing pearls. I did not know how the blood on my hands would affect the spell.

Fearing death was truly upon me this time, I realized I needed something beyond myself. I remembered seeing Erik pray.

"Erik, Devarim, Ma, I could use your skills right now," I whispered. "Yett Sorr, Creator of all things, Eternal One, if you exist, help me, please. Lag Giefan, Law Giver, they say you are merciful."

I knew not if the two were the same or not, or which one was true.

After an exhausting few minutes, I only got three pearls covered in the blood on my hands. The last leaf disappeared. No more chances.

I chewed them and swallowed, feeling a slight tingling in my wounds as they worked. My breathing eased. Maybe it would be enough.

Will I even have the strength to get out of here?

My bleeding slowed, but still trickled down my neck. My arm seemed better.

I looked around the lightless chamber, willing my heart to stop pounding. My elfin eyes revealed every detail except for color.

The numerous bones spoke of more victims than I had realized. Several bowls of coins rested on the floor and in nooks of the wall. Candlesticks of silver and lanterns of bronze sat among the bowls. These all seemed ancient, like from another time. Other coins lay piled in one corner. Most came from Lageheim, but some were the more valuable coins used by the Merchant Lords. A few other odd items like hunting knives, a wood chisel, a sharpening stone, and caps worn by the locals lay to the side in a pile. These had belonged to the gnoll's recent victims. As for the walls, unknown symbols and runes of ancient origins marked every side.

I wonder what they are? Lost records of mighty deeds or prayers to a forgotten god?

Small chunks of stone lay on the floor where time wore away the message. As I studied the walls, a fallen stone drew my eyes. The four symbols or letters on it started glowing.

Was I dreaming? Had I lost too much blood?

A bright white light appeared in the room, blinding me. When my eyes adjusted, a winged being stood over the marked stone, light radiating from his form. No hair grew on his head or anywhere on his body. His skin blazed like bronze, like molten metal still in a crucible. Feathered wings the color of pearls stretched across the chamber, and his right hand gripped a formidable two-handed sword. The tip of the naked blade touched the floor left of his bare feet. He dressed in robes of purest white, which shimmered more than the finest silk.

"Galieb! Galieb N'ethilion! Do not be afraid."

"Who...are you?" I asked, my body trembling despite his assurances. I did not shake because he threatened me. Instead, he possessed a purity I could never achieve, exposing my tainted heart.

"I am a servant of the Most High, Eternal One, He Who Self Exists." His voice was deep yet comforting. "I was sent here to you from those celestial halls."

"I... do not know of such things," I responded.

"Creation is far more than what can be perceived by those that dwell in the material world. There is much that is beyond even the senses of the elfin." He paused as I absorbed his words. "Galieb, you have experienced many fires on your journey here. Flames of passion. Fires of testing. Flames of judgment. Fires for reforging. Each of these trials had a purpose. As your sword, Angedon, once served evil, but is now reforged, so are you being reshaped to serve something beyond yourself."

Angedon, still in the beast's chest, briefly glowed a brilliant blue, then returned to normal.

"I...do not understand."

The being looked at me with eyes like fire. "More challenges await you. The battles in Lageheim have only begun. The one who now calls himself 'the Forsaken' will cast his shadow over all the land. Like the behemoth, he will crush all under his feet, even beyond Lageheim. By your own hand shall the Qoholet cease. Dark times lay ahead, but after the night comes the dawn. A light will rise that will cast away the shadows and overcome the darkness."

His words lay like a stone on my chest. I gasped to breathe. "Who is this Forsaken? What is this light that is coming? What must I do?"

"You will know what to do when the times come. Behold, even now, a helper has been prepared and awaits you. One who will give counsel. As for the light, He will be revealed to you at the appointed time."

"Will this light defeat this Forsaken? What can you tell me?"

"All that is written in the Lage will be fulfilled. As for the Forsaken, others once knew him and served him as Tyrir the Hunter. That is all I can tell you at this time. I have enhanced Angedon's power, but only against those who oppose the coming light. Now, go, do what you have been called to do. You will not be alone. Others will aid you and to them you will be an aid. Now, your helper awaits your call. Peace be with you."

The celestial being departed, leaving me alone once again in the shades of gray.

Many thoughts raced through my head and a shudder went through my body in response to all that had happened. Finally, I stood, my strength restored and my wounds healed as if they had never existed. Even my armor and clothes seemed like new. My sword slipped out of the body of the gnoll with ease. I wiped it on the beast's carcass, its fine fur cleaning the blade sufficiently, and sheathed it.

As I did so, my gaze went back to the stone with the four engraved letters. They no longer glowed, and the rock seemed perfectly normal. I walked over and picked it up. Each symbol was a vertical line with various angled lines across the vertical ones. Looking closer, I noticed the first and third symbols were the same.

"Maybe Maistren Lilke knows the symbols and can translate it for me." I put the stone in a pouch.

Somehow, I knew what to do next, as if someone planted the thoughts in my mind.

I began right away. First, I piled all the treasures by the exit, both old and new, then reverently put the victims' bones in the nooks. They would rest hidden here. If I had any say, the treasure would go to the victims of the eshkin and the gnoll. I put a few of the ancient coins in my pouch to show the Duke and Devarim. With much effort, I dragged the beast outside. He would not rest in the same tomb.

Outside, I placed the gnoll on his own altar for burning. I cut off the mane that ran down its back as proof of my successful hunt. After building the pyre up, I lit the fire using magic, rubbing my fingertips together. It came easier this time.

After washing in the nearby stream, I sat to rest, watching

the tall flames reach up as the first stars appeared in the twilight. A peace settled over me, a peace I had not felt in a long time.

I pulled out my axe and dug out my sharpening stone from a pouch on my belt. I worked the blade to a fine edge, pondering the words of the celestial.

Amongst the trees, I heard something approach. It moved from branch to branch in the darkness, staying out of the field of my elfin vision. Or perhaps, my elfin eyes only seeing shades of gray in the darkness caused its color patterns to match the forest. Surprisingly, I did not feel any fear. First, I saw just its eyes; the orbs reflecting the flames of the pyre. My first thought was of a cat. Then I suspected an eagle or an owl.

Do you demean me before we even meet, Ranger Galieb N'ethil-ion? a voice said in my head.

I had heard of creatures with the ability to speak to the mind, but I had never experienced it before. It came as a bit of a shock.

Slowly, the creature moved where I could see it. The head and chest matched that of a small eagle. Feathered wings of mixed browns stretched out as it glided without sound to my feet. Instead of a feathered tail beyond the wings, furred hind quarters of beige stood out, accented with a long tail. The hind legs bulged with muscles. It was not an eagle, but a griffin. The griffin's size, however, only matched that of a large tomcat.

"You know my name, but what should I call you?" I asked as we assessed one another.

Call me Rafnir, for I shall be like a shield to you. It is not unknown for rangers to have unique companions. Your mentor, Horten, has the wolf, Skelbrader. Shadow the panther walks with ranger Benito. You shall have a griffin for a companion. And counselor.

"I thought griffins matched horses in size? Even hippogriffs fear griffins, or so I've heard."

You are not ready for that yet. Do not let my size cause you to doubt my abilities. I need to be small enough to sit on your shoulder and whisper in your ear.

"We are talking in our minds. Can you speak, too?"

I have not the speech of men. But speech is not the only way to give counsel. I could bite your ear when you are foolish.

I looked at his hooked yellow beak. It looked as if it could take the points right off my ears in one snap. "Hopefully, that doesn't happen too often."

We will see, young ranger.

Strangely enough, the words brought me comfort. I disliked making decisions without someone to discuss it with, but I had made many since leaving home. The griffin curled up next to me as the fire burned down, and I fell asleep without fear.

The next morning, I woke filled with a new determination as Rafnir watched me from a tree limb. I felt as if I had matured more in the last few weeks than in all my nineteen years. Yesterday, most of all. The eshkin and the gnoll had showed me evil I did not want to admit existed. But now I knew of a goodness no one on this earth dared to hope was real. I had glimpsed something beautiful and pure and clear and clean. Something utterly wholesome. A veil separated the planes, but I do not think the celestial world was veiled, but our world. Those of us living in this material world are under a veil. We dwell within a fog that we cannot move beyond. But beyond is a perfect goodness that I now greatly desired to find. It was worth all that I could give to obtain it.

I knew all this was true and not just a dream because Rafnir was at my side, as promised.

The moment passed, and all seemed normal again. The

pyre sat cold with nothing left but ash and stone. I destroyed the altar and scattered the ashes to the wind. I took my axe, once again sharp, and slid it into my belt. The silver arrow, clean and unscathed, found its place in my quiver. Next, I took my bow, appreciating its fine curves before placing it on my back.

Finally, I unsheathed Angedon, the Undone, and felt the grip in my hand. I studied the runes of blessings Stakhiljan had cut into the blade and the faint lines in the steel, showing the discreet dwarfin weaves. The true artisan blade seemed no different despite the celestial's words.

"Time to get back to the camp, Rafnir," I stated as I slid the blade into its sheath. "Devarim may be worried. I can only guess what they will say about you."

"Yes, it is time to go. Much lies ahead of us, and today is just the beginning." The griffin hopped up on my shoulder as I marched into the forest.

The End

Watch for the next book
Ranger's Calling:
The Towers of Renweard

Did you enjoy this story?
Leave a review on Amazon or GoodReads

GLOSSARY OF NAMES

Accountable, the - according to the Lage (Law), some created beings are subject to judgment before the Law Giver and some are not (which have the same accountability as animals). Most of the intelligent races are considered "accountable" such as humans, elfin, dwarfin, gnomin, dragons, giants, eshkin, etc.

Aeryie -(Ear-ree) "nest in the heights" a Protectorate of Lageheim; known for hippogriff riders; rose, white and silver

Aelfred - (ALL-fred) legendary ranger and founder of the Qoholet

Adeline, Queen - (AD-da-line) queen of Lageheim, former Druen; infant son's name is Wilhelm

Aidan - (A-dan) squire of Wynchell under the knight Sir Bastain

Angedon - (An-GE-doe-n)- "the Undone" reforged sword of Galieb; originally a Kiavonian blade owned by his father; given to him by the Qoholet Council

Appointed - ruler of a dwarfin hall, appointed to rule by one of five dwarfin fathers

Aurel - wizard of Lageheim

Baldice - "Bold" a Protectorate of Lageheim; southwest corner, borders Volberg and VenKeth. (red and white)

Ballard - town reeve of Farrin's Crossing

Baralas (BEAR-a-las) -elfin bard of the "Royal Stag Inn"; master duelist and knife thrower (olive and black)

Bastian of Langbard, Sir - knight of Wynchell; red hair and beard, tall and broad

"between the waters" - area of Wynchell between the Gaderon and Kwit River

Blackmane Family - wealthy family that raises the best war steeds for knights; pure white horses distinguished by their black manes and tails

Blackmane, Erik - squire of the Defenders of the Lage.

Blesfyr - ("Lightning fire") name of Devarim's magical bow; small lightning bolt will strike where arrow hits target; three charges per day.

brigandine - a type of armor made of small overlapping steel plates attached to a coat or vest of linen, wool or leather.

Cat Paw Lakes - collection of huge and deep lakes south of Lageheim and Volberg; world center of trade and banking; run by Merchant Lords; known for giant dragon turtles and gigantic octopus.

Commons - copper coins of Lageheim; 5 commons equal a 'daily' or half silver

Colten - squire of Wynchell under the knight Sir Bastian

Cuthbert - lead healing cleric of Wynchell

Craven - eshkin leader who does not want to raid

Daily - half silver coin of Lageheim; equal to 5 copper commons; daily wage of a common laborer

Devarim (Dev-a-rim)- chief of rangers and mentor to Galieb; Wise Protector of Council of Qoholet; father figure to Galieb.

Defenders of the Lage - Order of paladins in Lageheim;

loyal to the king, but answer only to God (Lag Giefan or "Law Giver") and the Lage or Law. Highly skilled knights with some magical abilities; (blue and gold)

Delling/Delling's Find - first dwarfin to discover iron in Wynchell; location of iron forge

Derika - female Qoholet ranger acolyte that Galieb was attracted to but she was attracted to another acolyte named Jaegar.

Derleik -(DARE-Lek) - "forsaken, forgotten" wandering old man questioning everyone he meets; aka "The Wandering Eye," "Biting Fly" "Brown Robe"

Desolate Sea - large sea that forms the western boundary of Lageheim

Drinker - the name of Derleik's magical boar spear; needs to drink blood once a month or it becomes unwieldy

Druen (DRU-en) –(singular and plural) a secret society of magic users that live on a group of islands known as the Elemental Archipelago in the Desolate Sea west of Lageheim. Usually create natural sanctuaries, growing lots of plants, pets, gardens, woods, etc., to create power sources.

dwarfin - (DWARF-in; singular and plural) humanoid race of people; one of the Tolerated races; shorter stature than humans, long beards, known for craftsmanship, especially with rocks and precious metals; prefer to live among minerals in underground halls; worship the god Hamor Dammerik

Edhelwen - (ED-hel-wen) elfin name of Galieb's mother; took the human name of Sadima

elfin -(EL-fin; singular and plural) humanoid race of people; One of the Tolerated races; prefer living in more natural settings; live a thousand years on average; pointed ears, lithe builds, more attuned to magic; worship the goddess Amilye

Elfrieda - teenage girl who lives in Woodhaven; attracted to Galieb

Erdan and Enna Silverfrond - elderly innkeepers of the "Royal Stag Inn"; elfin siblings

Erian (ER-rain) - "ploughs" Protectorate of Lageheim, north of Gaderon River; (green and blue and white)

eshkin - (ESH-kin; singular and plural) humanoid raiders; gray skin, bald heads, broad flats noses, prominent brow, over-sized earlobes, an under bite with lower tusks; iron rings in the right ear lobe reveal rank; worship the god Eshek

Fae Lands - unique region of the VenKeth that is the home of many magical Fae creatures like faeries, fauns, noldin, dryads, unicorns, etc. Some say there are portals to other worlds within its boundaries.

Faeranduil -(FAY-ran-dull) elfin lord of HaerenVale; an elfin kingdom in the VenKeth

Faerie - race of tiny humanoid creatures; elfin bodies and dragonfly wings; harvest and live among mushrooms; each colony ruled by a queen who is mother of all; live for centuries. Defend colonies with bows and sword laced with homemade poison.

Fanalfin - (FAN-al-fin) blue skinned elfin with white hair that live in the far north

Farrin's Crossing - (ferry) town in Wynchell; river ferry located here

Fior/Fiorgyn - (FEE-or/FEE-or-gin) - less known 6th father of the dwarfin; deep underground dwarfin rejected by other dwarfin

Folami (FOL-la-mee) - "He who Commands Respect" master of arms at the Qoholet Abbey; former champion of the arena; mentor to Galieb

Forest Road - unused road that runs across the VenKeth

Fredric - town reeve of Woodhaven

Gaderon River -(Gad-er-RONE) "Gathering River" largest river in Lageheim; cuts across the center of the kingdom, east to west; all waters flow into it

Galieb N'ethilion -(GAY-leeb Neth-THIL-e-on) "Beloved, Son of the wicked man" main character, young half-elfin Qoholet ranger

gambeson - a type of cloth armor formed by multiple layers of linen

Giefanfeld (GHEE-fan-feld) "Giver's Fields" Capital city of the Providence of Erian

gnomin - (NO-min; singular and plural) humanoid race of people; One of the Tolerated races; small in stature, pointed ears, round faces; known for engineering and wisdom and prized as teachers

gnoll beast- upright humanoid like creature with body of hyena

Grimwald - a battle mage in the service of the Duke of Wynchell

Gwyn - female villager from Stonecrest, assisted Sadima with garden; Galieb was attracted to her, but she chose a local man over him.

HaerenVale -(HARE-ren-vale) elfin kingdom hidden in the VenKeth

Hidden Valley - Galieb's home; along the western edge of the VenKeth, between the forest and the kingdom of Lageheim. Qoholet Abbey and three small villages reside here; Hidden Creek runs through the bottom of the valley

hippogriff- half horse, half eagle creature; hawk-headed wingless breed has four hooves and hawk head only, not a true hippogriff

Horten -"hurt" mentor of Galieb; crippled ranger on Council of Qoholet; has a companion wolf named Skelbrader; likes to bake

"The Inn at the Forest's Edge" -official name is the **"Royal Stag;"** popular inn on the western edge of the VenKeth, run by elfin. Located in the Protectorate of Baldice in Lageheim.

Ivar - the Appointed of Sarengeld, dwarfin leader

Jarman - a hippogriff rider from Aeryie

Kean - a hippogriff rider from Aeryie

Kiavonians (Kee-a-VO-nens) - elite mercenaries use by the Merchant Lords as personal body guards; known for distinct basket hilt swords with cat paw pommels.

Kjell - (Chell) sworn ranger that sometimes is at the abbey; red hair, quiet; in his 30's; can handle a vek

Kwit River "white" (kwit) river in Wynchell that flows into the Gaderon River out of the Towering Mountains. Wild eastern boundary of the land "between the waters"

Lag Giefan - (Lag GEE-fan) "The Law Giver" generic name of the unknown god who gave the Lage, or law, to Walferd the Just

Lage (LAG-ga) - "the Law"; written law brought to the Tyrian region by Walferd the Just, first king of Lageheim

Lageheim (LAG-a-hime) mighty human kingdom ruled by knights and the Lage, the Law given to Walferd the Just

Lakeside - the central support village (one of three) in the Hidden Valley for the Qoholet Abbey; supplies fish, wool, crafts

lase n eck - (Laze-n-eck) "grace and death" specialized sword and dagger martial art of the elfin; a fast and fluid style

Lekhash - (Lek-HASH) gaudy dressed associate of the brown-robed monk, Derleik. Sometimes appears as a fox.

Lilke - (LIL-key) gnomin mentor of Galieb; Master teacher of Qoholet (Maistren Sabbis) ; on council; rumored to be a founder of the Qoholet; has many names-Lilke Obed Stavewielder Murnig Skholfounder Treestumbler Gottson...

Lil - goat found by Galieb in Wynchell

Lord Defender - highest ranking paladin of the Defenders of the Lage

Maistren Sabbis-(MY-stren SA-bis) "master teacher"; highest mentor of the Qoholet

Meinrad - (Men-RAD) middle aged, sworn ranger that sometimes is at the abbey;

Merchant's Common, Common Language, or Common tongue - a trading language used by most cultures and races to communicate

Morgrim -(MOR-grim) dwarfin stableman and guardian of the Royal Stag Inn

Mukluk - eshkin chieftain and shaman in Wynchell

Norir - (NOR-ear) one of the five remembered dwarfin fathers

Otto - beggar in Wynchell

Ottokar (OT-to-kar) ranger with the title of baronet; outlander

Outlander - ambassador or liaison for the Qoholet, informant or spy

Qoholet (KO-ho-let) "Gatherers of Wisdom" -brotherhood of ranger sages who study philosophy, wisdom, logic, martial skills, and survival skills; specialize in archery, swordsmanship, and wilderness survival skills

Qoholet Abbey (KO-ho-let)- The academy of the Qoholet ranger sages

Queen Chennai - (CHEN-nye) Merchant Lord from the Cat Paw Lakes; mother of Lady Zebah; not a true queen, but a self imposed title

Paladin - specialized knight with magical abilities and high martial skills

Pinnacle - heavy gold coins worth 10 regular gold coins (called crowns) per the Lakes/Merchant Lords minting system

Radbourn, Sir Lucian - (RAD-born) paladin, Defender of

the Lage, mentor to Erik Blackmane, relative of the Duke of Theomund

Rafnir - (RAF-nir) "ward or counselor" bonded cat-sized griffin companion to Galieb

Reeve - title; town master; appointed leader of a village or town; civil servant

Reinhart III, King - present king of Lageheim; father of Prince Wilhelm

Reinhart, Sir - legendary champion knight of Walferd the Just

Reyowin - (RAY-o-win) queen of the Fairy colony

Sabbis (SA-bis) - generic term for teacher, mentor among the Qoholet

Sadima (Sad-ee-ma)- "sad" (Tyrian), "peace" (Elven); mother of Galieb, human name taken by Edhelwen

Sarengeld -(SAIR-en-geld) dwarfin halls in Wynchell known for gold and iron

Seven Arches Bridge - easternmost bridge across the Gaderon, and the smallest of the three. Near town of Travailin; between Baldice and Erian

Skelbrader (Skel-BRAY-der) "shield brother"; bonded wolf companion to Ranger Horten

Stakhiljan (Stak-HIL-jan) 'made of steel' true artisan swordsmith for the Qoholet Abbey; dwarfin race

Stedgyr (STED-ger) "steadfast, trustworthy" - Erik Blackmane's prized stallion

Stonecrest - the support village (one of three) in the Hidden Valley for the Qoholet Abbey; closest to abbey

Tanyl (TAN-yill) elfin master of scouts from HaerenVale.

Thalassa -(Thal-A-sa) neighboring human kingdom south of Lageheim on the Desolate Sea coast. Known for fishing, shipbuilding, seafaring, etc.

Theomund (THEE-o-mund) - "wealthy defender" Protectorate in Lageheim; wealthiest duke in Lageheim; (red and yellow)

Theorn - (THEE-orn) capital city of the Providence of Theomund, at crossroads of the Kings Highway, Theorn Road, and the Thalassian Byway

Threshold Ridge - eastern mountain ridge of the Hidden Valley, western edge of VenKeth; stretches hundreds of miles from the Towering Peaks in far north to the Ven Marshes in the south

Torir - (TOR-ear) dwarfin ruler of Volberg Halls; ruler over all descendants of Norir

Towering Peaks - high mountain range stretched across the northern border of Lageheim and most of the VenKeth; aka "The Peaks"

Travailin (Tra-VALE-lin) - "Traveler's Rest" large town in the Protectorate of Baldice located at the junction of the Kings Highway and Theorn Road

Tyria/Tyrian -(Tie-REE-a/Tie-REE-in) name of region before the kingdom of Lageheim established; ethic group of humans who controlled the region before Lageheim; language of the people of Lageheim.

Ugalorian -(OO-ga-LOR-ree-en) human ethic group south of the Cat Paw Lakes; warrior society

Valda, Lady (VAL-da) - wife of Devarim, archmage; on Council of Qoholet; mother of two sons

VenKeth -(VEN-keth) "The Venerable Woods" Tyrian name for the mighty ancient and mysterious forest east of Lageheim; The Venerable Woods in the common language.

vek - small flying creatures that many of the intelligent races used to carry messages. They have long snake-like bodies with tiny legs and a dragon-like head. Small feathers run down the sides of their tail. Four dragonfly-like wings make them as maneuverable as the insect and they can travel hundreds of miles quickly. Can memorize and dictate short messages

Vigglod - (VIGG-lod) 2nd dwarfin commander at Sarengeld; trained guard and soldier; uses a silver horn

Volberg - (VOLE-berg) the neighboring human kingdom south of Lageheim between Thalassa and the VenKeth; known for dormant volcano and dwarfin halls and crafts; travelers from Lageheim must pass through Volberg on way to the Cat Paw Lakes

Vollyr - (VOLL-yir) mentor of Galieb; elder centaur on Council of Qoholet

Walferd the Just - (WAL-ferd) legendary first king of Lageheim; brought the Lage or Law to the people of Tyria; also known as **Walferd the First**

Wandering Eye - nickname of Derleik, an old man who wanders about asking deep philosophical questions; also known as the "Brown Robe" and "the Biting Fly"

Wattle and Daub - a composite building method used for making walls and buildings, in which a woven lattice of wooden strips called "wattle" is "daubed" with a sticky material usually made of some combination of wet soil, clay, sand, animal dung and straw. Sometimes whitewashed over with lime. Dark squared logs can be used for structure and accent

White Cliff - capital city of Wynchell

Wise Protector - title for Chief of the Qoholet Council and lead ranger

Wood Harvest - name of the wooded region in Wynchell between the rivers; trees have been harvested for lumber for centuries.

Woodhaven - the northernmost support village (one of three) in the Hidden Valley for the Qoholet Abbey; supplies lumber, wool, leather, food

Wolf's Nose - distinctive rock outcropping above the village of Woodhaven on Threshold Ridge

Wynchell - (WIN-chell) "drawer of water" Protectorate of Lageheim, NE corner; known for wood, iron, gold, and craftsmanship; (gold V on green field)

Yett Sorr - (YETT Surr) "The Self -Existent, Eternal One" name given by the Qoholet to the philosophical "First Cause, Creator of all things" eternal being who must logically exist.

Zebah of the Lakes, Lady - (ZEE-bah) daughter of Queen Chennai, Merchant Lord; betrothed to Archibald, son of Duke Theomund; "most beautiful woman alive"; (blue and white, swan feathers)

MORE FROM RAYMOND KEITH

Book 2: *Ranger's Calling: The Towers of Renweard*

The wall was supposed to hold forever.

After fighting the fierce eshkin raiders in Wynchell, Ranger Galieb Half-elfin and his griffin familiar Rafnir answer a call to the mountain fortress on the edge of the wilderness. For centuries, the Black Towers of Swartmael have guarded the kingdom of Lageheim against all threats from the north. But when Galieb scouts an army that stretches beyond counting, he realizes no wall can stand against what's coming. Eshkin warriors. Lumbering giants. Blue wizards wielding ancient magic. Terror birds and other fell beasts. And leading them all, a power that even the mighty dragon Shethar once knew and feared.

But the greatest enemy was already inside.

As Galieb and the knight Sir Erik Blackmane rally the defenders, they discover that the mysterious forsaken god is ready to reveal himself in a new terrifying form, claiming the land he once ruled. His followers have infiltrated every level of Lageheim's society, even corrupting sworn knights into treason. When King Reinhart III makes his final stand atop the dragon Shethar, the cost of heroism will be measured in the fall of the mighty.

Ranger's Calling: The Towers of
Renweard Book 2

Want more from Raymond Keith?
Sign up for my newsletter to get the latest updates and a free
short story:

Bandits abuse and enslave. Rangers rescue. Elfin endure.

"The Rescue of Edhelwen" is an introduction to the world of Veardalan—a place of knights and rogues, rangers and goblins, elfin and dwarfin, magic and swords.

Victims of a roadside assault interrupt Devarim's travels. Finding some dead, he soon realizes that the band of forest ruffians may be holding some victims captive. Severely outnumbered, the ranger will need all his skills to overcome the bandits and their ruthless leader.

Edhelwen left her elfin realm to enter the world of humans for the first time only to be taken captivity by cutthroats intent on selling her as a slave. As she wrestles with the idea of a hopeless future, she must not only think of herself. They have also taken a young human girl.

Newsletter sign and The Rescue of
Edhelwen free story

Find maps and more about the world of Veardalan on the
website:

Maps of Veardalan

ABOUT THE AUTHOR

Raymond grew up wandering the woods and fields of Pennsylvania looking for elves, goblins and dragons. He is fascinated with all of God's creation, both the natural and supernatural, talking to every animal he meets. To rest from reality, he would create stories for himself, but now shares them with others. As a servant of the True King, Christ, Raymond is currently assigned as a state park manager in southeast Montana. He lives with his enchanting bride and has been given an amazing daughter.